Joe's Quarry

Lynda Aylett-Green

First published in Great Britain in 2014 by

Bannister Publications Ltd
118 Saltergate
Chesterfield
Derbyshire S40 1NG

Typeset in Palatino Linotype by Escritor Design, Chesterfield, Derbyshire

Printed and bound in Great Britain by SRP Ltd, Exeter, Devon

This novel is a work of fiction. All names and characters are the product of the author's imagination and any resemblance to actual persons is coincidental.

My thanks go to:

Stephen Middleton for his advice on flora and fauna of the Peak District; Lyddia Green for her help; David Glasson for his help with cover photography; Jennifer Green for her encouragement and helpful suggestions; Peter Skipper for his attention to detail and valuable suggestions.

1

Storm Damage

Joe spent the night listening to the crashing and thundering of the storm and to whistling tiles, splintering wood and shattering glass. He would wait until dawn to assess the damage even though lightning lit up the groaning old house with stark white light. Let nature take its course then work with what you've got left. He trusted the stone walls of his farmhouse to protect him against the screaming wind and battering downpour; there was nothing he could do right now.

There was no such protection for the early clutch of Peregrine Falcon eggs that he had noticed on a rocky ledge the day before. The nest was a carelessly constructed affair, little more than a slight indentation scuffed out on the gritty ledge, its three eggs noisily guarded by the parent birds. Scrambling up the rock face to find the reason for their excitement, Joe would have loved to give them lessons in nest construction, some stout branches and dollops of hard setting mud. Such precious, speckled, fragile shells so negligently sheltered. Again, nature must take its course. If the eggs were destroyed the birds would set about mending the nest and laying another clutch but the foolish worry kept Joe awake for the rest of the raging night.

At first light the still air and watery sunshine seemed unreal. Perhaps it was a teasing lull until the stormy punishment began again. Far away peaks had a strange orange glow and the harsh rocky outline of Froggatt Edge was a menacing purple-black in the distance.

It was the old barn that formed the end of Joe's house that had suffered the worst of the fury. Its ruinous state, skeletal roof timbers

and broken panes had allowed the wind to rampage through it unchecked. It was much as he had imagined as he lay in bed, so he was relieved to find that the shuddering barn timbers had not dislodged the main structure of his farmhouse. It would live to fight another day.

He grabbed binoculars; no need to disturb the falcons by scrambling noisily up the rock face. He climbed a hill on the opposite side of the quarry and focused on the ledge. The female sat hunched and bedraggled but she perked up as her partner arrived with a beak full of food, setting off again on another dutiful search. They were large, muscular birds, yet they only amounted to a few ounces of feather and bone, clinging tenaciously to the narrow ledge without crushing the delicate shells they were fighting to protect. The falcons were stronger, more resistant than the slates and rafters of his barn.

No need to worry about the bats and owls wisely tucked away in caves and fissures. Returning home, Joe stoked up the log burner then had tea and toast next to it before going out again into the garden to tidy away the broken slates that had sliced through plants in the borders and littered the stone path. It was soon more orderly and the sun warmer, the world was a safe place again.

He set off for work, taking his bicycle rather than the car as it seemed easier to navigate the branch-strewn lanes by weaving about than stopping to move tree-trunks. As he left he felt the phone vibrating in his shirt pocket; unwise to answer as it was bound to be his mother fearing death and destruction and offering – again – to put his farmhouse on the market.

The offices were about ten miles away, a fairly easy ride with few of the punishing ascents of the surrounding peaks, and when he arrived at The Bugle offices, editor Fred Marshall was already hammering at his pc keyboard.

Fred grinned with satisfaction. 'Plenty of exciting stuff going off after last night. What a stinker. Did it get you?' he asked with relish, and then added callously 'I always imagine your place being swept over the edge of the quarry in a storm – that would be a good story, plus you'd be handy with your camera for some dramatic shots and a quick email with copy.'

'Sorry to disappoint, but there's not much damage to report. You'd be out of luck anyway because the power's cut off and the telephone line is down. And the crappy mobile that's all I'm allowed on expenses never gets a signal.' Joe poured himself a coffee from the thickening brew on the hotplate and sat down. He did not have his own office or even his own desk. He was humorously referred to as the Features Editor, or if visitors were about as the Environmental Editor, expected to bash out articles from home then send them in for Fred's approval.

'Just as well you're in one piece, Joe, because I need you fit and well to get down to the river. You did bring your camera? Flooding's the main story and that always makes for good photos. No casualties, fortunately,' he added virtuously, 'but the mill's several feet under water and the millrace is ...'

'Racing? Sounds as though you can write that yourself. No, I came in to give you the piece I mentioned last week, I've got some amazing pictures because the seasons have all gone haywire. We're well into March and yet there's some here that have normally still been in Morocco at this time of year to escape the worst ...'

'Joe, what the hell are you on about?'

'Butterflies. I told you, to have Painted Ladies over-wintering in their thousands must be a first, or ...'

Fred stopped typing and spat out 'Butterflies? Effing insects? I can't afford to pay you for pap like that when there's raging torrents and half the valley under water.'

'That's the whole point. The weather's been foul for months but these delicate little creatures are still here – in spite of giant sycamores uprooted and roofs off – the butterflies magically survive. We could do a whole page of the most amazingly colourful ...'

'Just leave me alone – get out and do storm damage shots for tomorrow.'

'I'm not the news reporter, Fred, and I don't do captions – I *write* for heaven's sake – in-depth scientific pieces that I ought to be sending out round the world instead of ...'

'If Bill isn't here to cover news, then you *are* the news reporter.'

'Where is he?'

'Don't know. He hasn't rung in.'

Joe dropped a paper copy of his butterfly article onto the editor's keyboard and went out, calling back 'I'll get you those flood photos now, but then I'm going home to finish clearing up. And you'd better check up on Bill. It wouldn't sound good if you hadn't bothered to contact him and he's dead under a tree somewhere. That wouldn't make a good story.'

He cycled downhill to the banks of the Wye, or to where the banks had now decided to be. The river was a brown bubbling torrent, battering its way down from Buxton. The riverside pub was several feet under water and it seemed an affront to photograph the landlord and his son baling out and dragging about useless sandbags. So he did not. A few shots of floating metal casks and a bus stranded with two happy schoolchildren should satisfy his news-hungry editor. Poor bugger, poor Fred. Years of filling pages with footpath disputes and well dressings, so a violent, destructive act of God was a god-send.

Joe set off for higher ground, up on the old railway line above the rocky gorge. This was the real news, the bigger picture, the muddy brown river that had changed its shape and proved how over millions of years water had triumphed over rock. The sun came out and changed the surge to silver. Joe took photographs and saw them punctuating his lovingly researched descriptions of Peak District rivers in all their moods. He saw them in scientific journals or richly mounted in severe frames and he saw them in heavy books by Joseph Wright, volumes on butterflies, on moorland plants and strange rocky outcrops. The smell of fresh glossy paper, the feel of embossed covers and the fragile tissue protecting each original plate and sketch.

۞

'What's happened to your telephone, Joseph? I mean your landline. Have you been cut off? If you can't pay, you've only to ask…'

'It was the storm, Mum. It was impressive, you can't imagine'.

4

'That's why I'm ringing, because it was terrifying here in Buxton, the lights kept going out and on the radio it said the river was flooding all over the Pavilion Gardens. I can't imagine how you survive in that dreadful ruin of yours. It ought to be demolished. Have you finally come to your senses?'

'It's only the barn that's a bit the worse for wear. When it's renovated it'll double the size of the house and the whole thing will be an impressive residence. Any money I spend on it will be a good investment.' Those were the words he knew she liked to hear – impressive, investment, a grand residence. Only this time it did not work.

'I was up all night imagining that great heap of stones collapsing with you buried underneath it. Or the whole building swept over the edge of the quarry, a pile of rubble at the bottom. It's no way to exist, you are nearly thirty-two, Joe …'

'Thank you, Mother. I'd been trying to work that out. Now I must go – I've just taken some impressive photos of storm damage and floods, really beautiful. Come over at the weekend and I'll show you.'

He almost felt her shudder at the end of the line.

'Joe, you know I have to steel myself every time I come to that place. It's no pleasure seeing you living in such squalor. It puts years of wear and tear on the Renault coming down that track …'

'Just take it slowly and mind the potholes.'

'Craters, more like. You'd better come over to me, Joseph, and bring the photos with you, though what possible artistic merit there can be in mud and water … and it's all been done before.'

'But not like this. You'll see.'

'Have you heard from Helen yet? Poor girl, I can't say I blame her if she can't …'

'Bye, Mum. See you later then.'

❧

Joe transferred the river photographs on to his computer then printed them on thick, matt paper. Fascinating how under heavy, low clouds the colours were sepia, black and chocolate, then lit up

by the sun they changed to silver and emerald. This was storm magic, not damage.

It was a fine afternoon, so he sat in the garden, sunbathing in late winter. The weather made up new rules every year. The only signs of the night's fury were branches split and jagged, some still hanging and rocking mysteriously in the now still air, some lying across hedges and flower beds. They would dry out in the barn ready for the stove next year. In a fit of generosity he emailed some text to Fred, to go with the flood photos he had sent that morning: the schoolchildren's names, the lessons they were missing, the publican's loss of income. That would do; he was not a reporter.

Reluctantly he took a broom and dustbin into the barn and started clearing up, admiring for the hundredth time the thick limestone walls and heavy beams, still standing after centuries of storms. One day he would put the old place to rights as it deserved. Done properly it would take serious money and probably years of hard work, but it would be done properly.

Once he had cleared the smaller shards and splinters he started to heave at some of the larger chunks of limestone that had once formed the barnyard walls and were now lying in the mud, marking them with chalk where he could see their old position.

Hard work. It was time for a tea break and the luxury of wandering thoughts. Thoughts of Helen and of how he would bring the farmhouse back to life so that it looked almost like some of those houses in the country style magazines. She'd like one of those useless, shiny kitchen ranges that belched out heat whether you wanted it or not and cream-coloured flagstones that never looked scuffed with mud.

Not many ramblers ventured near the quarry. Some strange local myth had swirled like mist around the nearby villages – the ancient striated rock face was crumbling and trembling, given to upheavals deep inside its fissures. Stories of houses tumbling over the edge (so where were traces of them now on the quarry floor?) or of a body once seen in the blue white water of the lake but never fished out because of the pool's legendary depths. It was, Joe had verified, little more than a large pond, about ten feet deep.

And of course there were tales of unholy rituals carried out, a satisfying broth of sadism, sex, depravity and wishful thinking. Wrong again, Joe often insisted over cider in The Miners Standard. The locals had so successfully wound up the evil legends that not even drunken teenagers with crates of special offers would dare go into the quarry.

So who was this now? Was it a rambler, or someone lost? Joe had been watching the hesitant figure for some minutes and it consulted no map or compass but slowly skirted his land then disappeared from view behind a rock formation. A man or a bulkily-clad woman?

Joe finished his tea then went back to the barnyard and carried on piling up stones. Those that had no obvious place in the walls he sorted into lots according to size, ready to fill in gaps. This methodical work felt like progress towards the day when new windows and insulation would welcome the barn as part of his house. Sadly he could see that there might not be enough stone to fill the missing gaps; some of it had been pilfered by the locals for dry-stone walls or for village garages.

'Is this your house?'

Joe turned to see a stranger, a middle-aged man with no rambler camouflage, no waterproofs or self-sufficient backpack but a grey suit under a heavy tweed overcoat caught up by persistent brambles. He might have expected to hear 'Is this a footpath?' or 'Is there a pub near here?' but the question surprised him.

The stranger felt his hesitation, 'I mean, do you live here?'

Not much better, so Joe ignored this and allowed a curt 'Can I help you?'

'I thought the place was derelict, couldn't see any signs of life.'

Lies. The man had been past the place twice and Joe's bike was outside the front door. 'It's mine, and I'm working on it. Renovating it.'

The stranger yanked his heavy coat free of brambles and found a drier patch on the path for his expensively-shod feet. 'I don't blame you, it's a lovely spot. Very peaceful, but the old place would be a money pit done properly.'

'It'll be done properly, I'll see to that. I've got plenty of time.' The old boy must be at least sixty and not up to tossing limestone boulders about.

'Good lad, glad to hear it. Did last night's storm cause you any problems? I've heard the rock face in the quarry is badly eroded. Do you worry about rock falls? Or subsidence threatening the farmhouse?'

'It's solid rock and the house is good for another few centuries.' Joe turned away, 'I'll get on – it'll be dark soon and I've no light in the barn. Mind how you go, they are always discovering old mine shafts round here.' Then he couldn't resist 'Not many of them are capped and covered with bracken, they're a real death trap.'

'Thanks, I'll watch out.'

From the barn door Joe watched the stranger disappear into the bushes, then a few seconds later from farther down the track the sound of an engine starting up.

❦

When Helen rang she said 'I've missed you, Joe. You promised to call in for a meal last week, you don't eat properly in that well-past shabby chic kitchen. And with that storm last night, thinking of you alone up there … I heard the news on the radio … there's been a lot of damage, and people injured. Are you safe?' She would let it sound like friendly concern, an offer of help that she hoped would not seem too needy, too intrusive.

Joe laughed and took the phone next to the log burner. 'Everyone seems to think I've been blown over the edge, me and this pile of stone.' He thought she sounded hesitant, uncertain how to bridge the gap that had opened up between them over the past months. He would help her out. 'It's lovely to hear you, and I've missed you too, though I enjoy thinking of you in your elegant flat in bustling Bakewell. I used to feel guilty when you were roughing it here with me.' That was overdoing it a bit; not really guilty, but something – uneasy, concerned, perhaps, that she did not enjoy the struggle against the elements as he did.

'So no earth-shattering damage then? You weathered the storm?'

Did she sound disappointed that the elements had not changed his mind any more than she could change it? Or than his mother could. Strange he'd had two doom-laden calls as though they were in league. 'All safe and sound, thanks love. And is Bakewell still there? Not flushed down the Wye? You must come over and see the fantastic stag beetle shots I did last week (what woman could refuse?) As long as you don't mind …the housework's been a bit neglected … but you know all about that. It's just that the place is even more quaintly distressed than usual.'

Helen hesitated, not because she dreaded the burnt offerings that usually came out of Joe's oven after several hours of waiting, but because it felt like sliding back into a relationship that was not right for her.

Joe said encouragingly 'The forecast is good for the next few days. You won't have to wade through too much mud. And I've mended the holes in the roof … only joking, the slates in the barn roof, I mean.' Now he expected a polite refusal, or a counter invitation to her luxury Georgian apartment for coffee and a friendly, awkward chat.

'I could come over tomorrow. Puppy would like it.'

'Puppy?' Had she already replaced him within weeks with some mutt?

'I found him. Someone dumped him in the field the other side of the bridge and no-one claimed him from the police. He's sort of growing on me.'

In a way he obviously never did, Joe thought.

'He isn't quite house trained, but really I don't suppose it would …'

'No, it wouldn't really matter in this tip, wouldn't notice. But you'd both be very welcome,' Joe added, to soften his remark. 'What's its name?'

'Well, Puppy, so far. I'll think of something if I keep him. He'll love your wilderness. He'll think he's gone to heaven after my patio and decking. See you in the morning then. I'll bring some curry.'

Well, that was all right then, because Puppy would love it. And, Joe admitted to himself, so would he. They'd go for a walk, Puppy

training, he'd soon get the critter into shape, then back for curry and cider and a catch-up chat. Lots more cider so she would have to stay the night.

❧

Joe went back to his computer and edited more of his flood photographs. The wet rocks looked like vast nuggets of gold in the sunshine. Funny, he'd never seen rocks by moonlight but probably they'd look like chunks of silver. He looked out across the field and over to the quarry but there was no moonlight. He must remember to try that some other time.

The phone rang again. Helen must have changed her mind about coming, regretted her weakness after saying they were too different all those weeks ago, too different to be happy for life, or even for a few days.

'Hello, I met you this afternoon while I was out for a walk. My name's Frank Webster. You'll think this is crazy, but I can't get your place out of my mind. Lovely spot, really peaceful. I know you said it needed a fortune spent on it …'

'You said that, Mr. Webster, I didn't. But it probably does.'

'Well, Mr. … sorry, I've forgotten your name.'

'Wright. Joseph Wright.'

'Could I make you an offer for the place, Joseph? I've been doing some sums and I'd be prepared to offer you more than any valuation a local agent would give you.'

'Kind of you, but I've never thought of selling …'

'No, I realize that, all a bit sudden and I apologise for my enthusiasm, so think it over for a few days and I'll get back to you. You wouldn't have to struggle to patch things up year after year, you could get yourself something easy to run, give you time to concentrate on your photography … or whatever you do. As I said, I'll be in touch.'

'Don't bother, Mr. Webster, I'm really not …' But the phone went dead, leaving Joe to wonder why Webster had the impression he was hard up and how he knew about the photography. Who was this guy? What was he after?

2

Kidnapped

Joe had to admit that Puppy was a charmer, a sneaky, unfair little charm ball. 'What sort is it?' he asked, showing a brief interest before giving Helen a long, close, full-length hug.

'I don't suppose we'll ever know. Some sort of terrier and a bit of labrador, perhaps. 'Isn't he lovely?'

Puppy looked up at Joe, glistening black eyes looking their loveliest.

'Mmm. He's running rings round you. A few weeks old and he's got you sorted. I'll make some coffee. I put the water on the stove ages ago so it'll be boiling soon.'

'What's wrong with the kettle? Or that microwave your mother gave you?' Helen looked round at the battered and sooty kitchen-ware, stifling her familiar irritation.

'Not so much fun as feeding the stove. Why waste free heat?'

'You just enjoy camping indoors.' She put her offering of tin-foiled curry onto the range hotplate and went to join Joe in the living room. 'I suppose I can understand the attraction of this place for you ... almost.' She sat next to him on the baggy sofa in front of the giant stove. Puppy tried to jump up to join them, bouncing on small hind legs to gather momentum.

Helen lifted him up. 'You don't mind him really, do you Joe?'

'No. But won't different rules confuse him? I seem to remember your antique chaise longue is cream velvet and the rugs are eau-de-nil. Or has he already got the run of your place too?'

'You're right, we must be firm and consistent. Be a love and get his bed out of the car, will you? I'll see if the water is boiling.'

Joe placed the padded dog basket behind the sofa.

'No, not there, put it next to us. I sort of feel he needs to see me as he's in a strange place.'

'But I'd rather he didn't watch what we are going to be doing,' Joe said, pulling her close and closing her mouth with his.

Puppy whined anxiously.

❧

'A walk would be lovely, but we can't go on your usual five hour expedition, Joe. His little legs aren't up to it yet.'

'Oh, hell. This pooch thing is crowding me. Put the little bugger in a backpack or something, like a papoose.'

'Certainly not. He needs to develop his muscles – another few months and he'll walk the legs off you. And you need to develop your more caring side, less of the wild woodsman image you like to cultivate. You spend your time photographing Nature, well Puppy is an animal, part of Nature.'

'Didn't know I'd got a more caring side.' Joe grabbed the thin miniature lead and hooked the ecstatically gyrating Puppy on to it firmly. 'I notice you refer to the next few months, so it's already adopted then?'

'*He* stays. It was seeing you two bonding that decided me. You look so good together, he'll love coming over here to see you.'

'Shit.'

'Not when I've finished training you both. Come on then, a short walk, and remember you are supposed to be some famous nature lover – butterflies and newts and wild orchids and stuff. Puppy is part of all that.' Helen took the lead and pulled the frolicking scrap gently away from a cow pat.

'I want to tell you about my idea for a book.' Joe changed the subject and walked down a gravely slope towards the quarry. 'Did you see my photos the newspaper printed about a month ago? Pretty good, I thought, and I'm planning a book about Blackridge Quarry, with illustrations and notes, not just a picture book with a bit of text and captions but a whole description of its unique insects and grasses, and why things are as they are.'

'Sounds a bit vague. Do we have to go this way when we could go over the fields? I never liked the look of it. It's just going down to the floor of the cave.'

'You know it's a quarry, not a cave, though it probably started off as one thousands of years ago. It all looks quite natural now, because nature has reclaimed it and created a whole small world down here – it has its own pool, there's even an island in it, and a copse with birches and alder. This is what I wanted to show you.'

'I've been down here before with you, I remember what it's like. I'd rather go up on the cliff top where you can see ranges of hills and peaks stretching for miles.'

'But that last time – and I remember it because it was the second time you visited the farm and I wanted you to love everything – you said you wanted to go back after ten minutes.'

'That was because you spent the whole time flat on the ground making love to some beetle, and it was snowing.'

Joe frowned. 'Can't have been. Snow and beetles don't mix.'

They were still walking downhill along a fairly wide ledge when Puppy stopped and sat down.

'Pull him along a bit. You've got to be firm,' Joe insisted, reaching out for the lead.

'Don't you dare, you'll hurt his neck.' Helen bent down, put her hands under the dog's tiny haunches and lifted him upright. 'Come on, Pup. You can do better than that, you show him.'

Puppy yelped, sat down again then tried to turn back.

'He doesn't want to go down there any more than I do, he doesn't like this place, it's creepy. Animals sense these things.'

Joe picked the dog up and retraced a few steps. 'You stay there, Helen. Bit of animal psychology going on here.' He put Puppy down experimentally and walked back towards Helen, but after a few yards the dog whimpered and sat down again. 'Thought so, it's the gravel. It's hurting his paws. We used to have a dog that refused to walk on stones. Until halfway down the slope we were on grass and he was fine.' Joe picked him up and continued downhill. 'I'll just show you something, and it isn't creepy, it's

beautiful. Look at those ferns and the caves halfway up the rock face. I found bones in there, wolves and wild boar.'

'No caveman remains? How disappointing. But I quite like the pool now the sun is on it.'

'There are bats and nesting birds, and flowers that only grow in quarries, and I think, though I need to do some more research into it, there are three varieties of grass that only grow in this quarry. Don't you think that's amazing, love? Plants that choose my quarry out of all the rocky places in the world. I know that sounds mushy, and that it's all down to certain minerals or the micro-climate, but it's wonderful all the same.'

Helen took squirming Puppy. 'Right, I'm convinced – this place is an undiscovered paradise with enough flora and fauna to fill at least two volumes. Now can we go because … oh, how odd. Look up there, there's someone on the cliff top.'

Joe turned and shaded his eyes to squint up at the sky. 'Can't see anyone. But why is that odd, apart from the fact that they are on private land?'

'He was watching us through binoculars.'

'A birdwatcher with binoculars. Why is that so amazing? I saw a falcon here a few days ago and it's got a nest up there, so our birdwatcher is probably hoping to get lucky.'

Helen kept staring at the high cliff face and the rim of shrubs that marked its edge, 'I'm impressed, that's a big, ferocious bird, a falcon. I thought you'd only get martins and pigeons. That's like an eagle, a falcon, isn't it? A huge bird of prey.' Puppy whimpered. 'It's all right darling, I won't let it get you.' She kissed the top of his head and the dog responding with frantic licking.

'Yuck, that's disgusting, Helen. He's just eaten half a cowpat. Talking of which let's get back and get that curry on the go.'

Joe was quiet as they scrambled back. He was always happy enough with his camera and computer, out walking alone for hours on end, but the computer screen didn't laugh and argue and tease him as Helen did. He loved the way she tried, without much luck, to tidy the living room in the farmhouse and to turn the old stone

fireplace into a kind of shrine with jasmine on the mantelpiece and a bit of candle she found in a drawer.

The old stove was roaring like a furnace when they got back and it belched smoke when Helen tried to calm it by opening the blackened glass door.

'Not exactly gracious living, Joe. Oh, sorry, Pup's done another puddle on the floor. It won't hurt the flagstones, and I'll put newspaper down …'

'So much for gracious living, and, bloody hell Helen, that's my pile of newspaper cuttings. And every time he pees you should put him outside so he gets the message.'

'Bit late by then. Besides, it's cold and getting dark.'

'I bet you don't let him crap on your parquet flooring in Bakewell, or on that cream fitted carpet in the bedroom.' Joe pulled back the heavy blanket on a rail that made the old door draught- proof. 'You check on the curry and I'll escort the lad outside for a bit of training.'

Helen stirred the simmering curry on the old range; the ancient house wasn't too bad once the fires got going and there wasn't a fierce gale that penetrated every crack and every rattling window. And when she knew she had her central heating and triple glazing in town to escape back to.

Joe came back in and put his arms round her, 'I've missed you, forgot how good and sexily lumpy you feel, but let's eat first.'

'First before what? And where is Puppy?'

'He's fine. I've closed the gate so he's got the front lawn to sniff around, and I'll give him a couple of minutes to get the pee message. We'll eat in front of the fire because the kitchen table's covered with photos.' He kissed her again. Even with that tiny scrap of a critter it felt like three was a crowd, the brilliant black fringed eyes watching him unblinkingly. It was good to be on their own for a few minutes.

'Puppy will start howling any minute, Joe, he always does if he's on his own. Pass me a can of cider, and the chutney. That was a bit of a find, lime pickle in your sparse cupboard.'

'Let me tell you more about my book.' Joe crammed a sustaining chunk of nan bread into his mouth then launched into his absorbing

project. 'The old quarry at the back here hasn't been worked for ages, since when my grandfather was young, and then it was just man and lad with pickaxes, not monster demolishing machines. So it looks as though Man hasn't ever smashed it up and blasted bits away. It's reverted to nature. In fact it's done even better, because the locals don't like going there so it has been left to grow in peace, and to try out new things, new plants and different birds nesting there.' He paused for breath and more curry. 'There's more wildlife in some of these old quarries than in the fields and woods around, but here in Blackridge things have really come back to life, like recovering from a terrible shock ...'

Helen laughed. Almost unwillingly she felt a surge of love at his raw enthusiasm. 'You talk about that quarry as though it were a person, when it's just a hole in the ground. New things, what does that mean? They must have come from somewhere, the newts you sit and watch for hours, and those weird white bats...' She stopped and stood up. 'Listen – Puppy would have started scratching at the door and setting up a fearful howl by now, but he's too quiet. It's dark, he must be too scared to move. You should have stayed with him.' She ran to the door and out into the garden.

'Joe! He's not here.' Then a few seconds later, a scream, 'You left the gate open. He's gone. Puppy! Puppy!'

Joe reluctantly put his plate of curry on the stove and took a swig of cider before going outside. 'He's got to be here. There's a strong latch on that gate, not much gate left but a hell of an iron latch, and I remember hearing it click ... fucking Ada ... how did that get open?'

'You didn't close it properly, can't have. You never do anything properly.'

They both rushed out into the field beyond the garden with Joe bellowing and whistling. 'He can't have gone far if he's as scared as you say. This is crazy. You said he couldn't walk far, so don't blame me. I'll go back and get a torch.'

He found two heavy duty ones that lit up the nearby fields and hedges in a wide arc. Looking for a tiny black dog at night, he thought, was crazy, but to suggest that they search in the morning

would be to ratchet up Helen's near hysteria. 'He's probably curled up in the bracken asleep.'

'With all the row we are making? And he hasn't had any dinner.'

'I used to find with the dogs I had that bashing a bowl with a spoon would do the trick,' shouted Joe, heading back to the house and another mouthful of curry. He stood at the door creating as much noise as he could with a tin plate. Helen had disappeared into the night, so he ran after her, shouting about watching her step.

'He's lost, Joe, wandered off and got lost. And those eagles …'

'Not at night.'

'Or foxes. Or badgers. He's so very tiny.'

Although this small drama meant she would have to stay the night, Joe knew that if the wretched animal wasn't found her mind would not be on making love to him and they would be out in this windy, moonless darkness all night.

Joe put his arm round her, partly to comfort her and partly to stop her dashing wildly off into the night. 'Let's think calmly. Or rather, like a puppy. Say he got a little bit disorientated, what would he do? You know, I'm sure I shut that bloody gate.'

Helen shook her head, 'I don't know what he would do. Why would he stray far from the kitchen where there's food and … and me.'

'I think he'd pick up our earlier scent and go the way we walked. I don't think the dark means much to animals, day and night are all the same to them.'

'But we went down there, to the quarry, and he didn't like the stones.' Her voice trembled. 'And you said there's all sorts of wild things down there.'

Joe was half-way down the quarry slope, running and slithering, the torch throwing out a broad, swinging beam. 'Yes, but nothing too scary. This is the Peak District not the Amazon.'

'It's no good.' Helen shouted after him. 'He wouldn't go down there, not that far. He wouldn't walk on those sharp chippings, they hurt his feet. Come back, Joe.'

But Joe had reached the quarry floor, his torchlight searching in a wide sweep round the cliff face, disappearing from time to time into a crevice or cave.

Helen caught up with him. 'We are wasting time down here, Joe. He'd never come this far, and he wouldn't go into those awful mines, they go on for miles into the hillside.'

'He might – it's raining a bit. They aren't mines, love …'

'Oh no, I've just thought. He could have fallen down a mine shaft, there are hundreds of them that haven't been covered over …'

'This is a quarry, not a mine. Keep quiet, we may hear something.'

No sound came from the quarry, apart from a trickle of water splashing down the rock face.

'Let's go back up to the top, Joe, and call for him up there. He could have gone back home by now.'

Joe did a final sweep with the beam of his torch and it lit up two bright disembodied eyes that glinted gold in the light.

'Helen! He's here. But how the devil … stupid little bugger, why isn't he barking?'

'Where? I can't see anything.'

'Do you see that small island, the one you said you liked earlier? It's really no more than a patch of mud that has grassed over. He's on that.'

Helen took her shoes off and stepped into the water. 'Don't move, Puppy, we're here.'

Joe grabbed her. 'No you don't. He may be only a few metres away but the water is too deep. And you can't swim.' He took off jeans and woollen cardi, waded for a few steps and then started to swim out but Puppy, after a few hesitant splashes, swam to meet him. Or rather, he swam to Helen on shore, neatly avoiding Joe's outstretched hand.

'Ungrateful little runt! He could have saved me getting wet.'

'Puppy darling!' She scooped him up. 'Isn't he clever? He can swim!'

'So why the hell didn't he swim over earlier when we were calling for him? Or bark when he heard us? Stupid mutt. Come on, I'm getting back to the fire. And the curry.'

The old house felt warm and safe, massive stone walls more than a match for the chill night air and determined drizzle. Puppy and Joe were toweled dry and fed.

'Don't you want the rest of your curry?'

Helen shuddered. 'I couldn't eat a thing. I'm moving on to your bottle of gin to recover from shock.' Puppy in one arm, she stroked Joe's back with the other and kissed him. 'You may be a prize idiot in most ways, but I loved the way you plunged into the lake.'

'My finest hour, though I could have done without it.'

They started to make love in front of the fire, and Puppy joined in, jumping on top of them and biting with tiny serrated teeth in jaws that seemed too big for his body.

'Get off you little bugger,' Joe growled, an unwelcome note of affection creeping into his voice. He picked Helen up and took her upstairs, shutting the bedroom door. Puppy howled outside but neither of them heard him, so after a while he went down and demolished Joe's slipper in revenge.

'It really was very brave of you, love, diving into that freezing, black water to rescue him. I know you like him really.' Helen climbed on top of him again, feeling an unusual mixture of hero worship and a strong need for satisfying sex. 'I don't know how to thank you enough.'

'You're doing ok.'

❧

He wondered, several gins later and with the log fire revived, how much to say. He was sure he had closed the gate, remembered hearing the latch click and remembered how the dog had sat on its haunches and refused to go down the slope to the quarry. There would have been no reason for him to swim out to that mud bank, no inviting smells, no remembered trails. Best to try to forget the scare as Helen seemed to have done as she sat next to him on the sofa, while Puppy rejected his bed and slept on her lap, whimpering and yapping in his dreams.

'I don't want to worry you, Joe, living way out here all on your own most of the time, but I think someone was prowling about and they tried to steal Puppy.'

Joe snorted, then laughed and tried to cover it by kissing her cheek.

'Don't laugh. I just know that he wouldn't have walked on those sharp stones. I've learnt a lot about him in these few weeks and he won't budge if he doesn't want to. Someone must have picked him up.' She shivered. 'And I do believe you when you say you closed the gate.'

Got me there, Joe thought, wishing he'd allowed for a small doubt about the latch to creep in. 'But if anyone wanted to steal your valuable mutt, and he's nothing special moneywise as far as I can see, why head down to ...' Joe stopped.

'Oh, Joe. They must have thrown him in. They wanted to drown him.' She startled the sleeping pup by hugging him close. 'I know you think I've got a bit unhinged, not my usual businesslike self, but Dad never allowed me any pets. Said it upset him too much when they died. He couldn't bear the trauma.'

'He's got a curse on him, your mutt. First abandoned in Bakewell, now this. Kidnapped. Pupnapped. No, we've had too much cider and gin, love. That's a crazy idea. What if we sleep on it?'

'Does anyone hate you?' Helen stared at him, trying to see him through a stranger's eyes.

'Not a soul in the world.'

'Perhaps you wrote something nasty in the newspaper?'

'Never. It's all birds and bees and sunsets. Besides, he's your dog. It's more likely to be one of your holiday cottage rental clients; you forgot to tell them about the next door cement works.' That was enough, Joe decided. They would end up scaring themselves rigid. 'I think we just had a visitor and we were making too much sexy noise to hear them knocking, or just someone who fancied cuddling your puppy and he wriggled free. And who would not fancy him rotten? Let's get some sleep.'

❦

Helen was up early, putting Puppy on his lead even though the gate was firmly shut and there were no holes in the dry stone wall or the fence, marching him round the overgrown garden then back into the kitchen.

'I'll be off soon, Joe love. I've got four cottages to inspect today and I need to get back home first to change into some clean clothes.'

Joe noted the 'love' – so he was still in favour after last night's drama. He had been lying in bed remembering Webster's telephone call and his offer to buy the house, probably for peanuts considering the remarks he'd made about its condition. He had decided to tell no-one, certainly not Helen who would nag him for months to jump at the chance and start negotiating. And most definitely not his mother, who would track down the stranger and most likely sell the place over his head if she could; he wouldn't even put it past her to forge his signature on the deeds. He ran downstairs and fell over Puppy.

'I'd hoped you were just a bad dream, mutt. Thanks for doing coffee, darling.' Keep up the love-words and perhaps things could get back to happier days. 'How's the holiday lettings market doing?' Show an interest. 'What cottages have you got to see? I bet most of them are real little palaces.' He could imagine welcome packs of tea and coffee, milk and supermarket bread, pot pourri on the pine coffee table, useless miniature soaps and pretentious brass decorated ovens.

'Yes, the first one is in Ashford, used to be an old forge, renovated to within an inch of its life but still lovely. They'll get over a thousand a week for that – the Peaks will be booked solid by April. I could almost see the attraction of this hermitage of yours – almost. If you did a bit of work on it.' Helen stood up and Puppy leaped about, peeing with excitement at the sudden activity. 'You must come down to Bakewell in a few days and give me a hand.'

'To do what? Dust the Hepplewhite?' Joe put his arms round her and gave her a long and satisfying kiss.

'No, to take up some stone slabs in the patio.'

'Burying someone? That nosey old girl who lives in the upstairs flat? That sounds more like it, I'll be round.'

Helen pulled herself slowly away. 'No, we need a bit of soil so that he can …'

'Yes, I got the picture. Just up my street. Romance is not dead. Give me a ring and I'll come right over and create a pee patch. And a poo patch with anaerobic digester.'

Joe waved them away down the long stony path, Helen's pretend off-roader veering about to avoid water-filled potholes of unknown depth. It had been a sweet few hours he thought guiltily, almost as if he had deliberately left the gate open to give him a chance for heroics.

❧

Joe printed off four of his flood photographs, stuck them into thick cream mounts and protected each one with a plastic envelope. It still gave him a sense of pride and wonder that fresh and immaculate images could emerge from his grotty old barn of a house, like the way little African children come out of mud-huts dressed in bright white cotton, lace and frills. Magic.

He cycled into the village to combine some marketing with a bit of shopping. The old village shop in Stoneybrook had closed two years ago, but now perched reincarnated as general store and post office in a wing of the Miners Standard Inn. This suited everyone, since on busy holidays there would be tables for tea and coffee in the courtyard and space made for ices in the deep freeze. Joe bought some groceries then headed over to the only other surviving shop, one scorned as useless by residents of Stoneybrook who seldom went in there. The Art Studio probably didn't make much of a profit, Joe reckoned, but tourists loved it, imagining that the pottery and knitting and watercolours were produced by smock-clad villagers working by the fireside during the long winter months. Stoneybrook was often cut off by snow for several days, but the villagers dusted frost off their satellite dishes and joined in the national grief over economic downturns and the millions wasted on football teams and bankers' bonuses.

'Amazing photos!' enthused Lauren, the shop owner and potter, running clay-thickened fingers through her short blond hair in Joe's honour. 'Have you touched them up – you know, filtered them or something?' She knew that would be sure to get Joe going. He was a good-looking fellow, but a bit of a recluse. And what did he do

22

with himself up in that isolated dump year after year? She was tempted to find out, especially since that elegant girlfriend of his clearly couldn't hack it.

'Have I ever done that in the past? Mucked about with my pictures? I'm a nature photographer, Lauren. The clue is in the word nature.'

'But that golden floodwater – and purple shadows.'

'Your trouble is that you never really look at the world. Your eyes are down on that pottery mud all the time inventing your own little shapes.'

'You're a fine one to talk, Joe. Your eyes are stuck behind a camera most of the time, looking for a prize-winning shot of disasters, while the rest of us down here in the dale are fighting the floods and trying to save our hard-earned possessions. You could come down from the heights and give us a hand next time.'

'Good idea, and I could get some action shots of the local peasantry battling the elements as they've done for centuries. Just the sort of thing The Bugle loves to print. It might even make the Derby Telegraph.'

Lauren threw a wet lump of clay at him. 'Have you got time for a coffee?'

'Sorry, I'd love to, but my editor has got some idea I'm working for him. Keeps pestering me for prize-winning journalism on Peak District floods.'

'Well, you can make me one next time I venture up to Blackridge. Meanwhile, these river photos of yours will sell like hot pots.'

Or very much better, Joe hoped, getting on his bike. Who did buy all those pots and bowls and mugs that seemed to spin off wheels in every converted barn, mill and old forge in the country? He'd had the same four mugs and assorted plates for years; he could only imagine other people broke more stuff than he did. 'I'll leave them with you then. Give me a ring when you want some more.'

'I'll be wanting some more prints of your snow scenes, visitors love buying those in summer. Glad they weren't here and snowed in, I suppose. I'll come up and choose some.'

Joe fixed the bag of groceries more firmly to the handlebars to stop it swinging and set off.

Alan Wood the publican of The Miners Standard called out to him as he went past. 'Did you hear about the quarry, Joe? Well, I suppose you must have done, seeing as it's yours.'

Joe stopped. 'Hear what?'

'Park up for a bit and I'll tell you about it. I just need to move these sandbags before some customer falls over them and sues me.'

Joe went in and bought a drink. 'Is this some new way of getting customers, Alan? Making up gossip.'

'I was hoping you could tell me a bit more. We had some bloke in here this morning said there'd been an accident up at the quarry yesterday. A rock fall, and a twitcher got hurt. It's a dangerous place, always has been.'

'What sort of time? I didn't hear anything.'

'Not sure, but it was getting dark. There were two of them and one had a nasty fall when the cliff face gave way. They tried to phone for help but couldn't get a signal. After a few hours his mate managed to drag the injured one out. It must have been getting late by then.'

What with Puppy yelping and the pair of them being noisy in bed, Joe reckoned they could easily have missed a few cries for help.

'We didn't hear anything, but it's a bit strange we didn't see anything of two people wandering about earlier. And then, later, no-one came to ask for help. How did they get back? What the hell were they doing up there in the first place?'

'That's as much as I know. I thought you might fill me in on ambulances or rescue helicopters. You're the one we rely on to spread the news, you and that Bugle lot.'

'There was nothing like that. Certainly not an ambulance – you know it would have trouble getting up my track. Perhaps they never did get a mobile signal, poor buggers. I often try for hours. Or more likely your customer got the whole thing wrong and there never was an accident.'

'Never mind. I expect it'll be in the paper next week, but I'm surprised they didn't contact you, being the landowner. And I'm

surprised your Ma didn't hear anything. She's a sharp one, doesn't miss much.'

Joe remembered he had said '*we* didn't hear anything' but he wasn't about to explain. No point in getting local gossips talking and saying what a nice girl Helen was and how glad they were she was back and why didn't he buck himself up a bit?

'I'll give you a hand with the other sandbags out the back, Alan, then I'll be off. Sorry I couldn't oblige with a murder or at least a fatal accident.'

'Thanks. Maybe see you this evening then? In the village hall I mean.'

'What's on? Is it film night? I tend to lose track.' He always intended to go, even if it was foreign with subtitles, because it was great the way tiny villages made their own entertainment. Visitors often said there was more happening in Stoneybrook than in their town suburb even if it was only competitive dominos, Wakes Week or Well Dressing.

'No, the meeting about the houses. There's a plan afoot to build a block of social housing on Painter's Field and a row of affordable semis. The Parish wants to nip the idea in the bud. Haven't you seen the yellow planning notices up in the village? There'll probably be the usual village whingers sounding off about social security scroungers, then they'll be down here getting pissed on their pensions.'

'First I've heard.'

'Now that really has been in the local paper, but I suppose if it hasn't got fur or wings then you don't notice anything.'

Joe smiled. 'And I reckon that's the best way. Critters never cause as much trouble as folks. Strange that Lauren in the craft shop didn't mention it, though.'

Alan grunted. 'She's been keeping her head down, sitting on the fence.'

'Uncomfortable position.'

'She probably thinks more houses means more customers, but I don't reckon them in social housing would buy her arty pots.'

'To be fair,' Joe countered 'she sells my stuff as well, and May Vernon's intricate knitted sweaters. We need all the trade we can get.'

Best not to comment about new housing, Joe thought as he pedalled away. He wasn't sure how he felt about it. People deserved houses, but buildings needed wood and stone, stone from beautiful Peak District landscapes. More hideous scars on the hillside – it did not bear thinking about. No wonder there were disputes among villagers. He'd only been in the village just over an hour and discovered insurrection in the village hall and drama in the quarry.

3

A Mysterious Accident

Joe rang Fred at the newspaper. 'Did you get anything in about an accident in the quarry last night?'

'What quarry? There's dozens of the things.'

'My quarry, the one behind my farmhouse at Blackridge. I heard in the village – Stoneybrook that is – that there had been an accident.'

'No, nothing's come in to me. But how come you didn't hear stuff going off if it's right behind you? Why ask me?'

'Because we didn't see or hear anything, and we were out there last night.'

'We? Who's we?'

'Long story. But don't sound so grudging, Fred, I'm giving you a hot tip. You could check the police and the hospital.'

'Who told you about this?'

'Alan at The Miners Standard – no apostrophe.'

His boss snorted. 'That whole village is inbred and barking mad, and their publican's the worst. He's always seeing alien aircraft and spy planes, but I'll ring round and see if there's anything in it. If there is, I'll expect a story from you in the morning.'

'How many times have I told you, Fred, it's not my kind of ...'

Fred rang off.

It was a day of generous bursts of sunshine, so Joe got out his deckchair and sat in a sheltered spot out of the cold wind. It was warmer here than it was in the old house, and he wanted to think about yesterday, to re-live the moments with Helen and compare his feelings with when he was alone. There was certainly a warmer, livelier feel to everything when she was around. But she could be demanding. Or perhaps he was being unreasonable, too quick to

judge and doubting whether his precarious way of living and working could ever make life comfortable enough for her.

Even that exuberant Puppy and his night time adventure had been almost enjoyable, though the water had been paralyzingly cold.

Joe suddenly remembered Helen's sighting of the binocular man, and he went and got climbing boots and set off for the quarry. He took his camera and notebook so that the afternoon walk would have a pleasurable purpose rather than just checking up on a nervous Helen and gossiping villagers. He would do a circular walk round the edge of the quarry and look for signs of rock fall. As usual he had not asked enough questions when Alan gave him a lead, he hadn't got a reporter's ferreting instinct. Had the mystery accident happened on the ridge with the victim falling down when the edge gave way, or on the quarry floor with the victim hit by rocks? What had the publican said? Either way any disturbance in rocks or soil would be easy to spot and photos of the disaster spot would earn him a few gold stars from his editor. It was all probably a rumour, or illegal lampers hunting at night, although he'd had many a set-to to with that lot before and they usually made a row with shouting and klaxons and dogs. Last night had been quiet apart from him and Helen shouting for the mutt. There had been no sign of anyone. No sign? He suddenly thought about footprints. Talk about the bloody obvious. If the pup hadn't walked then he'd been carried. If people had come to grief in his quarry, there would be footprints. The place must have been as busy as Bakewell on a Bank Holiday.

The quarry was vast, so that at times you lost sight of the other side of it as the cliff edges curved round. It had once been a natural fault, a rocky hollow exploited and deepened by both miners and quarrymen in times beyond local memory, but now bushes and trees softened not only its rim but the rock face too. Joe always thought it looked like a setting for one of those surreal films set in vaguely prehistoric times where unconvincing dinosaurs lumbered out of caves and pterodactyls flapped on too-small ledges.

In spite of local belief that children had vanished over the crumbling edges and sheep and goats mysteriously disappeared,

no doubt rotting in the lake, the rim of the quarry was firm. It would take dynamite to shift it, as it often had. The sun reflected heat from boulders and sitting in a sheltered spot you could forget that it was early spring. Joe was distracted from his investigations by a sturdy clump of aconites and a wild hellebore; he would get lovely pictures but it was a pity that no camera could capture the warmth burning through his jacket and the scent of fresh spring growth.

His phone rang and Fred's harsh tones insulted the peaceful afternoon. 'That publican was talking out of his arse and I've wasted a good hour checking round hospitals, GPs and the police. No-one knows a thing.'

Joe had only covered about a third of the quarry but he did not want his show of initiative to be wasted. 'I'm up at Blackridge now checking for signs of an accident. Alan at the pub did say that one of his customers had told him about it, so you could ask him who it was. It wasn't a local.'

'Or perhaps I might just not bother. Most of the villagers are soft in the head and usually pissed so I'll save myself the trouble.'

'There was something else,' Joe said slowly. 'My girlfriend thought she saw someone on the cliff yesterday evening.'

'You didn't mention that before.'

'That's because I didn't believe her. Or I thought it was just a twitcher. Nobody screamed or shouted for help.'

'Well, let me know if you find a body. Photo and text in before six. And no more sunsets or bloody snowdrops.' Fred rang off.

Joe went on walking; it was several years since he had done a complete round of the quarry because he usually aimed at a particular rock stack to watch for nesting birds or a small copse to wait for deer. Now he was surprised to note how gorse and birch and thick undergrowth had colonised the cliff top. There were few sheep to graze and control new saplings these days and no cows. Two of the local farmers had sold up due to poor livestock prices and falling subsidies. There was now so much vegetation to grab and hang on to that you would have to be suicidal to fall over the edge. An hour later and he was back at his house with no photos

of landslides, corpses or footprints. False alarm. He did not bother to report back to the office.

❧

Puppy was getting to be a problem. Helen worked her way round the holiday cottage inspections, making sure that the owners had done everything to create an almost unnatural air of calm and tradition and had provided all the comforts listed in the brochure. She had no trouble imagining the arrival of those holidaymakers who were often on their first visit to the Peak District. They would stare spellbound at the distant grey-blue hills framed by stone-set windows or be daunted by the sheer cliff that rose at the edge of the courtyard, its splintery face softened by ferns and rock roses.

She met the Health and Safety inspector for the two cottages that were new on their books. Puppy slept in the car for hourly naps, so she was getting used to working round cottages in the time he allowed her, then getting back to the car. Inspectors and mainte-nance men were deftly organised so that she could leave them to finish their work; much longer than an hour and a bored dog would chew his way into the upholstery. She couldn't blame him if he peed on the seat or started to howl in a heart-rending pitch that suggested abused and neglected animal to indignant passers-by.

She hoped her frantic timetable would not last for long. In a few months Puppy would be fully grown, house-trained, calm and patient, guarding the flat. Exactly how this transformation would take place she was not sure. The only certainty was that Puppy would grow and eat, eat and grow, and they would learn to accommodate each other. Until that time tasty oriental rugs and antique chairs were put into the spare room. It shouldn't be that difficult to second-guess his antics.

After work they went for a walk by the river and Puppy chased the geese and ate the tourists' duck bread. One of these days, Helen feared, a total stranger would shout out 'There's our puppy! You've got our Jasper.' Or Rufus, or Sam. Because surely no-one could have dumped such a wonderful creature? They must just have lost him. At least those careless strangers she was imagining would have given him a proper name. She took to taking their walks a different

way, along the water meadows towards Haddon Hall where fewer people went; in two or three months he would be a different, unrecognizable, fully-grown dog and they would be safe.

At home Helen wrote up fanciful notes on the holiday cottages ready to take into the office the next morning to send to the printer, then she curled up on a bean bag next to Puppy's bed. He wasn't allowed on the cream linen sofa, but there was nothing in her self-imposed rules that said she couldn't get down to his level. Of course, this silly behaviour would stop when Puppy grew up and didn't look such a helpless scrap. A scrap that within days – hours – had completely dominated her flat. Was he a Joe substitute? Crap psychology, she knew, but when she had decided not to live with Joe any more the small animal had taken the edge off the dead silence in her flat.

The facts had to be faced, she was not the right person to share Joe's spartan existence, his lack of desire for basic creature comforts, lack of real ambition. She had hoped that by leaving him he would feel the emptiness of his cold stone pile – surely the occasional rescued stoat or hare wasn't enough company? But instead she missed his undemanding good-nature even more, and the way he teased her and the way he … Puppy lay on his back and begged to be tickled, as though sensing that Helen's attention was somewhere else.

Not that she was doing much better than Joe in the ambition stakes; her Sheffield degree in English and the inspiring revelations of the set books on the literature course had not aroused any deep story-telling desire. Teacher training had luckily involved some early work experience, soon enough to warn her that she was no match for cynical and heartless teenagers or even manipulative six year-olds.

Now she worked in the Bakewell holiday lettings office on the Buxton Road with a newly discovered sense of purpose. The little cottages where once lead miners or farm hands had lived were now pressed into service with log burners, espresso machines and floral duvets to attract the world to the Peaks. Helen found that she cared in a way that surprised her when she welcomed holidaymakers

who smiled with delight at ferns and foxgloves in dry-stone walled gardens and at the views of peaks, high ridges and moors from the deep-set windows. Why would they ever want to go anywhere else?

Time for an after-supper walk; she almost missed Joe's isolated farm garden where Puppy could leap and stalk early gnats in the tall grass. From her flat it needed an expedition past the pudding shops, post-card stands and pubs to the floodplains. At least he would not get lost or stolen, clipped firmly onto his lead and tugging her down to the banks of the Wye. She had got used to the regular walks routine, so that after only a few weeks she could not imagine her day without the familiar pattern that the dog imposed. The three tiny meals a day and valiant attempts at house training that frustrated her and left him puzzled by her angry looks.

The flat had a small patio garden with old paving stones keeping a cluster of shrubs at bay; digging up three or four of those slabs would provide a small dog-friendly space. It was a good idea for now, but how big would Puppy get? Perhaps she could persuade Joe to adopt him, to train him not to destroy his beloved wild flowers or interrupt his long bird-watching hours.

They walked towards the river and out of town, disturbing cows and other dog walkers whose sedate, obedient pets seemed offended by the leaping pup, but half way back, sensing the return journey was now under way, Puppy refused to go any farther and had to be carried. Back in the small garden Helen tried to decide which slabs to take up. Would her landlord notice if she hid them behind the shrubs?

'Heard anything from the police yet?' Mrs Bonsall, her upstairs neighbour returning from market, rested her shopping bag on the wall.

'Why the police? What's happened?'

'I mean about that dog. It doesn't seem right you should have the trouble of it. I could hear it whining all yesterday evening.'

'Yes, he loves your radio. Started howling as soon as the Archers' music came on.'

Mrs. Bonsall was too intent on rescuing her shopping bag from a leaping dog for Helen's defensive note to halt the indignant stream

of complaint. 'What sort is it anyway? He'll get too big for our apartments, you can tell that by the legs he's got on him. He'll be too much for you, what with you working and being out most of the time.' She spotted some holiday cottage brochures that Helen had left on the garden table to sort through, anchored by a chunk of limestone. Mrs. Bonsall loved a good neighbourly chat, but never found the generosity of spirit to hit the right note.

'Those holiday cottages ruin villages. In my sister's village half the houses are empty most of the year and she says looking at all those dark windows depresses her. No-one to talk to and a person could easily die and not be …'

'Shall I take your bag up for you? I think the light on the stairs has gone again and it's getting a bit dark.' Helen hoped that when she got to Mrs. Bonsall's age she would have found more reasons to be cheerful.

❧

Joe answered the phone, hoping it was Helen.

'Did you go to that meeting in the village hall last night?' his editor asked.

'No. The whole village was in such a ferment over the thought of a new estate that I thought the debate was in safe hands and I didn't need to go.' He hesitated, 'and to be honest I sort of feel sorry for people who couldn't even afford to buy my old place.'

'Yes, from what I remember you could do with a new house. But that wasn't why I rang. Rumour has it that if developers get the go-ahead for a new estate then your old quarry might be re-opened for limestone. It would mean that heavy lorries loaded with stone wouldn't need to clog up the main roads, they could just use the track past your farmhouse then straight down to the building site in the village. I rang the Peak Park Authority but they wouldn't comment. Could you find out who started that hare running about your quarry? Joe? Are you still there?'

'Yes, still here. They wouldn't dare dig this old place up. It's only just started healing over. It's taken over sixty years…'

'Healing? That's a bit emotive and spiritual.'

33

'Sorry Fred, but it won't happen, and I'll tell you why if you want me to be prosaic and practical, like your bloody boring headlines. New houses in Stoneybrook just wouldn't sell. There's no jobs, no shops to speak of, no transport. There's no gas, power cuts every other day and snowed in for weeks in winter. It's sad, but this is no place for young families.'

Fred Marshall whistled down the line, 'Whew! Write all that down for me and that bit about Old Mother Nature in the quarry, plus a few more facts and figures to balance your embarrassing emotion. Headline: "Peakland Village is the Pits. Not Fit for Human Habitation" slams Naturalist Joe.'

Joe put the phone down. It rang again. 'No Fred, it's not a joke, conservation may be an easy target for media types like you, if The Bugle qualifies as media …'

Helen said hesitantly 'It's me. I really loved yesterday. I want you to know that. I just wish we could work something out, talk about what we both want.' She did not have the heart to add that whatever they worked out would have to involve a more comfortable lifestyle than the one Joe enjoyed. She would have to persuade him to move. They said love could move mountains, but nothing about quarries.

'How about a talk now, Helen? I could do with a drink but not on my own. I've just had a bit of a shock. I'll be over to you in about half an hour. See you outside the Red Lion?'

Helen found her boots and coat and tried not to look at Puppy who knew these exciting signs. 'Best not,' she explained 'I may need to concentrate on Joe for a few minutes without you playing up all the time. You stay and howl at the neighbours.' She hid a few biscuits in his bed, playing for time, and fled.

Bakewell was deserted and frosty, black hills in the distance under a bright moon with a fuzzy halo. It had been a sunny day, so pubs and tea shops had ventured out onto pavements with benches and tables ready for the spring visitors. Helen sat for a few minutes on a bench laced with frost watching the Buxton Road that was really the A6 in denial. Then gave in to the glow of the welcoming flames she could see through the pub window and went in to stake

a claim to two armchairs near the fire. Joe had sounded … anxious? Disturbed? Definitely unlike him. He must be worried to be tempted into the tourist metropolis of Bakewell without being driven by lack of provisions. Just for an evening drink and a chat? Now was probably not a good time to mention heaving up paving slabs. She guessed that Joe's unbusinesslike relationship with the editor of The Bugle had led to harsh words. He'd probably had a favourite wildlife article rubbished.

Joe came in with a burst of icy air and kissed the top of her head. 'What, no mutt? He'll be destroying the place in revenge.'

She stroked his cold, bristly cheek. 'Dry cider, please and some sort of chocolate in a fair sized slab.' No questions, she'd just wait to find out what the problem was.

'I needed to get out of the village and see a friendly face.'

She noticed his pint was already half gone before he got back to the fireside. 'I always thought your Stoneybrook locals were quite friendly, but I'm sure I can do even better if it's sympathy you want.' That sounded all wrong, like gushing friends meeting by chance. 'I mean, I was going to ask you what the shock was, but … well, I was giving you a bit of space.'

'And I suddenly found I didn't need space, I needed you. I got a bit rattled earlier. I had an upsetting phone call.'

Helen got him another pint. 'Tell me what happened. Unless it makes it worse.' Perhaps it was his mother nagging him about what a mess he'd made of his life, but that would not come as a shock.

'You know I've been working on a book, a photographic record and the story of an old quarry – my old quarry – returning to nature.'

Joe gulped his beer and Helen kept quiet. She knew all that, so what was his problem? She couldn't quite see the attraction of such a spooky hole, but she'd seen his quarry photos and they were spectacular and had almost persuaded her that a hole in the ground could be a place of beauty. Had someone else beaten him to it? Stolen his pet book project?

'They want to build a new estate in Stoneybrook …'

'Oh, I heard about that. It'll never happen; it would double the size of the village and developers will back off once they realise

what's involved – new roads and gas and drainage for that flood-plain on the Wye.'

'That's what I told my editor when he rang me about it, but developers are short of work these days and hard up. They'll do anything …. what if they … I should have gone to that meeting in the village. The worst thing is they want to take the limestone from my quarry, blasting and digging and killing everything.'

Soothing words like never mind or it'll be all right wouldn't convince Joe or anyone these days when government and councils were obsessed with building quotas. Helen could only put her arm round him and say 'Getting planning permission would be almost impossible. Finish your drink and I'll make you a coffee at home. Leave your car where it is.'

'One minute I feel it's unthinkable, such destruction in a National Park, next minute I worry that the bastards always seem to win in the end. No-one has the guts to stand up to them.'

They walked back in silence, waiting for the right moment for Joe to face his fears and work himself into a useful state of anger. It took Puppy an age of leaping, gyrating and nipping before he calmed down after the excitement of seeing his rescuer again.

Joe had never liked her flat, saying it was too grand, too enclosed, facing a row of pretty stone cottages with only a distant view of hills towards Hassop. Bakewell, sitting comfortably and smugly in its valley, protected from the moors and edges with their icy blasts, was only fit for tourists.

'Bastards!' Joe helped himself to a digestive biscuit and aimed one at the dog. 'They've got no idea what they would be destroying, and they wouldn't care even if they did know.'

'That's better, love. I've never seen you look so disturbed before and it unnerved me. You are usually so calm and … solid. Anger is better. Those meetings are all talk, just so Peak Park can say it's arranged a public consultation. They don't want more quarries any more than you do. Nothing will happen.'

'Why do we need to keep blasting great holes in the countryside? What's wrong with timber houses, or mud huts like the old wattle and daub? They lasted for centuries.'

'Now you're being daft. Haddon Hall wouldn't exist without quarries, nor would Bakewell.'

Joe gave a hrrumphing sort of laugh. 'Quite. But oak beams, timber frames and wattle and daub look great and cost next to nothing, so why not use them?'

'And nor would your ancient pile exist, with its great stones cut from the rock and dragged up the hill.' Helen poured more coffee and got some brandy to soften the edges of logic. 'I often wonder about quarries.'

'You do? I'd never have guessed it.' He put both arms round her and held her close. 'Tell me what you wonder.'

Puppy barked frantically, not sure whether this was attack or play, and Mrs. Bonsall banged on her floor above making him even more excited.

'It's as though everything is turned inside out, the rocks excavated just to scatter the Derbyshire Dales with a jumble of rough-hewn villages. And I can't find it in me to say I wish it hadn't happened. Except,' Helen hesitated, 'when I'm looking across to distant hills and there's a great scar of excavation or a cement works. Was it worth it? I don't know what I think.'

' I think it's time we knew better. The old stone villages are lovely, but they belong to the past and it can't be allowed to go on. It's time we used wood or made some kind of recycled plastic out of all our great landfill waste, stuff like those mock-wooden park benches are made of. Or go back to medieval times when villages were timber framed. Did you know that there weren't any of your pretty stone cottages before about fifteen hundred?'

'Please don't come out with ideas like that if you do go to any public meetings, Joe. They'll think you're a crank and they won't take you seriously. I'm the only one who knows you're not completely barking and even I'm not sure sometimes. You are staying the night, aren't you? Tomorrow you'll find out that your editor was just winding you up. He's a trouble-making old bugger, it's the only way he can stir up any scandal.'

&

Over breakfast, Joe, becalmed amid an array of pale oak fittings that disguised dishwasher, food blender and puzzling gadgetry, admitted that permission for a new estate in his village was unimaginable and unlikely. But even so ...

'The worst thing is my editor wants me to investigate the quarry rumour and come up with a story. Even if he is bullshitting just to sell papers, if I start investigating in order to prove him wrong it will be like admitting that there could be some truth in it. I can't face it.'

Helen put beaten-up eggs and milk in the microwave then did some toast. 'Just be your usual immoveable self and refuse to do it. Or, more subversively, we could find out who the developers are and what their plans look like, then we could ...'

'You keep saying we, Helen.'

'I fancy having a day off and doing a bit of sleuthing. After all, it isn't entirely unconnected with the holiday cottage business. The company's got three properties to let in Stoneybrook and who'd want to spend their holiday next to a building site?'

'I know what you're doing, Helen, and you're a love to think of cheering me up, but I still don't feel ...'

'We could write our own version of the story for the press, play your Fred at his own game and find some of those endangered newts on the development site or discover an ancient curse on the meadow so that no builder would want to go near it. Make the facts prove whatever we want. Isn't that what you reporters do all the time?'

Joe ignored the provocative reporter label and ate his eggs.

'Time is money,' Helen announced profoundly, 'so if we confuse the issue by telling enough lies about floodplains and marshes, underground mines and subsidence, the developers will lose interest and go for the easy money somewhere else.'

'I thought you said it wouldn't happen, so why would we need to go to all that trouble?'

'It won't happen, but I was just enjoying the idea of wielding a bit of power. It makes a change from writing holiday brochures. Now eat up before Puppy pees lovingly over your foot because it's

time for morning walk and we have our routine. I've got responsibilities these days you know.'

Joe stood at the window finishing his coffee and staring gloomily at the townscape of souvenir shops and the Co-op. 'What's that woman doing in the front garden?'

'That'll be Mrs. Bonsall from upstairs doing her morning inspection for chip papers and beer cans. She'll probably want to know if I had a man here all night. Give her a wave.'

'Helen, were you serious about rubbishing the plans for the new estate?'

'Better to know the facts,' Helen persisted as they walked, 'than just to hope it will all go away. And if there aren't any facts then we'll invent some. You're the writer. We'll start by finding someone who was at the village meeting, someone with a few brain cells.'

Joe sighed miserably. It was not his kind of work but perhaps he could just scribble down a few lines for The Bugle, a few negative lines about the cruelty of plonking young families down in the middle of nowhere. Phrases such as family break-up, mental illness, stress and delinquency. At least Fred would be pleased if he and Helen produced some half-true, lurid copy. He only had his half-job to lose. The idea began to cheer him up. 'We could give it a try. I'll go back to my place first to get camera and notebook. We've done our doggy duty for today, so does it have to come with us?'

'Puppy, the 'it' in question, will be fine for up to about an hour in your old tank while we do our interrogating. He can't make it much worse.'

4

Scare Tactics

Helen left a message for her boss explaining the value of thorough research into the threat of a new housing estate next to his holiday cottages and they bounced up the track to Joe's farmhouse.

'I'll come in and give Pup a drink. I forgot before I left home.'

But Pup wouldn't move far from the car. He got out but refused to go past the gate, just sat and barked and whined.

'No drink then, he's obviously not thirsty. I won't be a minute, I'll change my … Christ! My front door's open!' Joe's muffled voice came from inside. 'There's stuff thrown about all over the place.'

Helen shut Puppy in the car and ran into the house. What did Joe have that anyone would want to steal? The living room was a very thorough and deliberate mess; some photos of kestrel chicks on a rock-face ledge had been torn in two, and a close-up of a plant labelled mouse-eared hawkweed was the object of even more anger. Or hatred, or spite.

'What have you done to annoy someone?' Helen shouted. 'This doesn't seem like an ordinary burglary.' These were only photo prints, and horrible though the destruction was, surely these days it was easy enough to … she heard Joe give a wail.

He had rushed upstairs to the box room he used as a study. Another wail, 'Bastards, I'll kill them,' before he launched himself downstairs. 'They've got my laptop. Could have been anytime last night.' Joe stopped at the front door with its broken lock. 'I've no idea which way to go. Or we could have passed them today on our way here and we wouldn't have known.'

So it was just a break-in, rather than hatred. Helen clicked on the Bakewell police station number on her mobile. 'Tell the police.'

'What can they do?'

'Not much, but tell them anyway. They know who fences electrical gear.' She handed him the phone.

'Fences? You've been reading too many … hello officer, I'd like to report a break-in.'

Helen went upstairs and started to pick up discs and notebooks thrown about the floor. Another destroyed photo, this time of an owl, its piercing gaze turned harmlessly towards a pair of socks. These torn-up creatures were more disturbing than the chaotic room. But something was not right, did not feel right. Something she had seen.

Joe called from downstairs 'I think we ought to go into the village to find out if anyone saw or heard anything.'

'You've got copies of everything? Discs and memory sticks?'

'I think so. And my camera was safe in the car.' Joe put his arms round her and held her tight. 'Sorry, it's a nasty shock for you too. Coming in like that with the front door open and not knowing who was about, whether they were still lurking about in here.'

'The clock is still there. That's what puzzled me; I knew there was something that didn't seem right. The old carriage clock that's worth far more to a thief than your laptop, it's still there in full view on the mantelpiece.'

'But kids wouldn't know it was worth much. Come on, your mongrel is destroying my car.'

'What about the front door? We can't leave it hanging open.'

'I'll find something to wedge against it. Shouldn't be difficult to find a few boulders.'

As they looked around the garden for a weighty object Helen suddenly grabbed Joe's arm. 'Look! Over there on the water butt.'

Perched dangerously on the rotting lid, shiny glinting metal against the blackened oak, was the laptop, a carelessly abandoned 21st century relic.

Joe rescued it carefully from above the slimy water. 'Someone's been playing silly buggers.'

'Someone with a cruel, unbalanced sense of humour. They could have ruined your book plans, destroyed your photos and discs for

ever. There's some kind of weird message in balancing a laptop on that pile of festering timber. We'll still need the police to look into it.' Helen tried to stop Puppy ricocheting round in the car as Joe bounced it over the old miners' paving slabs and down into the village. 'What do we do now? Burglary investigation or inventing newspaper stories?'

In Stoneybrook they started off at The Miners Standard where the small group of regulars was always ready for fresh local gossip. Puppy was introduced to the exciting possibilities of the bar room floor. Joe's phone buzzed as they were about to start on their pints. It's the boss,' Joe groaned, looking at the familiar number. 'Shall I take it? He'll be grinding on about the meeting I failed to get to.'

'Yes, take it. Give him the same spiel I gave my boss – important research in the line of duty. We're in the right place for informed opinions. Hold the phone up' Helen suggested, 'so your editor can hear the lively debate.'

There was a cackle of approval from the merry drinkers and a few loud comments on ingenious ways of recycling the local newspaper.

The editor's irritated voice filled the low-beamed bar. 'Joe? Are you listening? I need some copy by tomorrow. I don't need stuff I can get from the minutes of that consultation meeting, they'll be online on the council website. I need the villagers' reactions. Get some names and make it a bit personal. See if you can wind them up a bit … it could turn into something big, a national protest like with the Tree People at Nine Ladies on Stanton Moor.'

'I'm on the case, Guv, doing some interviews in the village, but there's been a bit of a hold-up. Well, more a break-in, really. Someone ransacked my place and seemed intent on destroying my wild life stuff, photos, discs and chapters for the new book, so I've not quite finished working on the piece about the meeting …'

'Your place was broken into? Never thought there was enough security out there, no alarm or decent locks even. Is it worth a story?'

'Thanks Fred, I'm fine. Kind of you to ask. Not hurt at all, in fact. Don't you worry.'

'Strange though, it sounds kind of vindictive. Anything valuable taken? Did you have anything worth taking?'

'They dumped my pc on top of the water butt, like a kind of threat. The lid is all rotten, it could have ...'

Fred broke into journalese: 'Famous wildlife writer and photographer, frequent contributor to this paper, targeted by mystery intruder intent on cruelly destroying a lifetime's work ...'

'It was no joke, Fred. Horrible sensation wondering if the intruder is still in the house, and finding some of my best work torn to shreds. I'll be in touch.' Joe clicked off the phone abruptly.

Helen took his hand. 'Drink up and forget about him. You are still in shock at seeing those torn-up critters. Kind of symbolic of something. In a demented way.'

The other customers had gone quiet, until one said 'Couldn't help hearing that, Joe. Nasty business you having a burglar, and one intent on doing senseless damage. Sounds a bit mental, like.'

Helen looked round at the small circle of eager faces. They would welcome any scrap of excitement to delay another boring potter round the village criticizing the neighbours' vegetables or muttering about incomers' expensive new extensions.

'Did any of you see anything or anyone? You don't miss much when you're sober. Could have been yesterday evening or early this morning. Any strangers in the village or anyone heading for Joe's place?' Helen stood poised, notebook and iphone ready to record.

They all looked suitably thoughtful but shook their heads. The landlord came up and joined the group.

'I didn't see anyone, but then a burglar wouldn't come in to the local pub when he's about to do a job, not if he's got his wits about him. I'll ask more of the other regulars this evening when we are busier. No-one can keep anything secret in this place – except when you need some useful information, then they all clam up.'

'Thanks, Alan.' Joe invested in another half-pint and a scrumpy for Helen. 'On another problem, did anyone go to the meeting about the new houses?'

There was a general outburst of heated opinion.

'About time we had some new development in Stoneybrook before it disappears up its own stuffy arse.'

'We don't want a new estate of social housing or we'll have break-ins every five minutes and kids hanging about.'

'You can't say things like that, it's some sort of discrimination. You can be done for that.'

'I can and I did. It isn't discrimination if it's only kids. If there's no jobs and no buses to get out anywhere, what else is there to do except thieving and vandalising?'

'But what about the meeting?' Helen tried for a few hard facts. 'Who was there from Planning? Was our MP there, whatsit McAndrew? What was the general mood of the other villagers?'

Joe got his camera out, switched to video and the opinions faltered into silence again.

'Who really went to the meeting?' Joe suspected that most of the comments were the result of rumour and gossip. His notebook page stared blankly up at him.

'I certainly went, because a new estate would ruin the character of the village.' This from Simon Gent, an accountant who ran his business mainly from his converted stable block.

'All very well for you lot with money, Mr. Gent, but my Samantha needs a new home. The flat she's got in Chesterfield is too small for her and the twins.'

'It's people like your daughter demanding houses and benefits …'

'What was the general mood of the meeting?' Joe interrupted before class war broke out.

'Hardly any of the residents bothered to go.' Simon Gent glared at Joe. 'So they'll get what they deserve. Public apathy in this country makes a mockery of democracy.' He drained his Courvoisier and went out.

Helen glanced at Joe's nearly empty sheet of notepaper. The snatches of conversation they had managed to record were mainly uninformed, resentful opinion. She tried again: 'I heard your local councillors were in favour of the development.'

45

This provoked a mainly unprintable torrent of accusations, of greasy palms, snouts in troughs and other stock phrases culled from the popular press. One said more soberly 'You'd have thought they'd have learnt about building on floodplains after all the disasters this year. That brook turns into a raging torrent at the drop of ... well, when it rains. Can only be offers of backhanders dulls their wits.'

'Greed, sheer greed, and bugger the rest of us.'

'Folks desperate for a cheap house don't think about flood insurance until it's too late.'

'Cheap? You must be joking! "Affordable" just means easy pickings for landlords.'

The publican said 'I went to the meeting because I don't know whether it's good or bad for the village or for me, but I reckon it's a foregone conclusion. The planning officer was talking about government targets having to be met. They don't listen to reasoned debate when it's all about targets. Councillor Ible didn't say a lot. I suppose he didn't know which way would affect his votes most.'

Joe scribbled a few notes then kissed Helen's cheek in gratitude and there was a cheer of approval. 'Thanks folks, but before you get back to your pints, did anyone see any suspicious characters round the village late last night or early this morning?'

There was a muted rumble of uncertainty and shaking of heads. He guessed that no-one in the bar had their wits about them much after nine o'clock in the evening.

'How about this morning? You're up round your farm by about six, Ted.'

'There was only Hubert in the milk tanker, same as usual. Nobody making a fast get away. If nothing got nicked then sounds like some looney. Could be anybody round here.' There was some laughter and a general feeling that computers were best put out of action and what did a few torn photos matter?

Joe took Helen's arm and steered her towards the door. 'We won't get any more out of this lot. I'd like to ask around the village about my break-in. We'll go and start with Lauren in the Art Studio.

Her place is on Main Road so she's got a good view of any vehicles heading for my track.'

'I thought she spent all her time making mud pies round the back of her studio.' Helen pulled a resisting hound out through chairs and stools where he'd been on the trail of a crisp packet. 'Though I don't know why she bothers. It's your atmospheric photos of the landscape and endearing furry critters that customers go for, not her boring brown pots.'

'So let's be especially grateful to her.'

Lauren appeared through the back door of the shop, slicing chunks of clay off her fingers with a dangerous-looking blade at the prospect of customers, then as usual running nearly clean fingers through her short hair. The result made her look like a medusa with Etruscan-style pottery waves.

'Hello Joe. Got some more great stuff for me to sell? Oh, hello Helen.' Then seeing Puppy dancing on hind legs to greet her, 'Oh, isn't he the sweetest little thing! I always wondered why you didn't have a dog up at your farmhouse, Joe.'

'He's mine,' Helen put in, deliberately letting the lead slip. 'Joe only likes wild animals but Puppy is working on that.' Lauren might do her best to ignore her but there was no ignoring a whirlwind of sharp claws and friendly nips.

'What a little darling. Can I pick him up?'

Joe feared a distracting love-fest. 'Lauren, did you see any strangers around yesterday or early this morning? Someone broke in to my place and turned it over, tore up some of my best pictures.'

'Joe! You poor thing! That's horrible.' She clutched his arm, smearing his jacket with a mixture of clay and green paint and at the same time trying to free her jeans from tenacious jaws. 'What a frightening experience. Were you there when it happened?' She turned to look at Helen, 'I mean, were you both there?'

'Of course not, or we'd have stopped it,' Helen snapped.

'Well, there could have been several intruders, they could have been armed.'

'So did you see anything suspicious or not? We need to act fast,' Helen persisted, trying to inject some urgency into the situation. 'If not, we'll ask others in the village.'

Lauren screwed her pleasant face into a thoughtful frown. 'I wish I could help, I'll try to remember. I didn't do pots yesterday, I was rearranging the shop window. I only had three customers, but none of them went off in your direction, and I don't suppose burglars buy ceramics on the way …'

Joe retrieved the dog lead. 'Get him to heel, Helen. If Lauren wanted distressed jeans she'd have bought them ready chewed.' Joe walked off up Main Road calling back 'Thanks Lauren. If you think of anything later, give me a call.'

'Oh, I certainly will. And your pictures are safe here with me.'

Joe took Helen's hand when she caught up with him and pulled her gently to a stop. 'You were rather sharp and grumpy with Lauren – she gets a good price for my photos and doesn't take much commission. Her little shop seems to fascinate visitors, for some unfathomable reason. They watch her slapping mud about and churning out endless identical pots and then they buy my pictures, and I need that money. You weren't helping with Joe Wright Marketing, so what was all that about?'

'She's so vague and dithery. Impossible to get any sense out of her. All she does is stare adoringly at you as though rendered speechless, gob smacked in other words, by your good looks and talent. Which is understandable, but most women manage to hide their infatuation a bit better.'

Joe threw a handful of wet grass at her and tripped over Puppy who joined in the fun. 'Now I get it. You're just about managing to hide your hots for me, and the strain makes you a bit of a cow. But getting back to my break-in, we aren't getting sense out of anyone. My intruder seems to have been invisible. Last try will be Margaret down the end of the ginnel.'

Two elderly residents sitting on a bench next to the horse trough said they had seen and heard nothing. They looked scared. 'Last year there were gangs of kids on bikes terrorizing the villages,' one said. 'The police can't stop them. I heard them again last night. The

yobs tear off up footpaths on those fat wheels. Off-roading they call it. There's going to be a law against it soon.'

'No, Olive. That's when it's jeeps. You must just have heard motorbikes in the distance, on the A6.'

Helen walked off.

'I think that was probably a bikers' rally from Matlock Bath. They look like leather-clad orangutans, and that's just the women, but really they are quite a pleasant and harmless lot. They are only interested in drooling over each other's bikes, and anyway, you'd have heard a load of motorbikes in the village last night. This is useless, Joe. I think we ought to go home and print off some posters to put up round the villages.'

'Margaret's house is just down here. She's always got her wits about her.'

Margaret Byron was a retired maths teacher who now worked part-time in the shop-in-the-pub when Alan and his wife were busy. Her cottage of jauntily random limestone and thick, stone-tiled roof was up a narrow pathway and then up the hillside by way of two flights of mossy steps, the curse of most elderly Peak residents. The climb either kept them fit or put them in expensive care homes in Bakewell.

'I don't know how she does this with a load of shopping,' Helen stopped for breath, 'but the view is worth it. There's Chatsworth one way and Yorkshire the other.'

'I've heard she gets it all delivered and spends her time playing the Stock Market online, with great success.'

Margaret had the kettle on by the time they reached her door. 'Lovely to see you both, I need some interesting distraction. Footsie's lost two percent today and the Nasdaq's even worse. You need to be up in the City watching ten screens at once, and even then the computers beat you to it. No chance for the ordinary punter. What a lovely little dog, he can have that wooden gnome, I never liked it. Are you out taking your lovely photographs, Joe? I've got two in my conservatory, the one of brown hares boxing and a misty one of Cheedale. Works of art they are, and a good investment.'

Joe explained about his break in.

Margaret shook her head. 'You'd think I'd see everything from up here, especially as my PC is in the window recess, but I didn't see your villain. What a mean, senseless thing to do.'

She turned to Helen, 'Lovely to see you, dear. You must feel quite exposed at the farmhouse, down that long track and with no neighbours. Let's hope your lovely puppy will be a good guard dog when he's bigger and can sort out any crims.'

She thinks I still live up there with Joe, Helen realized. Or does she think I ought to and that I don't know a good thing when I see it? Margaret was another of Joe's admirers.

'Puppy is loving that piece of cake.' Margaret had cut the iced fruit cake into four equal slices and given the dog one large indigestible chunk which would probably be spewed up in Joe's bone-shaker on the way back. 'It's delicious. Did you make it?'

'Lord no. Get them delivered from M&S in Chesterfield. Have some more.' She opened a glass-fronted bookcase and selected a green and gold tin from the stacks of shortbread and oatcakes.

They drank tea in front of a vast traditional Derbyshire stone fireplace, one of those that seem far too big for the room and more suited to a stately mansion. If Margaret had that impressively hewn stone monster in her modest cottage, what would Joe find, Helen wondered, behind the brown Edwardian tiles round the range in his farmhouse kitchen?

'I'm sorry I can't help you catch your criminal. It makes me feel angry just thinking about it. Give me your phone number, Joe, and I'll let you know if I see anyone suspicious. We ought to warn the rest of the village.'

'The trouble is,' Joe was into his second chunk of fruit-held-together-with-brandy cake, 'how would we know what's suspicious? Not all burglars helpfully wear balaclavas or hoodies.'

'I've developed a good eye for miscreants. Some of them are my ex-pupils and,' Margaret added with pride, 'they are quite professional.'

'Before we go,' Helen remembered, 'Joe's meant to be writing a piece for the Bugle about the plans for a new housing development

and he needs a few quotes. I suppose as a teacher you'd welcome young families into the village?'

'But would we get young families? If it's just affordable housing councils always seem gutless when it comes to setting out rules for purchasers. They ought to say the property can't be sold on for twenty years. That would stop speculators making a fast fortune. No, we've got six derelict cottages in Stoneybrook, let them start by renovating those. Get the council to buy them up, fund the repairs and give the local craftsmen some work. That's my quote.'

୭

Back at the house they felt a need to exorcise the intruder with some loud music, an extravagantly piled-up fire and a warm bottle of red wine. Torn papers and photographs of dismembered critters were cremated.

'We could do some posters about the break-in and I'll take them back with me. The trouble is, we haven't got many clues or sightings, no scary identikit images, but I can easily pin some flyers up in Bakewell and Ashford and some in villages on the way to Buxton or Sheffield – a getaway route. I could even stretch to a small reward. I feel a need for action,' Helen explained, 'but without really knowing what to do. We can't even guess at a motive. I just need to do something useful.'

'So do I,' said Joe, unbuttoning her shirt. 'We won't bother with anything else right now, just this. Warm skin and wine to help me recover from the shock. I could even need counselling.' He tried to lift her breasts out of her low-cut bra.

Helen pushed him gently away and filled up their glasses. 'Just the wine then for now, because the longer we leave it the colder our sleuthing trail will get. It's no surprise that the police aren't interested in torn up art photographs when they've got homicides in Derby to deal with. It's up to us.'

'There's no point, love. I've been thinking about the goings-on of the last few days and nothing makes sense, or perhaps I mean there's a kind of sinister sense. Someone is trying to worry me, but I haven't a clue why.' He consoled himself with kissing the creamy skin pushed up by the unyielding bra.

51

'Why do you say 'goings-on'? Have there been other burglaries you haven't told me about?'

'No, but there was some man who tried to be friendly walking past here and he was no rambler or holidaymaker. Then he rang me wanting to buy this place and he seemed to know things about me, as though he'd been watching me. Then there was that figure on the cliff top that you spotted who was out too late to be a twitcher. All that in the past few days.'

'And that terrible Puppy scare. We still don't know how he got in the lake.' Helen clutched at the sleepy pup at the thought of his disappearance. 'Now this senseless break-in with nothing stolen, just spiteful damage. Put it all together and things just don't seem like normal Derbyshire life. Even that strange rumour in the pub that you told me about – someone falling down the quarry face. Where did that come from?'

Helen looked pale and tense, so Joe lightened the mood. 'I think I've worked it all out. You have a half-crazed lover who wants to get rid of me. Or scare me into clearing off.'

She appreciated the brave attempt. 'Why would he go to all that trouble? Right now a cheap holiday somewhere hot and sandy and I'm anybody's. But let's think – what can we do? Do we just sit around helplessly and wait until the next bit of nastiness?'

Again Joe appreciated the 'we'.

'I could leave Puppy here with you for a few days; at least he'd bark – he's got amazing hearing.'

'When he isn't asleep and having exciting dreams.' Joe put his arms round her and kissed her neck. 'But I know what it cost you to make the offer. It seems that runt is part of the family now.'

'Do you think I'm getting paranoid about mystery strangers, Helen?'

'A bit. Strange things have happened, but I'm not sure that they are linked. Apart from spooking you, I can't see any reason behind them all, any common element. It might be worth asking your newspaper boss if you've upset anyone. Any complaints, or Letters to the Ed.'

'Meaning my writing is a crime against the English language? Most of the time I'm writing about bluebells, bambi and bunnies. The worst thing I do is slam the thoughtless public for dropping rubbish or disturbing nests – and thoughtless dog owners with dangerous beasts.'

'Newspapers – even local ones – provoke a lot of cranks with weird motives. Please Joe,' Helen took his head in her hands, forcing him to look at her, 'promise me before I go that you'll ask Fred the Ed and get him to headline your break-in. And you must keep on nagging the police. Even if they can't solve the crime, it will remind them that there is a problem that they haven't done anything about. Ask them to keep an eye on the place for the next few days at least. I hate leaving you. I feel we're being watched.'

'Are you going right now? Do you have to? Can't you stay and protect me, the pair of you?'

'I'd love to stay,' Helen found herself admitting, 'but I'll have a busy day at work tomorrow to make up for skiving off today. Though I think Adrian will understand when I tell him about your intruder. He's very hot on security in remote cottages, he's got cameras up in the most unlikely places.'

'There's a joke there somewhere but I can't quite work it out. Your boss can afford to muck about like that. He probably sets it off against his taxes.'

'Right now, love, you need to get that article on new housing out of the way, then write something about mysterious criminal happenings at Blackridge Farm, including the hideous attack on Puppy.'

'I expect Fred has already squeezed every last drop out of my burglary story. He'll reprint some of my best photos without paying me a penny.'

'But you can write it from a personal point of view – years of creative artistic genius destroyed, valuable archives, intimidating strangers, living in fear ...'

'Abduction and attempted murder of helpless pup.' Joe grabbed his camera and took a picture of sleeping Puppy, head on remains of slipper, tiny fangs gleaming in the flash. 'You're right. Perhaps

I need to be thinking more like a reporter, getting all the goings-on out into the public as a kind of protection. Watch this space.'

When Helen had gone Joe settled down to write. It wasn't his usual style, but Fred would use anything sensational in the Bugle if it livened up pages deadened by auction prices and charity runs.

Fred rang. Joe answered irritably: 'Bloody hell, it's nearly ten. We need to establish some sort of rules here, because you can't just …'

'You've won the jackpot, laddie. Millionaire at least. Your place will be worth a fortune if you play it right.'

'What are you on about, Fred?'

'I joked about them blasting up your old quarry – but now it's true. My squealer on the council says planning permission has been given for ten houses and, just as I said, the limestone comes out of the nearest hole – your hole, your quarry. I'll bet the houses are just an excuse for massive extraction rights.'

'But there hasn't been another meeting. I was determined to get to the next one and nothing's been …'

'No need,' Fred said, gleeful at the imparting of horrible news. 'They had a special meeting this evening and didn't need councillors or consultations. Delegated Powers it's called, and nothing's supposed to be made public for a few weeks … but I have ways …'

'Do shut up Fred, there's nothing clever or subtle about handing out a few tenners. You must have it wrong – Blackridge Quarry hasn't been worked for over sixty years. There's no access for hefty modern machinery and there's a lake to drain. Just for ten houses? It doesn't add up – you've been had.'

Fred was silent for a few seconds. 'Wishful thinking my son, and I can see you'd be upset. I can't understand how anyone could be fond of your windswept, derelict pile but once you realise the price you could get for that bit of land as a car and lorry park, not to mention the quarry itself …'

Joe switched his phone off. Fred must have been fed misinformation by some troublemaker, but now there was even more reason to send him a lurid story about the strange chain of events. Helen was right – work up public interest and put the place on the map

in a way that he had never wanted to before. His mother always said he was too secretive, never explained himself so that people could understand him better. Joe could never see why they would be interested, but now he'd make damn sure they got the full story.

His mother. The burglary. Oh hell.

❧

Sylvia Wright lived in an elegant terraced villa on the outskirts of Buxton. Although the moors stretched out across the Dark Peak from her small garden, she preferred to think that she lived a cosmopolitan life – life in a busy spa town that had a real Opera House, wealthy tourists and a Whiterose supermarket. Although Buxton has the reputation of being the coldest town in England, there were enough warm, sunny days for Sylvia to enjoy the café culture. If she sat on a pavement terrace for a while making a cappuccino last for half an hour she'd be sure to collect a group of friends ready for gossip.

Joe knew his mother's habits well enough. He would have to tell her about the break-in before she read it in the newspaper or was told about it by eager friends chatting in the Pavilion Gardens. Telephoning her was no good, she would have to see for herself that her son had not been attacked by intruders in his wilderness retreat. He would introduce it jokingly – as if any burglar could find anything worth stealing, probably felt sorry for him when they saw the state of his place and would never come back etc.

Joe went to her house first rather than scour the coffee shops; the fact that her car was in the drive meant little, because his mother was the new and furtive owner of a bus pass. The house – or villa as she insisted on calling it – was a grand early Victorian pile, built when Buxton Spa waters attracted the wealthy worried well. It had a breakfast room as well as a dining room and parlour, four bedrooms and an attic room for a long-departed maid. It had been a comfortable size for a family of three, but Joe's father had left when he was two and Joe did not remember him. He would, he felt sure, have traced his father to Dorset and his new life with Gerald, a wealthy hotel owner, but invitations to seaside holidays from the couple had gone unanswered. His mother explained later that the

pair of them would have been a bad influence on a boy, as if he might catch their gayness like a cold. The grown-up Joe imagined the scene over and over again, the chance to see a happier father and spend warm summers on the south coast but his father died when he was ten so he did not get the chance. He often wondered about visiting Gerald after his father died just to talk about his father with someone who had loved him but it seemed a difficult compulsion to explain to his mother and his courage failed him.

Joe stood in the hall at the bottom of the imposing staircase in a puddle of stained-glass sunlight and shouted, not expecting a reply. It was eleven fifteen on a sunny morning with no breeze so a quick tour of the pedestrian precinct should find her. He did a slow jog down the steep hill to the town centre glancing in the windows of the many small tea shops and coffee bars. There she was, at a table in the window ready to tap on the glass at any passing friends or neighbours.

'Joe, dear, how clever of you to track me down! Your usual mint tea?' They did not kiss, they never did, but Sylvia smiled at her son delightedly.

Joe was pleased that none of his mother's many acquaintances had been waylaid because he needed to get in there first. Once he was settled in at the little table Sylvia's friends would not like to intrude – strange how gossip went in generations and they would not feel comfortable chatting in front of a thirty-something youngster.

'Is this a special visit or are you shopping? I hope you can come back home for lunch. What about a few croissants now with your tea?'

'Thanks, I'll have a slice of Bakewell pud. You're looking well, Ma, I've always liked that stripey suit, I know spring's on its way when that suit comes out. I had a bit of a shock yesterday, someone tore up some of my best pictures.' He knew this would not register as great drama.

'How nasty for you. Uncalled for, even if they didn't like them … was it in that little shop in Stoneybrook with all the mugs and vases? Customers can be so difficult, I'd hate to have to deal with

the general public. I expect it was children, totally out of control most of …'

'No, someone broke into the house, but nothing was stolen.' Joe gave her vague and reassuring details. 'The thing is, no-one seems to have seen or heard anything, so I'm going to use the Bugle as a means of investigation. I may write up the event and make it sound a bit more traumatic than it really was, just to get some interest and reaction. We don't think the police have much to go on. So if my article in local papers sounds alarming, don't worry. I just wanted to warn you.'

'We? You said we.'

'Helen was there. She encouraged me to make more of a fuss and get some publicity, keep on at the police, put up some posters.'

'Sensible girl.' His mother thought it best to say nothing about her son's short-lived relationships at this moment. 'Two heads …'

'So don't panic, Mum, when your cronies tell you we were nearly murdered. I know you don't read the local press but it might be on the radio or even regional telly, "*Famous Wildlife Photographer Robbed of Valuable Artwork.*"'

More worrying than pointless burglaries was Fred Marshall's inside information about quarrying again at Blackridge after all these years but he certainly was not going to tell his mother about his editor's second-hand gossip. She wouldn't be able to hide her excitement at the thought of her son being seduced by a tempting offer for his hovel. Not only because of the cash but more importantly the thought of him and Helen moving back to fill the empty space in the Buxton house while they made plans to spend his fortune.

❧

Margaret Byron felt that she had failed. Her cottage overlooked the village, overlooked the little Main Road which was the only way up to Joe's house, but she had seen nothing. From her window she could also see the track leading off the road and up to the quarry a few yards farther on. Of course, she could not be expected to be glued to the window all day but when Margaret was faced with a problem she liked to find a solution. The easiest way to Blackridge

Farm from the village was on foot and ramblers often parked on the verge to set off on a strenuous march past the quarry to link up with the Limestone Way, taking perhaps half an hour before they were out of sight over the next hill. Yesterday there had been no parked cars and no walkers, though she couldn't be entirely sure. Her computer screen had been unusually fascinating with riots in the Euro Zone spooking stock markets across the world.

She loved reading Joe's nature articles in the paper and admired the grainy photos that only really came to life when Joe printed them on thick textured paper and framed them in beech or maple. She was looking at two of his pictures on the wall now, and there were more on his website, safe from malicious thugs. It was difficult to destroy images completely these days when everything was safely online; she loved her computer and its friendly winking lights connecting her to the world and to life, but she doubted whether even a desperately pleading Twitter would spark a reaction round Stoneybrooke. There seemed nothing she, or logic, mathematics or technology could do to help Joe find his intruder.

Margaret poured herself a vodka, positioned herself in the window and thought about the day's events. A neighbour had called in on his way back from the pub at lunchtime and repeated the story of Joe's break-in, recounted by a fellow drinker. It was interesting how descriptions grew wilder and more colourful – Joe had grappled with an intruder who escaped in a getaway van with his computer and a load of valuables and only a few nights ago there was a strange van parked up there in the dark with no lights on. She had almost switched off, cut short the excited gossip saying 'That's all wrong, they didn't see anyone, and I'm sure Joe never had ...' when she remembered the words 'in the dark.' She went down the steps and along to her neighbour's.

'We were talking about Joe's break-in ... you said something about a conversation in the Miners, about "it being in the dark". What was all that about?'

'This lunchtime, after Joe and his young lady had gone, a mate of mine came in and by that time we were all telling about strange goings-on over the years. My mate said funny stuff was still going

off, and that was only three days ago. He was getting firewood out of his shed late that evening and he saw a chunky sort of wagon, silver coloured, the sort you can get about ten people in, going along the track towards the quarry. Weird thing was, he said, it had no lights on but he thought it stopped just short of Joe's place.'

'How could he tell, if it was nearly dark?'

'We all asked him that, and he said he could tell by the engine noise in the distance, or the dodgy exhaust, then it stopped. Odd thing was, Joe didn't mention that when we were talking about seeing strangers about the place. He didn't mention having any visitors.'

'If it was a friend calling on Joe, then he wouldn't bother to mention it.' Margaret declined the offer of a beer and went back to her vodka. She rang Joe: 'Here's another little puzzle to add to your collection, though it's on the wrong night and comes from one of the regulars at the pub.' She repeated details of the sighting and added 'it would need checking, you know what that lot are like, but he seemed sure about a few details, silver off-roader possibly with a faulty exhaust.'

She heard Joe whistle into his mobile.

'Thanks Margaret, that could tie in with something else about that time, someone kidnapping our pup, well, that's what Helen thinks happened. I'm just writing a lurid piece about the break-in for the Bugle – if I say Margaret Byron is on the case that should scare intruders off.'

Later that evening Margaret switched on Radio Derbyshire and heard that planning permission had been passed for ten houses in Stoneybrook – when new houses were planned in the Peaks it could even make the national news. The ramblers and holidaymakers who returned to the hills and dales year after year felt each new incursion into their bit of heaven like a personal blow.

5

The Power of the Press

Joe was pleased with the piece he had written about the break-in. He had sensationalized it, overwritten it and told lies – valuable artwork, especially old prints and paintings collected over the years, had been destroyed, together with months of work for his new book about quarries as wildlife sanctuaries with Blackridge the richest haven of them all. There would be a substantial reward for useful information. It was all very nearly true; it was emotionally true, he felt, because the intruder had broken the thread of his story. Now he had been sidetracked into putting his energy into dealing with his anger and this article would help. The lies did not matter; the intruder could hardly complain about damage he had not done, or about distress he had not intended to cause. Joe wrote about a campaign of intimidation and violence: the old house he was hoping to renovate had been violated, doors and windows smashed. A young puppy had been stolen and left for dead, and prowlers had scared his girlfriend away just when he needed her support ... reading it all was enough to make you cry. He rang Helen and asked her to take a particularly soulful photo of Puppy, the one he had taken with the slipper made him look too contented.

'Could you do it now and email it to me? The photo needs to show how small he is. Perhaps do it when he's asleep and not destroying stuff.'

'What's the hurry, Joe? What are you up to? You want a picture of Puppy for your bedside table? You haven't got one of me.'

He read out his article in a stop-press voice. 'You gave me the idea, love. Publicity is what we need. Readers will see the photo

first and wonder what happened to the sweet pup. What do you think?'

'I think it's cynical to exploit the poor creature for your own ends, especially when you don't love him. He feels that, you know. Your editor will have you writing up every hard-luck story in the Peaks from now on. It's heart-breaking stuff. I won't tell anyone that you've made most of it up.'

'Splash a bit of water on the hound so he looks a bit bedraggled before you …'

'Why not just throw him back in the lake for an action shot? There's a criminal streak in you that I never knew was there, Joe, and it's making me wonder …'

'No time for that – just do the photo like an efficient accomplice. I'll make it up to the mutt by taking up those paving slabs for his piddle patch.'

'Wait, Joe. We can't do a photo. Someone will recognize it and claim him back.'

'No danger there. He must have changed a lot in the past few weeks. He's twice the size now and, I hate to tell you this, Helen, but I don't think they want him back.'

Joe went off to photograph the few torn photographs he had kept as evidence, and some shots of his ransacked studio, his mind composing dramatic headlines "*Please Help Find This Heartless Maniac …*' or perhaps, descending to the literary depths of Fred Marshall, '*Talented Young Wildlife Artist's Work Destroyed in Senseless Rampage …*' He could hear Helen snorting an ego-puncturing snort.

Helen was worried about the photograph. She wanted to help Joe, but he was hoping for popular sympathy and public interest which meant that locally hundreds of readers would see appealing photos of a defenceless pup. She refused to believe that the dog was unwanted. What if his original owners saw him and came to claim him and take him away? But how could they if they had not even bothered to report him missing?

The photo reached Joe a few minutes later, a tiny, vulnerable scrap of Puppy with no white fangs or vicious claws showing – surely one she had taken three weeks ago when he was even

smaller? Joe pasted the photos into his article and sent the lot off to The Bugle, closing his laptop with a feeling of satisfaction. The public may not give a damn about Joe Wright and his book, but they'd certainly care about some lunatic shredding his pictures of brown hares near the quarry, frogs in the pool and a small hound nearly drowned in it. All around the villages there would be watchful eyes alert to sightings of silver vans and suspicious strangers. The laptop gave a closing-down grunt and he kissed its shiny lid. Revenge.

When the phone rang Joe said 'Thanks, love, that'll do fine that shot. Just the job.'

'Is that Joseph Wright?'

'Speaking – and you are Mr. Webster. I remember your voice from when you wanted to buy my house, and the answer is still the same. I don't want to sell.'

'Apologies for troubling you again, but I realised after I rang you before that I had not mentioned a price. I fell in love with the spot and your old farmhouse is charming … romantic almost.'

'That's not what most people call it.'

'I simply could not get the property out of my mind – it really spoke to me, and sympathetically renovated … well, to get back to my offer. I would be prepared to pay four hundred and fifty thousand pounds for buildings and land.' Webster said the sum slowly, the vowels fat and rich.

Joe nearly dropped the phone at the sound of such wealth. Then he laughed, 'Blackridge Farm is a listed building, Mr. Webster, and if you are imagining luxury renovations with extensions and conservatory and swimming pool or whatever, well Peak Park Planning will never allow it. You are offering nearly half a million pounds and you'd need another two hundred thousand to repair it to conservation standard. You think it's a charming old ruin, but you haven't thought it through.'

'My offer is a serious one and my money is in place Mr. Wright. I've set my heart on Blackridge Farm.'

'Then stop now before you get too heartbroken. My answer is no. I'm happy here and intend to stay and work here.'

'Are you really sure about that after all your problems? You could be much happier ...'

Joe switched off his phone and took a deep breath. The fellow was unhinged, one of those obsessive, time-wasting types that make offers they can't follow through.

He cooked himself a herby cheese omelette on the range and celebrated his journalistic venture with several pints of dry cider. Strange how satisfying writing so many exaggerations and lies was; not like the pleasure of writing that chapter on discovering falcons in the old quarry for his book of course but still sort of gleeful. He could understand the pleasures of what used to be called the gutter press – you could get the punters to believe anything if you found the right words, a strange and heady power.

The cider was working well, but after several hours of polishing prose Joe needed some air and something more active. There was still clearing up to do after the storm, so he wandered out into the garden and looked back at the house. Half a million! What a nutter! He could see sunlight shining through holes in the barn roof and again through gaps in the limestone walls, shafts of light cut with beautiful precision. Pretty, but the gaps had to go and he seemed to have run out of useable pieces of slate and stone. Helen had once said he bodged things instead of doing an elegant job and he could hear her sighing over his bits of reclaimed limestone, none of which quite seemed to fit the gaps he thought they had come out of.

Joe was turning a puzzling bit of limestone round and round when a voice said:

'It'll look lovely when it's finished. How lucky you are to have a place like this to work on.' Lauren had been watching him work for a few seconds before speaking, admiring his careful selection of stone and his loving concentration on the old building as well as his tall, strong figure juggling huge chunks of rock. His old baggy trousers reminded her of ancient labourers, sinewy and tough, like the ones in the old sepia photos she sold in her shop.

'It's like a jigsaw puzzle, Lauren, and I'm never any good at those, no patience. But all these bits came out of these walls somewhere and they are definitely going back in.' He smiled at her, a fellow

craftsperson with dirty hands, except now she had scrubbed up and most of the clay had been scraped off her face and back into the tubs ready for tomorrow. 'Can I get you a drink? There's some good dry cider on offer and I deserve another break.'

'Cider sounds good.' She followed him in to the farmhouse and watched while he livened up the fire in the stove. 'I envy you this place. Your barn would make a great pottery. I love walking up here and round the top of the quarry, but I do have something I feel I ought to tell you. The trouble is, I don't know whether it's true or not.'

'So I'll bear that in mind and you can let me judge.' Lauren was not the sort to gossip or even to make casual conversation and now she seemed to be making an effort to find the right words.

'My brother works for the council – the County in Matlock, not Peak Park – and something he said worried me, but I don't want to get him into trouble.'

'Then let me guess, and it won't be your fault.' Joe topped up her glass and hoped the cider would help her to relax. 'I've heard the news. Permission has been given for a few houses to be built in the village and the easiest place to get stone from is this quarry,' he said in a forced matter-of-fact tone. 'But it won't happen.'

'It's a horrible thought. It makes me sick to think of it.' She sank down onto the old rag rug in front of the fire, took a big swig of cider and looked up at Joe with a sincere expression of concern. 'Miserable for you and for the village, with blasting and sirens and lorries rumbling through Main Road. You'd have to move, and all those lovely photos you take   '

'I said it won't happen, Lauren. I know it's been on the local news but the media gets everything wrong.' He wondered why she was bothering to repeat all this, but he was touched by how concerned she seemed.

'But my brother said he'd heard that the council   I got confused between what Peak Park does and those two councils in Matlock – were backing the plan. They use words like strategic and vision and planning policies. They want every village to take its quota of new

housing so that they can add them all together and say what a valuable contribution Derbyshire is making.'

Another long draught of cider and Lauren drooped dejectedly, almost lying at his feet on the rug. 'It's you, Joe, that I'm really worried about. You and your birds and insects and things. You love this place so much.' Lauren's voice faltered. Men did not like emotional women who thought they could understand other people's feelings when they probably did not want to be understood. She sat silently staring into the flames.

Joe sat down facing her but at a comfortable distance and said reassuringly 'Of course I love this place, you're right. And I've got plans for it. I know the quarry like an old friend – an old and ruined friend. It would take millions to drain the lake, to make an entrance, roadway and parking for modern equipment. I know that plans for houses are viewed favourably by officialdom these days but cash decides plans, not committees. Getting planning permission is one thing, finding the capital to build stuff is another. It just wouldn't be worth it, not for ten affordable houses.' Joe smiled at her; it gave him a warm, comfortable feeling to know that villagers thought about him, even if they were slightly pissed on cider. 'It's very kind of you to be concerned ...'

'My brother said it isn't just the planning permission. He heard his boss talking about your quarry being the nearest source of stone, about it being more environmentally friendly to dig up the stuff locally. He knows of other cases where once a bit of stone is quarried the owners get permission to keep on and on, for decades sometimes ... our quarry could be supplying the whole country.' Lauren had visions of the Peak District disappearing into a great hole. 'He says no-one can stop multinationals, they can afford to spend whatever it takes.'

'Hang on a minute, Lauren. It's just ten little houses, and the country's in such a state no-one can afford to build anything much, in spite of a tiny bit of an upturn. It can't last. Shall I put the kettle on and make you a coffee?'

Lauren rose slowly, settled into an armchair and for the first time took in chewed up slippers and a shredded teddy bear. She stood

up again. 'I must go before Helen gets back. Is she out with that lovely little dog? She'll think I'm over-reacting and making you worried.'

'You were quite right to come, Lauren,' Joe soothed, keeping quiet about the Helen situation, 'the village has got to stick together on this.'

Joe went back to his lumps of stone feeling uneasy. That phrase of Lauren's 'they can afford to pay whatever it takes' made him think of Webster and his crazy offer. Perhaps others were beginning to see the value of his run-down farmhouse. He stood with the heavy stone in his hands, a lump of rock that seemed to be worth more and more. Webster was no emotional lover of the Peak District, he thought he'd spotted a good investment that big business would pay even more for than his crazy offer. Or what if Webster himself was big business? An agent for international quarrying? Joe put the rock down again without finding its right place in the puzzle. That was the trouble with money – just the thought of it made you suspicious and paranoid.

&

Mrs. Bonsall watched her downstairs neighbour from her window. She wondered whether to get her mobile phone and use the little camera in it, something she had never done before. They said you could send photos straight from it, and she'd dearly like the landlord to see what was going on in the garden. As it was, she'd just have to ring him and ask him to come round as a matter of urgency, because the girl downstairs had called in some strapping great fellow to churn up patio. That new dog (did the landlord know about that?) was dashing about all over the flower beds, cocking its leg up the sundial, which would soon smell disgusting. No answer from the landlord so she had to leave a message.

'Mrs Bonsall's watching us,' said Helen, waving up to the window and smiling sweetly. 'Probably reporting me.'

'I feel she might have a point, but do you mean reporting us to the police for burying something suspicious or reporting us to your landlord for rearranging his property?' Joe stood a flagstone up

against the dry stone wall of the garden. 'I feel we shouldn't be doing this.'

'No problem. As soon as I got the glad tidings that you were dashing over to create Puppy's pee patch ...'

'I'm not *that* keen ...'

'I rang Lennie on his mobile and promised that I ... we would put the slabs back as soon as Pup is fully trained.'

Joe laughed. 'That'll be the day. That dog takes no notice of you whatsoever and he can't understand why you don't join in the fun.' He picked the puppy up and planted him firmly on the fresh soil where he started to dig frenziedly, sending mud flying.

Mrs. Bonsall tapped on the window and Helen waved and smiled again. Joe picked Puppy up again and waved one of its paws up at the old lady.

'That's enough pantomime for today, Joe. Let's go in and get cleaned up, then you can tell me what you are really here for. I'm deeply suspicious. Take your boots off while I wipe his paws.'

Mrs. Bonsall appeared in the front garden with a broom and Helen mimed her intense gratitude with gestures she hoped conveyed despair at the antics of young critters.

Joe gulped down some tea and filled his mouth with scone to delay the moment of admitting 'I really needed someone to talk to. We've worked out that there's something odd going on, but when Lauren called round with something even more worrying ... I ought not to tell you how she found out ...'

Helen shrugged. 'I wouldn't want you to betray her confidence and let out any secrets you both have.'

Joe ignored the acid tone. 'Last time I came over I was worried about those new houses. Now it's even worse, first my boss, now Lauren. She's found out, from sources inside the council, that HGVs can't use the B roads and the turn into Stoneybrooke. Which means they've got to get the stone from somewhere closer, just as we feared. She's heard the ten houses could be a sort of Trojan horse ... or a red herring.'

'Or a pig in a poke? Or dog in a manger? We guessed all that, Joe, now just because your Lauren's finally got the picture ...'

Joe stood up angrily and started to walk out. 'You've never taken my interest in the quarry and the wildlife in it seriously, just because you can't see a big salary in it and the farmhouse renovated to destruction. Now you're having a go at Lauren. Well, she's part of the village and some of them are worried for me.'

'I'm listening, love, but just tell me what's worrying you and cut the daft imagery, horses and herrings. I'm sorry for joking when I can see you are upset.'

'It gets worse. We suspect that the houses are just an excuse to get the quarry opened up again, then once it's up and running, with roads and site offices and car parks it will develop into a full-scale operation. Huge works, international exports, railway lines even, like the sites that have ruined the Peak Park round Buxton.'

'And your old place demolished in the national interest?'

Joe glared at her, suspecting sarcasm, but Helen put her arms round him and held him close. 'Now I understand why you look so distracted but believe me you really are imagining the worst. This isn't London. I know a bit about property round here and people are letting out cottages, barns, cowsheds and pigsties because they can't sell and builders can't build. The housing market is in such an unpredictable state that there's no demand for materials like stone. Your old house and quarry are quite safe, thanks to the poor wretches round here not being able to afford a mortgage.'

Joe looked doubtful. 'So my future depends on economics? On the housing market? What if it picks up, or whatever markets do? And don't developers buy up land just for the hell of it?'

'That's a bit dramatic.' Helen kissed him then released him from the reassuring hug because as usual Puppy was trying to wriggle between them, nipping their ankles for a quick result. 'You need publicity again; write more articles about the special wildlife in the quarry, things that can't be found anywhere else. Lots of photos of rare beetles that have to be protected. Or better still, find some dormice or something furry. Something that gets a protection order slapped on it, like they do with trees.'

'Like Special Scientific Interest? SSSIs? You're right, that always causes developers problems – and costs them a lot in lawyers and specialists to fight it.'

'You've got the ear of the editor of the influential Peaks Bugle. Now you're nearly laughing. That's better. '

Joe only managed a watery smile. 'Now I know you're joking. But you're right, I was getting into a spiral of depression. Unfair of me to dump on you.'

'But we got our pee patch done, didn't we Pup? Talking of dumping, I think the wee mite needs a walk along the river. It'll do us all good.'

Joe cheered up at the thought of more obedience training. 'I'll take his lead and get him to walk to heel. And Helen, do you think that at his advancing age you could at last choose a less wimpish name for him?' Wandering down by the river, Joe thought the three of them presented a happy family image. Why, then, hadn't he been able to tell Helen about the vast amount of money the Blackridge land was suddenly worth?

6

Fire at the Farm

'Any news about your burglary, Joe?' Fred Marshall asked, hoping to fill up his newspaper with *'Further Developments in Attack on Young Naturalist'*. 'Because no-one's written in to the paper or called us.'

'Only one anonymous phone call blaming the drunkards coming out of The Miners Standard throwing up in the horse trough and terrorizing the village in their search for drugs money.'

'Vivid imaginations some of these old gits have got. Sorry there's nothing helpful, Joe. The police haven't got anything either.'

'They did come round to the farm and dusted everything for fingerprints. Nasty silvery stuff they used and I can't clean it off.'

'Do you worry much about cleaning and housework though?'

'No, but every time I open a cupboard or a drawer I see this sinister shiny patch that reminds me strangers have been poking about. But I've been a bit preoccupied by something else, Fred. Someone on the Council's got definite proof that the planning permission for a few houses is the thin end of a big rocky wedge. Take a few tons of limestone from my quarry to start with then open it up on a national scale. Bulldoze me and my house down.'

Fred slammed his fist down on his desk and gave what almost seemed like a cheer, which Joe felt was deeply hurtful.

'Didn't I tell you last week that's what they were up to? Trust an old news hound to scent these things,' Fred crowed 'Please tell me it's a council officer leaking confidential decisions and not some dim-witted councillor who's got the long words all wrong. Not that it would stop us printing the story.'

'I can't say how I heard; I don't want to get a friend into trouble so I'm protecting my sources.'

'You aren't supposed to use that old line against me, that's pissing into the tent.'

'Did you start the rumour, Fred? You hang around County Hall a lot, and some of the newer councillors believe whatever you tell them. Was it just to get the council rumour mongers going and creating a scare story for the Bugle? After all, you did come up with the idea a few days ago.'

Fred shook his head sadly. 'That was just my fertile imagination. Don't worry, Joe, much as I'd like to have a Peak Park national interest story with London court appeals and big money, I think you are quite safe. Even with permission for a few houses some wealthy village landowners with influence will appeal against it and in the end it won't happen, in spite of housing targets.'

Joe frowned, 'I hope you're right, but I can't leave it to chance. Too many strange things have been happening lately. Odd characters prowling about, and someone's made me a crazy offer for my farmhouse.'

Fred yelped like an ageing adolescent, 'They'd have to be mad! How much? Or is that secret info as well?'

'Afraid so. But it was enough to make me suspicious. There's a shedload of money to be spent on it just to make it comfortable by most people's standards, so who would want to buy it unless they wanted to own the quarry?'

'Now you really are beginning to wonder if I was right! If your council squealer knows something about you and your place being rubbed out,' said Fred, switching from teenager to gangster.

'Over my dead body.'

'Now that really would be a story.'

'Which is why I came in to see you. About a story.' Joe thumped the drinks machine into action then pulled up a chair opposite Fred. 'Let's suppose it's all true, international mining company, megaton lorries, farmhouse blasted to kingdom come and so on ...'

'Hang on, I do like to have a shred of evidence, even for The Bugle...'

'Put your incorruptible moral values aside for a minute, Fred. We thought it was time we controlled events instead of just …'

'We? Who's we? The village?'

'Probably. The villagers will support me when they hear about the quarry. My friend … partner … Helen, thought we … you … could publish our story saying I'd been approached by an international company to buy up my farm and my quarry. To flush out the true facts, if there are any.'

Fred leaned forward, showing unusual interest in what Joe had to say, 'you keep saying *my quarry*. I thought that was because you're always down there talking to the animals. Do you mean you really own it? Not just the land at the top?'

'Haven't I ever said? Yes, it's all part of the old farm holdings. The deeds go back over three hundred years, well before the locals started digging bits out of the ground to build their houses.'

Fred said nothing, deep in thought.

'As I was saying, it was Helen's idea, but I'd do it in my name. Write an article saying I'd had an offer of a million for the land …'

'And the rest. All the time I've been laughing at you and that ruin next to a bloody enormous hole in the ground …'

'That's all it is, really, but lots of amazing wildlife seem to love it. Stop interrupting. We'd dream up this story of untold millions, of plans for hundreds of jobs for surrounding villages, new roads, a bigger school, doctors, infrastructure they call it, a new railway line…'

'Now you're getting carried away. You'd want me to publish this fairy story?'

'Helen says the more exaggerated the better. You'd get hundreds of Letters to the Ed. to choose from, it would hit the national press, or at least the bits that matter, and it would flush out anyone who really wanted to get their hands on my land. Plus the planners would be forced to state their position.'

'And then what?'

Joe hesitated, stood up then went to look out of the window at the Wye flowing sedately past the mill that housed the Bugle offices. 'I don't know yet.'

'So these international moneybags come out of the woodwork when they read your article and then you turn them down, if I've read you right.'

'Yes. Then I'll know who they are.'

'Why not just wait until they make a move and then make your self-righteous lunatic gesture of refusing their generous offer?'

'Because we are worried,' Joe admitted slowly, then added 'I want things out in the open so I know who I'm up against, before more falcons get torn up and puppies get drowned, or worse.'

'I think living in that isolated spot has got to you,' Fred said, standing up to end their talk and thinking that Joe was sounding hysterical. 'But put your article together and I'll think about it. Try to make it almost believable – there are limits to credulity, even for Bugle readers.'

'I'd need space in the paper – at least two pages – to make it clear why my quarry is so valuable, and to make a feature of all the plants and animals that are unique to places like Blackridge Quarry – tawny owls, kestrels, pyramid orchids, frog orchids …'

Fred put up his hands to stop the flow. 'Spare me the list.'

'… and to print my photos of them, to stress their ecological value and protected status.'

'Ecology, environment, diversity, sustainability – shove all the buzz words in, except hardly anyone listens anymore,' Fred said wearily, opening the office door.

'And I'd want paying.'

❧

It made you angry, Joe thought, how burglars changed your life. Going home now he scanned the doors, windows, outhouses for signs of attack relieved to find the doors still stoutly defending his possessions, his place of comfort and safety. He fed the stove with logs then went through to the kitchen to see what kind of warm food he could invent without going shopping, perhaps a creation of soup reinforced with chick peas and garlic. After that he could settle down to a few hours planning his article on the threat to his homestead, perhaps even a couple of days of comfortable creativity when he did not have to worry about Fred sending him off to

74

photograph more floods or landslides. Sorry, he would say, but my quarry piece is far more important – for me, the Peak landscape and The Bugle.

He froze when he saw a shadowy figure looming in the grimy stone-framed scullery window.

'Margaret! What are you skulking round the back for? I'm so edgy these days you nearly got a crack over the head.'

'Sorry Joe. Just catching the last bit of sunshine while I waited for you to come back. I haven't been round the back here for years and I'd forgotten what a lovely collection of rockery plants you've got. It's sheltered but there's a view right across the top of the quarry and over to the Dark Peak.'

'Come in and have some soup, I'm planning an original recipe. More a kind of broth of whatever's in the cupboard to keep me going for the next few hours.'

'Then this should come in handy,' Margaret extricated a brown and seedy loaf from her string bag, 'only a quick one from my bread machine, not exactly farmhouse baking. You do the soup while I tell you about unrest among the natives.'

'About the new houses?'

'Lots of the villagers think it's unfair to dump young families in an out-of-the-way place like ours. Really, of course, they're worried about their renovated mansions being contaminated by the closeness of first-time buyers, but they'll never be that honest. The final straw was when Adrian Hucknall – he's your Helen's boss – was scouting round the development site and met one of the planners from Peak Park. Two of the so-called houses are in fact going to be three-storey and divided into flats. There's nothing like the word 'maisonette' to get the local squirearchy apoplectic.'

Joe chopped up the seedy loaf and added it to the tray of soups. 'Come and have a seat by the fire while you tell me about the uprising.' He decided not to tell Margaret about his fears for the quarry or its amazing value, although she would probably guess.

'What's the stuff in the tomato soup? It tastes good whatever it is.'

'Chickpeas – underrated little devils – and some early wild garlic shoots from down by the brook.'

Margaret handed him a greasy sheet of paper. 'I printed off a list of people who want to protest, about twenty so far. Adrian even got the vicar to sign because it would mean moving some old gravestones. That's the Church for you, never mind the living – the old bones are said to be thirteenth century plague victims who still do their bit by attracting a few generous tourists to the church charity box.'

Joe scanned the list. 'So you've contacted all of these by email? It didn't take you long.'

'Good lord, no. We are all on Facebook, apart from the vicar. And you, I should imagine. So add your mobile number and email address, and get your editor to print my letter this week. It should be possible for a few dozen members of the protest group to get an appeal going if we include three neighbouring villages, ones the extra traffic would disturb. We could even get hundreds of supporters because there's villages all over Derbyshire, all over the country in fact, who get alarmed at the word quarrying.'

'Great stuff, Margaret. You seem to be relishing all this trouble-making. Let me fuel you up with a brandy.'

'I must admit village politics take my mind off watching the Footsie and the Nasdaq, which are thoroughly depressing these days.'

Margaret was outraged when Joe offered to walk her home. She'd been treading these village paths and ginnels for over fifty years and no sighting of strangers in a pretentious truck was going to stop her. He watched her wavering torch disappear down the track then settled down to start his article.

7

'Ripping the Guts Out of the Peaks'

"Blackridge Quarry has more protected species than the Galapagos but is under attack from multinationals intent on ripping the guts out of the Peaks…"

He would make it follow on from his article about the break-in, so as to wring the last drop of sympathy out of Bugle readers, then if Margaret and her Letter to the Ed provoked an avalanche of Twitters or new Faces … but could you say an avalanche any more now that no-one used paper? Perhaps it ought to be a mob of Faces or a flock of Twitters. Joe had reached the limits of his hazy knowledge of social media and with vague thoughts of such exciting possibilities he dozed off.

When he woke up it was past midnight. Time for another coffee before he confronted the patiently waiting screen with only two lines of writing on it. In the past a blank sheet of paper had seemed guilt-making enough, but now that winking little cursor urging him on was far worse. He switched his laptop off and put the tin kettle on the stove to heat some water.

He reached for a sheet of paper; he would make a list of contents for this important piece of writing, things that were dear to the hearts of millions of country lovers. Hedgehogs always seemed to get people going, but the trusting little creatures were rare in the Peak Park – not enough hedges, he supposed, and they were far too canny to go wandering about near quarries in the dark. He needed loveable, furry mammals and preferably endangered ones; there were certainly bats in the caves but bats never seemed to get people's hearts racing, though he thought they were sweet little

creatures. Much would depend on his choice of photographs. On the grassy slopes around the quarry there were always plenty of rabbits and hares – he started his list with hares, plenty of people fell in love with hares – and then there were mice and voles, not an obviously cuddly choice, though pictures of sleepy field mice might do the trick. Strange how people had a soft spot for owls, and there were several of those, especially Little Owls and Tawny Owls on the quarry face as well as his pair in the barn. The owl appeal must be due to their huge encircled eyes and quizzical head movements, though he'd better avoid pictures of their beaks and talons tearing at the flesh of aforementioned furry mammals.

He noticed a chewed-up slipper and an old beanbag used as a makeshift dog bed. Puppy had been the most usefully appealing furry mammal so far; he felt a small wave of affection followed by regret that at the time he had not felt much sympathy for the mutt's kidnapping ordeal. Mongrels were not a rare or endangered species.

He'd been writing by the light of the burning logs, but there was no point in feeding the stove at this hour. Joe got up to switch on the light and noticed an unusually bright orange glow coming from the scullery. Strange, because although he had used the range to heat up the evening's soup the fire in that should have died down. When he opened the door there was an explosion and a rushing whirl of smoke so thick that he could not see where the fire was coming from. He slammed the heavy oak scullery door and rushed outside to peer through the window. The flames were certainly coming from the large recess where the range stood and a door would have to be opened unless he was going to stand outside and watch his home ruined.

Joe rushed round to the back of the house and connected his hosepipe to the outside tap, and as the tap was next to the back door that was the way in he had to use. He turned the jet full on. Just as well there were no expensive carpets to ruin, no white electrical goods to blacken and rust. The flagstones would dry out and the old range would come to no harm, so he inched forward, directing the spray to the side of the range where his precious stack of dried

logs was now well alight. A smaller fire had run along an ancient rag rug and was now attacking a cupboard.

Smoke made it difficult to see farther into the room and after what seemed like hours of dousing flames that died then sprang up again Joe knew that his puny hosepipe was losing the battle against the fire. He'd heard a lot about death from smoke inhalation and had tied a tea towel round his face, but what could you do about streaming, stinging eyes that refused to focus? And a stinging, choking throat that made you gasp?

He was suddenly grabbed from behind by a strong pair of arms and dragged back out into the yard.

'Leave this to us, Sir. You'll only be in the way. Stand back.'

❧

Joe never discovered who called the firemen. They had the fire put out within minutes and left with a lecture on keeping a can of petrol in the house. Joe slept in his car because the back door had been damaged and could not be closed, though he could not remember getting any proper sleep. He felt safer locked in his car with his laptop on the back seat. The farmhouse was now beginning to feel like a trap, the dodgy front door still not repaired from the break-in and the blackened, cindery back door liable to crumble at a touch. He felt certain that someone had tried to kill him. He did not own a petrol can.

He slowly became aware of an urgent tapping on the car window. Lauren was shouting something at him, so he unlocked the door and climbed unsteadily out, the cold air hurting his swollen throat.

'There's a group of us from the village mopping up inside your place. It took us a while to realise you were asleep in the car and not wandering about somewhere semi-conscious. That's a nasty cough, Joe, you're probably full of smoke.'

'What's the time?' Joe asked pointlessly.

'About half six. You look dreadful, although I suppose it is mainly soot.' Lauren took his arm and tried to drag him down the track. 'My car is just down here, come back with me to get cleaned up and have some breakfast.'

'I need to see how much damage there is. I don't remember anything after the fireman dragged me out.'

'Why not wait until they've mopped up a bit more?'

Joe ignored her and went up to the farmhouse which from the front looked innocent of all traces of inferno, its cream and white limestone sparkling in the morning sun. He ran round to what used to be the back door, now only a few charred planks. Alan Wood, the pub landlord was directing three villagers with mops and buckets but Joe ran past them, through puddles and bits of charred furniture and into his living room. 'I must get my folder … it's got the stuff I printed …'

'You've been lucky there, Joe. The fire didn't get past that inside door, so it's only the kitchen that's a mess. Sorry, I didn't really mean lucky, but it could have been worse.'

The living room was much as he had left it, except for a few fingers of sooty water that had crept under the heavy door and stained the flagstones. His notes about quarry wildlife and his camera were still on the armchair.

'Sorry, Alan. I shouldn't have rushed past you all like that. How did you know about the fire?'

'When a fire tender hurtles through Stoneybrook at two in the morning and up this track it doesn't take much working out. A couple of us followed it up here then went back for our buckets, mops and sponges.'

Joe stood in a puddle, dazed. 'I didn't call the fire station; they turned up just when … ' He covered his face with his hands, shaking. 'I couldn't stop the flames and smoke, then suddenly there they were, the firemen.'

'Just as well they were quick.' Alan put his hand on Joe's arm to steady him. 'Why not go back with Lauren? Get a drink and a shower and some more sleep. The police will be turning up later, but until then there is not much you can do.'

Lauren appeared in the doorway and led him out to her car, her arm round him as he clung to his laptop like a child guarding a favourite toy. He noticed what strong hands Lauren had. Potter's

hands, he supposed, firmed up by slapping and pummelling great mounds of clay.

Margaret called out to them as she emptied a bucket of black sludge 'What about a trip to A and E in Chesterfield? Smoke can do a lot of damage to the lungs if it ...'

'I'll take care of him' Lauren said firmly, slamming the door on her prisoner then clamping the seatbelt round him and his pc.

'I ought to tell my mother before she gets wind of it' Joe wheezed, feeling more helpless than ever. 'First the break-in, now this ...'

'All sorted. Margaret rang and left a message. I don't think your mum was awake, which meant a nice, soothing version of events was waiting for her and she couldn't ask any awkward questions. That's the good thing about leaving a message.' Lauren's hand gripped his thigh and squeezed it reassuringly, painfully. 'I'll ring her later and let her know you're in good hands.'

'I'm not desperate to talk to my mother, she's always wanted me to sell the place and now ...'

'Maybe she's right.' Lauren swung her car into the small court-yard in front of her pottery. She had a sensation of coming home to a life with Joe and it felt good.

'I'm being pathetic, Lauren. There's really nothing wrong with me and I ought to be back with the others clearing up my own mess.' He had begun to notice, in spite of streaming eyes and choking coughs, that Lauren was enjoying taking energetic control.

She ignored his mutterings, wrested the precious laptop and camera from him and lowered him on to a roomy sofa. 'I'm something of a brandy buff and there's a twenty-year-old Courvoisier waiting for this occasion.'

What occasion? Attempted murder by arson? 'I'm more of a cider man,' Joe said in the same strangely jovial tone.

'Not this morning you aren't.'

She even had brandy goblets, or whatever they were called, big as goldfish bowls, and the mellow liquid felt good and soothing trickling down his throat. 'I'm making a sooty mess on your linen covers.' Her workshop may be a mess of paint and clay and broken pots, but her sitting room was an oasis of pale oak flooring and

oatmeal rugs with art pottery in earthy colours displayed on a low table.

Lauren put more brandy into his bowl before she said 'I'll run the bath so you can get cleaned up.'

Having swallowed several generous mouthfuls of the unaccustomed liquor in the belief that it was good for him, Joe began to appreciate the taste and the warm out-of-body feeling it gave him. It was so very kind of her to help him as he swayed happily upstairs, to undress him gently – though he told her he was tons and oodles better – and to help him into the warm foamy water with her strong potter's hands.

'No need to … I can …' he began as she soaped and massaged, 'that's lovely but I feel like a baby.' He couldn't help a weird, gurgling laugh as he looked up into her face and saw her eyes closed, mouth open and a dab of foam on her nose.

'Big, big baby,' she cooed, diligently cleansing parts that smoke had never reached. She lifted him up out of the bath, holding him against her while she reached for a towel.

They both jumped when the doorbell rang and Joe, unsteady on the polished granite floor, slipped and knocked his head on the washbasin as he fell.

He lay quite still, a peaceful smile on his face, and Lauren panicked. She could manage him happily pissed, but splayed and floppy on her floor he was too heavy to lift. She'd have to get help. The doorbell rang again so she ran downstairs and opened the door to Helen.

'Joe's Mum rang me about the fire, then they told me he was here.' She threw her arms round Lauren, 'Thank you, they said he seemed in shock, it's wonderful of you …'

Lauren pushed her away and ran back down the hall, thinking fast. 'Quick, I've just heard the most terrible crash from upstairs. Perhaps Joe's fallen … he went upstairs to have a bath. My fault, I should never have left him to …'

Helen pushed past her up the stairs and into the bathroom where Joe, still grinning hugely was now trying to haul himself up.

'I'm fine, ladies, welcome one and all,' he laughed, putting a soapy arm round each of the women.

Lauren reluctantly handed a bath towel to Helen and went downstairs to make some coffee, double strength, hoping it would work quickly to counter the effects of a triple brandy.

'You mustn't blame yourself, Lauren,' Helen said soothingly when they were all downstairs, 'brandy and a hot bath always sounds just the thing, I know it works wonders for me, but they say smoke can do strange things, worse than flames, so probably the whole lot together knocked him out for a while.' She kissed Joe's cheek.

He smiled at the women and stroked his pc affectionately.

Lauren poured more coffee. 'I've made things worse,' she admitted, hoping that concussion, smoke and brandy would help Joe forget her bathroom passion. Damn Helen, just when things were feeling good. She felt a small erotic tug deep inside her. No need for her ever to forget that soapy scene.

'I was just saying,' Helen repeated, 'that we'd better get back. Joe needs a good, long sleep. Our bedroom,' she said slowly, 'doesn't seem to have been damaged by the fire. And thank you again, Lauren dear, you've been a real friend.'

The police were waiting when they got back up to Blackridge Farm. Joe had dozed off, lulled by the swaying of Helen's small car as she drove slowly over the rocks and cobbles of the old farm track; brandy fumes and the smell of scented bath oil filled the car. Helen left him and walked up to the front door where two constables looked as though they were just about to leave.

'Sorry, officers, Mr. Wright … Joe … had to spend a few hours with a friend. He's suffering from smoke inhalation and isn't making much sense. Could you come back later? Or could we come down to Bakewell?'

'We'll come back, Miss. We've had a good look round and can see there isn't much damage, but we need to discuss the matter of keeping a petrol can next to the range. It's illegal, you know.'

'Joe hasn't got a petrol can, or not one that I can ever remember, so you must be mistaken, officer. We only … he only ever burns logs so why would he need …?'

The officer held up a blackened object in a plastic bag 'Definitely a petrol can, Miss. But I can see Mr. Wright's the worse for wear. We'll be back tomorrow.'

Helen walked through the house to the kitchen. It had always looked bare and uncomfortable to her, but now it looked desolate, the walls and ceiling blackened, the stone floor damp and grey. The solid pine table could probably be stripped back and salvaged, but two wooden kitchen cupboards had collapsed and the team of village helpers had piled plates and saucepans neatly in the stone sink. What a miserable mess. Helen felt unreasonably angry and when Joe appeared at the back door she made no attempt to help him. Living in a half-derelict hovel attracted fire-raisers and burglars. It was partly his own fault.

Joe did not seem too disheartened by the soggy mess. 'They've done a good job of cleaning up. It isn't as bad as I feared, a bit of lime wash on the walls and ceiling, and Mum's got loads of chairs she doesn't need. It'll look fine. Sorry I kept passing out round at Lauren's. I ought to have waited for the firemen, except I didn't call them. I don't think I did. How did they know I needed them?' He still wasn't making much sense.

'You think all this will be fine with a coat of paint? With another load of crap old furniture out of your Mother's shed?' Helen turned away and walked into the living room.

'This room isn't much better. Never was. Pity the fire didn't …'

Joe caught up with her and put his arms round her. 'Give me a chance, love. I'll put it all right. And I can't get over how kind people are, coming round within minutes, Margaret, Sid, Alan and especially Lauren.'

'Oh, especially Lauren.' Not that she could blame her, who wouldn't want to get the dozey hunk into a soapy bath? 'Lauren's a real star. She didn't even mind getting her jeans and tee-shirt soaking wet. I wonder how that happened? But this place, Joe, can't we talk about it? You can't go on living like this.'

Joe wasn't listening; he had heard the feeble hoot of his Mother's car some way down the track. She abandoned it to come stumbling up the path.

'I came as soon as I could, Joe – you look terrible, haven't you had time to change? I mean, are you all right, dear?' She gave him a quick hug then pushed past him to inspect the fire damage and gave a shriek of horror when she reached the kitchen. 'You can't live like this, you'll really have to move now. Hello Helen, talk some sense into him, will you? He listens to you.' Sylvia put her arms round her son, as though checking him for damage. 'What a fright that message gave me, I could hardly drive over here.'

Helen unearthed an electric kettle from the shed and made some tea. She could best help Joe by reassuring his mother that her son was not a complete failure whatever her own feelings were about his lifestyle.

'It wasn't Joe's fault, Sylvia. Someone must have …'

'Someone said it must have been an electrical fault,' Joe interrupted loudly. Insurance money should cover some repairs and redecorating.'

'You're insured? Last time I asked you said it wasn't worth …'

'No problem, Mum. I'll get on to it tonight. Does anyone fancy a takeaway? I'm suddenly hungry.'

Mrs. Wright looked round the untidy room and out to the pile of grimy plates in the sink. 'I can't stay, much as I'd love to help you clear up. Got badminton this afternoon, so I'll eat later. Call round to the house when you get time both of you, I've got some lovely old Windsor chairs in the shed that would look charming here.' She kissed them both. 'Joe's so lucky to have such a treasure, Helen, he just doesn't …'

'Bye Ma, thanks for coming. I'll be over later.'

When they were alone Helen picked up the computer from the charred kitchen table. 'Executive decision. The most important thing now is to get that article written about the break in – and now this fire – and to get as much publicity as possible. When I saw you round at Lauren's you looked in a terrible state. Someone's trying to kill you.'

Joe grinned. 'No, Lauren didn't mean any harm, getting me drunk and trying to drown me, she's just lusting after my amazing ..,' he ducked too late as Helen hit him.

'Hasn't he been through enough without you assaulting him?' Fred Marshall appeared, focusing a professional-looking camera on the burnt-out kitchen. 'Stand over there, Joe, next to that wreck of a back door. I can get the first report of this into tomorrow's edition. Presumably it wasn't an accident? It just confirms what we've been saying about a dirty tricks campaign.'

'The police mentioned a petrol can, but whoever started the fire must have used it then left it to cause even more trouble,' Helen explained. 'Hurry up and finish your photos, Fred, because Joe's coming home with me for a few days and I won't let him out of my sight until he's written several thousand words on the sinister and murderous goings-on at Blackridge Farm. And about the threats to an unworldly young naturalist who is struggling to save endangered species.'

Joe muttered about two bossy women dragging him off in one day, when he was perfectly capable …

Helen interrupted firmly ' I hope you won't be offended, Fred, but as well as asking you to publish it in The Bugle I thought we ought to try to get it into the nationals – The Guardian and Independent readers are usually up for campaigning to save endangered wildlife.'

'As well as the animals, you mean,' Fred joked, nudging Joe, whose sooty face had escaped Lauren's attentions.

Helen ignored this. ' Have you got any contacts in their offices, Fred?'

'No offence taken, my dear. We provincial hacks are always looking for an excuse to hobnob with the quality. I'm flattered, but I don't have any friends in Docklands. Might have to make do with Newsnight.' Fred had finished taking his photos and was leaving hurriedly. He'd had a quick look round the farmhouse and thought that the general disrepair of the building made it difficult to tell what was fire and water damage and what was decay, but there was still a good story in it.

Helen said firmly 'Get a change of clothing together, Joe, and we'll get back to Bakewell. 'I've got an endangered species of dog at home needing food and upsetting the neighbours.'

ॐ

In the hallway of Helen's flat Puppy had nearly demolished an envelope of thick, expensive paper embossed with a London solicitor's pretentious-looking crest. It was a formal offer of six hundred thousand pounds for Joe's farmhouse and quarry.

'There's a handwritten note from Webster with it, saying how much he loves the place …' Joe handed the soggy remains to Helen. 'How the hell has it got here, to your flat?'

'So Webster wasn't to blame for the fire, because it only happened early this morning, and this letter's got a London address on the notepaper. Unless …'

'Unless the fire was all planned days ago and they expected me to move out. To here. And the solicitor's in it as well.' Joe pieced together the tooth-marked envelope. 'There's no postmark, it's been delivered by hand.'

'That's a whole load of money, Joe, so that means the place could be worth … even more.' Helen looked dazed.

Joe reached for his computer. 'And this email says the answer's still no, and they'll be hearing from my solicitor on even thicker embossed notepaper, saying that I suspect Webster of harassment and criminal damage. Harassment because somehow they have found out where you live, Helen, and brought the letter round here because they didn't expect me to stay in my burnt-out shell. I think that's more than sinister.'

'Careful – you've got no proof. Have you got a solicitor?'

'Not yet.'

'I think we should go back to the police and tell them the full story. About trespassers and poor Puppy,'

'As you said, love, we've got no proof. We can't prove he didn't just fancy a swim and I can't prove I've never had a petrol can. And this letter is just a simple offer to purchase. I can't prove anything, but I can threaten to build up a case of intimidation. Perhaps the newspapers have got more punch than the police.'

87

'Did you see Joe Wright's article in The Bugle?' Alan the publican of The Miners Standard interrogated each of the regulars as they came in. 'I got some extra copies in if you didn't.'

'I didn't see it. What's an SSSI? It says here the old quarry could be one of those.'

'Some sort of Special Secret Information place that needs secret bunkers. They choose quarries and old mines if it's hush hush. Like they used the caves near Matlock and some near Buxton in the war. Got them all ready to bring all the generals and Churchill and their papers and wirelesses up from London in case Parliament got bombed.'

'Bollocks, Ethel. You do talk such crap. What's the use of wirelesses hundreds of feet underground? I can't even get a signal up here for my mobile. Joe's place is only about plants and animals – newts and water beetles usually, though I can't see why the SS whatsit bothers about them.'

'I've heard he's been offered a couple of a million for the old place, so there must be something fishy going on. Fishy! Get it?'

'Now you're talking. Loch Ness monster in Stoneybrook, that would be fun. Do you think Joe's pond is deep enough?'

'Deep enough? Those old quarry pits go down thousands of feet. I heard somewhere Joe's poor dog got drowned in it. Takes a lot to drown a dog.'

'Margaret reckons that fire Joe wrote about was arson, to try to smoke him out. Or kill him.'

'What's the point of that? His mother would inherit the place and she's in some posh town house in Buxton. What would she want a quarry for?'

'Exactly. She came in here for a cream tea once, said she hates the place so she'd flog it soon as look at you. But I never knew there were rare birds and animals up there in that dingy hole.'

'Joe's photos make it look a real picture, like something abroad, the Amazon or the Alps. And the way he described the eagles and orchids, real poetry.'

'Thank you.' Joe came in and ordered a dry cider. 'All the stuff I've written over the years that no-one's even noticed, so I'm glad a few of you have read it.' He feared it was talk of big money rather than tiny frogs that had fascinated the reluctant readers.

There were about twenty customers in the pub, all speculating on the value of a hole in the ground.

'Who made the offer, Joe? Your article doesn't say. Who wants to buy it?'

'I'm not sure yet. Someone calling himself Webster, but I think he's just a front man. My boss at The Bugle, Fred Marshall, thinks it's a big mining company, a multinational even, and he thinks my article will soon flush them out. Get a bit of competition going, then I can say no to all of them.' The more wild rumours the locals spread the better. 'I expect the media will be all over Stoneybrook wanting your considered views on the matter.'

There was a sudden, uneasy silence, then Janet, the publican's wife who ran the shop at the end of the pub, started to laugh. 'That Fred Marshall is having you on, just to sell his papers, making it sound like some Midsomer Murders conspiracy on the telly.'

'It's a free rag, Janet, so why would he? Try reading it.' Alan threw her a copy over the counter. 'Fred was in here yesterday and told me the Derbyshire Times is printing the article, and so is the Buxton Herald. Stoneybrook will soon be famous. Good for business. Sorry Joe.'

Joe frowned, 'Seriously, how does everyone feel about all the publicity? I had the regional television on the phone just before I came out. They are coming to film the quarry in the morning, and they'll probably be roaming round the village too. Perhaps I should have asked around before I wrote that article.' Hypocrite, he thought. No grousing villager would have stopped him writing it.

'Publicity is what you wanted, so let's keep it going.' Margaret Byron drained her vodka and Joe bought her another.

'That's for helping clean up the farmhouse after the fire.'

'But you've already given us all bottles of wine.'

'That was Helen's idea, not mine. Nasty acid stuff, wine. I suppose publicity for the quarry and the village will help the "Stop

the New Housing" petition. I still feel bad about not bothering to come to the meeting.'

Lauren came in to the bar and someone whistled. 'Doesn't she clean up lovely? Going anywhere special dear?'

Joe bought her a double brandy and kissed her on the cheek. 'I'll never be able to thank you enough for helping me after the fire.'

There were cheers and calls of 'Go on, try, Joe. Bet you'll think of something' until Alan behind the bar shouted over the noise 'Gentleman here looking for Joseph Wright.'

Joe turned round and saw Webster, who came over and greeted him like an old friend. 'Good evening, Joseph. What is it, cider?'

Suggestions as to how Joe could thank Lauren died away at the sight of this smartly suited stranger who said firmly 'Could I have a word with you outside?'

Joe followed him out to the small courtyard. 'I haven't got anything to add to my email, Webster. And I don't like you following me about like this.'

'Just having a friendly drink. And I owe you an apology: it's quite true that I find your old farmhouse charming …'

'Especially the quarry.'

'Even more so after I'd read your splendid article. I'm a bit of a nature-lover myself …'

'What's the apology for?' Joe turned to go back in to the pub. If Webster was going to admit to any dirty tricks he's like a few witnesses.

'I work for Stonecraft Mines and Quarries International. You'll have heard the name? I didn't quite explain the situation.' Webster had not bought a drink at the bar, but he drew a silver flask out of his pocket and took a sip, leaning up against an old stone mounting block. 'As I said, your farmhouse is delightful. I'd like nothing more than to lavish time and money on it but the national, indeed world-wide, appetite for building materials means that sentimentality is an indulgence mankind cannot afford.'

'What a pompous little speech. Why didn't you say all that when you spoke to me the first time? When you were creeping round in the undergrowth up at my place? And how did you know I'd be in

here? Why did you leave that letter in Bakewell? It's beginning to feel like harassment.' Joe's voice rose; he could see eager faces peering out of the pub window. With the two men facing each other in the yard it felt like some corny Western. 'And you can leave my partner out of it. Or there'll be trouble,' he added lamely.

'If it were to come to a compulsory purchase order then you would get a less generous offer.'

Joe walked away shouting 'All this just for ten affordable houses, Webster? Do you think we are all fools in Derbyshire?'

The customers who had been crowded round the two small, deep-set stone windows returned to their seats.

'Who was that, Joe?' Lauren asked, sitting next to him on the pub's baggy sofa. It was an uncomfortable reminder of another drinking session when Joe had slipped from her grasp like a wet bar of soap. 'Was it another offer for your place?'

Joe nodded. 'It's been a big mining company behind it all along. He suggested they could force me to sell, but it's probably a bluff.'

Margaret stood up and addressed the drinkers: 'Things have gone far enough up at Blackridge Quarry. We all remember Great Longrock and the terrible destruction of vast stretches of Longrock Edge. Peak Park Authority and the local groups had a big fight with the mining company, it went on for years with High Court Judges and appeals ...'

There was a rumble of reluctant agreement; if it could happen at Longrock it could happen anywhere, even with all Derbyshire against it.

'But Longrock won in the end, didn't it?' Joe felt the mood was getting too despondent.

'Not really. I'd heard the company's gone to appeal again and that the case could rumble on for years, and all the time they go on digging and blasting away. No-one's got the power, the guts or the cash to stop them.'

'We need a proper meeting, not like that last one when none of you bothered to turn up. We need a big hall, and all the villages,' Margaret waved her arms in a global gesture 'all the villages fired up because of noise and dust and lorries.'

'And the rare bats and grasses in the quarry, those are just as important,' Lauren insisted, smiling at Joe.

'It won't do no good' said one elderly villager coming back in after having a smoke. 'Them big companies always wins in the end 'cos our local councillors got no balls.'

'They'll soon grow some if we refuse to vote for them. But you're right, Bill, councils can't afford to go to appeal so in the past big business has won. But this time it will be different.'

'How's that, Margaret? What will be different about Blackridge? You mean about it being of special scientific interest?' Joe looked hopeful, but no-one heard him.

There was a loud cheer as Fred Marshall came into the pub. He held up his arms like a champion fighter. 'I thought there'd be a good crowd in, nothing like a bit of controversy to give you a thirst. I hear your little piece has worked, Joe. We've flushed out the big game, only it's rushed off in what could have been an Aston Martin. It was having trouble with the cobbles.'

Conversation drifted off into little groups arguing about what to do next, then about the shortcomings of the council, of the government, the cancellation of the late-night bus to Buxton and the price of diesel.

Joe looked grim. 'I keep saying no to offers for the quarry, but is that enough? I don't know what to do next.'

'One small step at a time,' Fred advised. 'Did you get the name of the company?' He was fiddling with his smartphone.

'Stonecraft International. I had a letter from their solicitors. I should have got Webster's card, or address, but I just didn't want anything to do with him.'

'Doesn't matter. I've found it but there's no local head office address, only one in London and one in South Africa. They've got three workings in Britain, one's in Derbyshire so we could have a look round that to see how they run things. Great! One step at a time, and this is enough info for our next edition, just to keep things on the boil. The Bugle's doing well with extra advertising – I don't know whether it's the dirty tricks or the furry critters but copies are in demand.'

The publican flicked at the bar with his soggy little drip towel. 'Are you buying a drink, Fred, or just using the place as an office?'

'The Bugle and Joe have doubled your clientele tonight, Alan, and saved on your heating bill with all this waffle. I'd better just have a cup of your fresh-ground, fresh boiled instant coffee before I go back to my lonely office and work into the night on this exciting development.'

'Which will take you all of twenty minutes to bash out. And don't forget the payment for my story and photos.'

Fred turned to go. 'Who's that well-built lass in the orange dress? She's been staring adoringly at you, Joe.'

'That's Lauren, and I don't want to join her or she'll expect me to go back to her place. She's a great girl. Scares me a bit. Keep talking business Fred.'

'You fight your own battles, I'm off as soon as I've finished this coffee.'

Margaret saved him. 'Come back to my place, Joe, and we'll decide on a date for a public meeting and compose an email to book a venue.'

'How do we decide on a date? What if it isn't right for other people?'

'It's your quarry, your land, your fight, so you're in charge from now on.'

8

An Offer He Can't Refuse

'We'll take Puppy for some long walks across the moors, love, strengthen his little legs.' Joe was using base, underhand tactics on the phone because he hadn't seen Helen for over a week. 'The back door has been replaced and I've painted the kitchen walls and ceilings. You wouldn't know the old place. And I'm missing you, love.'

'Could we come for the weekend? Mrs. Bonsall's reported Puppy to the landlord again, for barking this time, so it would be good to escape for a while. The weather's not bad so we could take picnics, and there's a play on in Tideswell on Saturday. See you Friday evening, then.'

She hadn't said she missed him or loved him, Joe reflected, although there had been pleasure in her voice at the thought of a busy weekend spent with him. Why hadn't he thought to look for village merrymaking and planned picnic hampers with baguettes and champagne? He had visions of wicker baskets, linen tablecloths, wine glasses and bottles cooled in streams, or did that only happen on film sets? He certainly couldn't fit all of that into his backpack.

His mother had been over the previous day with some new kitchen curtains, followed by a man with a van bringing a pine corner cupboard, two chairs and some old units that had been in her shed since her last kitchen refit years ago.

'Thanks, Mum. They'll do fine until I get round to making some fitted cupboards.' How had she lived so long without realising that furniture wasn't that important?

'I'm sure you'll do a good job, you always were good at carpentry. Trouble is, it will take you another two years to get round to it and meanwhile you need something to sit on.'

Joe had shown her the first chapter of his book on quarry wildlife and she had to admit that his photos were stunning: rock formations and the blue frozen lake with skating geese and glowing sunsets that turned the cliff face orange. Beautiful, she had said, thinking how clever her son was, except that all that beauty never made him enough money to buy security. She felt she was a nagging old misery but how could she stop worrying?

She took away a wad of posters advertising the quarry meeting to stick up in strategic places round Buxton; she certainly didn't want more quarrying blasting away, who did? All that dust and thundering lorries. Joe had not told his mother that he'd been offered nearly a million for the despised farmhouse and land. In fact, he could almost name his price the company had said when met with another 'no'.

On Friday Joe finished an article he had promised Fred for the past few weeks 'The Secret Gardens of the Peak District' then put it to one side for Helen to read through when she arrived. She loved 'secret' gardens hidden away up ginnels or high on hillsides and though Joe could admire their ingenuity and feel the love packed into their tiny confines, he always felt they could do with a bit more wilderness and neglect. Now he stared out of the window and down the track, waiting for Helen's small car to lurch its way to his gate. The evening seemed suspended in a cool spring mist and for once the old house seemed empty, seemed to be waiting quietly without even the usual creaking beams and whistling draughts, waiting for something other than the sterile clicking of his computer keyboard. Joe lit the fire and pulled the bean bag dog bed out from under the sofa.

At last there was the sound of wheels on stony gravel and Puppy launched himself at Joe.

'What a monster! He's grown even in the last week.' Joe gave the leaping hound a brief pat then pulled Helen to him and gave her a long kiss. 'I've been looking forward to that all day.' He buried his

face in her hair. 'You look and smell wonderful … to a hermit who hasn't seen a woman for weeks.'

'And you feel warm and baggy,' Helen smiled, running her hands over his chest under an ancient fleece.

Puppy made the most of this lull in attention by sniffing round the room at fresh smells that had matured since his last visit. And there was that old slipper that he had made his own, waiting to be shaken and killed, and a pile of old paper on the floor waiting to be shredded.

Joe reluctantly released Helen and hauled the dog off his journalistic masterpiece.

'Have a look at my Secret Gardens article while I open a celebration bottle, and tell me who's going to be upset by being left out of my gushing prose.' He felt pleased with himself – he had calmly rescued some pages from Puppy's jaws without swearing and had avoided the tiny white fangs that were playfully turned on him. 'Lie down,' he growled masterfully and, for a second, Puppy did.

Helen wandered into the kitchen to inspect the clean-up. The effect was a bit like the back room of a charity shop. 'You've certainly made a difference. It's sort of … retro farmhouse,' was the kindest encouraging phrase she could think of. 'My holiday cottage visitors love this kind of look.'

'Oh, shit, I've got a look. Retro. Is it that bad? Well, blame Mum and her storage shed.'

They settled into the depths of the old sofa and a weekend of no deadlines, no holiday makers, only warmth and wine and lovemaking.

Helen woke up when Joe prodded the log fire into life. 'Puppy's being good, considering that I haven't fed him. And he's fast asleep.'

'He cleverly fed himself. Didn't want to disturb us.' Joe pointed to her empty shopping bag, and a trail of mangled quiche and cheesecake. A tub of stuffed olives had been tried and found wanting. 'Fortunately he won't fancy my very hot mushroom curry with lime pickle, so we won't starve.'

'I saw Fred Marshall's report on that mining company in the paper … Stonecraft Mines, was it? It said that they had made you another offer to buy the quarry, and upped the offer again. How much has it got to now? You've been keeping quiet. You don't trust me not to be impressed by big money, do you?' Helen watched him carefully for signs of guilt.

Joe shrugged. 'It was just another offer. I've lost count.' He waited for her to repeat how much this time, and why didn't he sell up and buy something more comfortable?

She kissed his cheek. 'I think your book is going to be a big success, and I'm beginning to understand that you need to be here, fortified by trips out to that wilderness,' she jerked her head in the direction of the quarry, 'in between attacks of the creative urge. I couldn't ever live like this, but I can see …'

Joe took her face in his hands and insisted 'Just wait until I've made a fortune and turned this place around. And talking of urges …'

The phone rang and Margaret's voice boomed down the line. 'Tell me you won't cave in …that's a good one … you won't cave in over the quarry and sell up, will you Joe?' she dropped her voice slightly. 'The village spies said that Helen was with you. Lovely girl, but she'll try to make you change your mind. Do you mind if I call in for a few minutes?'

Joe covered the receiver. 'Margaret Byron wants to come up, she thinks you'll weaken me with your lascivious desires …'

'I heard her. That's fine.' She added loudly 'I'll get another glass out.'

'I expect she wants to talk about the meeting … I meant to tell you but we've been too busy doing more important things.'

'I know all about the meeting, and in fact I knew about the mining company's offer because my boss, Adrian, was down at The Miners Standard when that Webster person collared you. Adrian's all fired up and will probably be chief agitator in the save-the-old-quarry campaign. We've got holiday cottages in Stoneybrook and several more in nearby villages, and tourists don't come to the Peak District to see HGVs and hear blasting all day. Adrian fears he'll lose money

if people start cancelling. And I'll be out of a job,' Helen added bleakly.

Margaret arrived with a bottle of brandy, fending Puppy off with it. 'I won't stay long, you young people have better things to do. But nipping this quarry business in the bud is important for poor Joe's sake, don't you think so, Helen my dear?' She made herself comfortable and poured brandy absent-mindedly into their half-full wine glasses, then produced a crumpled paper from her cardigan pocket. 'I've had a stab at an agenda. Don't want anything too formal, too technical. It would frighten the horses.' She handed the list to Joe.

Helen plumped down next to Margaret on the sofa as an expression of solidarity. 'My boss, Adrian, is right behind us, he's worried ...'

'Oh, he's already been in touch with an offer of cash for printing leaflets and advertising costs for the meeting, which I imagine he can well afford. He says a brace of MPs and a clutch of County Councillors should add weight if not substance.'

'And we need that petition to have thousands of signatures, there's nothing impresses politicians more than armies of voters.' Helen's voice rose and Puppy leaped excitedly on to the sofa.

Joe, riddling the stove as a distraction, looked uncomfortable. 'Aren't we going too fast? The company may back down. After all, I have said no to their last offer. We'd look pretty silly organizing a public meeting without a cause ...'

Margaret snorted. 'We need to be ready. The meeting is not for another few weeks, time for Stonecraft International to make their intentions clear as to whether they are going to go against local public opinion, and if so, to get their solicitors to put stuff in writing.'

'But we don't need to reinvent the wheel, campaigns like this have been fought before. I've been looking some up in the County Records in Matlock. The petition is a good idea but remember Stanton Moor and the Nine Ladies protest? We'd only have to threaten Stonecraft with a big national demonstration like that and I'm sure they'd back off.'

Margaret sat up straight and raised her glass. 'That was a wonderful campaign – we put a caravan up in the trees – can't quite remember why we did now but it was great fun.'

'And remember that Skycraft high up, with layers and layers of platforms going up into the trees? And you could stay up there for weeks on end without ever setting foot on earth, hauling up your provisions on a whole network of ropes and pulleys. That's the kind of spirit that wins.' Joe waved the poker aloft in triumph.

Helen stared at him in amazement. 'You were there! I can just imagine you as an eco-warrior! How exciting!'

Joe frowned, 'It was deadly serious. The media – press, radio, television, all grilling us and insisting on interviews. And we won, after months of hardship and struggle,' he gulped a mixture of Cognac and Bordeaux, 'we won.'

'I'd heard that it was the Druids who won it.'

'You're right, dear.' Margaret jotted down notes. 'Nothing more scary than a circle of robed figures chanting and imprecating on a dark night. Casting spells and curses up there on the moors. It was a famous victory, but we can't be too careful, just think of Foolow. That was a scandal, the quarrying there was said to be in the national interest, just to produce a few roofing tiles. National need, my arse.'

Helen looked thoughtful. 'So what we need is a site oozing with religious symbolism and stuffed with newts and bats. Sounds more like a coven of witches. I did hear of a quarry near Cromford where a religious sect meets to offer up sacrifices to something or other. A friend of mine went, but she got thrown out for giggling.'

Margaret glared at her. 'It's no joking matter. Any hint of amateurism and big business will have us for breakfast. We need thousands of signatures from Peak Park lovers all over the world. Longrock Edge is not really safe even after the powerful campaign all the locals mounted; we'd have to do even better.' She stood up with a crusading gesture, wobbled and sat back down again.

'I'll walk back with you,' Joe insisted.

'You'll do no such thing. I've been walking these village paths man and boy for over sixty years…'

'Puppy needs a little walk before it gets dark, Joe,' Helen suggested diplomatically. 'I'll get some supper on. I would invite you, Margaret, but the pup has eaten all the pud.'

❧

It was a calm and relaxing weekend, reminding both of them of good times they had enjoyed in the past. The weather was mild, so that a walk to Cheedale, a picnic, and then planting some vegetables in a sheltered spot in the garden all seemed more than enough to make their bit of the Peaks feel like the centre of a comforting world.

'Puppy and I are going to sit in the garden, Joe, while you spend a few hours working on your book. I know we don't need to import Druids and wild boar to make the quarry a special place, but more people need to know that it is worth saving. So off you go. Two thousand words before supper.'

It was what Joe wanted to hear, and he hugged her gratefully. 'It didn't seem right, me ignoring the pair of you and drifting off into my own world.'

'I quite like the cosy thought of it. Me out here in the sunshine while you write a book to change the world.'

'Keep the mutt off the seeds.' Joe collected together the notes he had made over the past few days and opened his laptop. The phone rang.

'Joe, dear. Something very strange has happened.' His mother's voice sounded unusually hesitant. 'I've just had a call from some gentleman about your quarry. He says, and I'm sure there must be some mistake and he means some other quarry, that he is offering you a million pounds for the farmhouse and the land. He must be mentally disturbed. I know it can't be a genuine offer or you'd have told me about it.'

Joe covered the mouthpiece. 'Shit. Webster's got to mother, the conniving sod. 'Sorry, Ma, what did you say? Helen's here and she's making a racket in the kitchen.'

Helen pulled a face and rattled some mugs together. 'She'd have read about it in the paper soon enough.'

'Mr. Webster. Says he's from some big company, but I expect you've looked into that. Is it a fraud, Joe? If you didn't take it

seriously, do you want me to investigate, just in case there's something in it? Some people have more money than sense.'

Joe chose his words carefully, 'Mr. Webster and the company do exist, but your instincts are right, Ma. I wouldn't trust them, wouldn't turn my back on them for a second. Webster called round here once. A nasty-looking piece of work.' Wrong words.

'You can't stay there, Joe, it isn't safe. I don't want to alarm you even more, but now I think about it that Webster sounded very unbalanced. He seemed to be warning us, saying it would be safer to accept his offer because his associates would stop at nothing … then I remembered that fire, Joe, and the place being burgled. Perhaps he's right – he may be off his trolley, but if he's got money … or you could sell to someone else now we know how valuable it is … get a bit of competition going.'

'Stop, Mum, please. That's crazy and dangerous. Webster and his company Stonecraft International are not to be trusted.'

'But you could test the market. With a million pounds you could buy something safe, and quite grand, and still have …'

'A bidding war is a dangerous game. Webster wouldn't play, he'd get the best lawyers and claim that quarrying at Blackridge was in the national interest, you don't know …'

'Of course, I never know anything, Joe. But if you think you can handle it …'

His mother hung up abruptly, which meant she would not let the matter drop, and now he felt too distracted to settle down to writing. In the last patch of sunshine at the end of the garden Joe could see Helen throwing sticks then running to pick them up, while Puppy looked on in surprise then got on with his job of digging up the lawn. Joe laughed and went out to join them. Monday tomorrow, that was when the working week should start.

That night, when Joe was nearly asleep, his leg spread heavily across her stomach, Helen asked 'Do you think your mother will sort Webster out? I'd lay odds on her any day.' But there was no reply.

At breakfast she tried again.

Joe sighed, 'I was hoping you'd forgotten about that. Mum sounded strange, half scared and half seduced by the thought of millions. I'm worried because she'd do anything to make me sell this place.'

'I don't think that's true.' Helen finished her coffee and put on her coat. 'Look at the way she's brought furniture and curtains over for the kitchen. Some thought went into that, even though it probably isn't her taste.'

'Too right it isn't! When Dad left home nearly thirty years ago she stuffed all the old furniture into the shed and it's been there ever since until she shipped it round here. That's why you think it looks cleverly retro.'

'Ungrateful wretch. Mothers are always in the wrong. I must be off, someone's got to work to pay your pension.' She gave him a deliberately domestic kiss.

'Are you taking mutt into work?'

'I was thinking of leaving him here, to keep you ...'

Joe handed her the lead and picked up his notes again.

9

"Save Blackridge Quarry's Rare Wildlife"

Helen's boss read out the article in The Bugle:

"Over two hundred people packed Bakewell Town Hall to voice fears that ancient Blackridge Quarry, for centuries the undisturbed home of rare flora and fauna, would be devastated by quarrying on an international scale. Margaret Byron, Stoneybrook resident, chaired the meeting and called the outraged villagers to order with all the authority of a former maths teacher. Members of the public attended from as far away as Buxton, yet although invited, officers of the Peak Park Authority and local County Councillors declined to turn up on the grounds that no formal planning application had been lodged.

Joseph Wright, landowner, writer and photographer, showed copies of letters from Stonecraft International offering to purchase the land and played a recorded telephone conversation in which a Stonecraft agent implied that the farmhouse was unsafe due to subsidence. Copies of an email were also in evidence in which the agent threatened Mr. Wright with compulsory purchase 'in the national interest due to a need for building materials.'

Publican Alan Wood from the Miners Standard in Stoneybrook insisted that it was dangerous to wait for a planning application – the group must act now and sign a petition which could attract thousands of signatures from Peak Park lovers across the nation and indeed the world.

Local artisan Lauren Postlethwaite reminded the audience of decades of campaigning in the fights to save such iconic landmarks as Longrock Edge and Stanton Moor.

Mrs. Byron recalled exhausting efforts to preserve peaks, dales and edges amid hordes of lawyers and barristers, the Court of Appeal, High Court rulings and threats of the European Court of Human Rights. The Peak District, she said, was not safe in the hands of a toothless government and a cash-strapped Peak Park Authority. 'It is up to us to save the Peaks' she urged.

Two speakers, one the son of a lead miner, were shouted down as they suggested that quarrying would bring much-needed jobs and that the Peak District was not an adventure playground for tourists. It was stated that the real interest of the quarrying company was the extraction of fluorspar, which accounted for less than one percent of employment in the whole of the Derbyshire Dales.

Joseph Wright, owner of Blackridge, showed spectacular photographs of the ecological delights of the quarry, including kestrels, owls and rare orchids (prints available from The Bugle, price £5) and shared with the audience his vision of a future with no quarrying, where new buildings were all of sustainable timber and recycled waste. 'The Scandinavians,' he mused, 'have for millennia built charming and sturdy houses of pine. Close the quarries and stop blasting the guts out of the Peak District.'

One dissenter branded Mr. Wright 'a f*** ing nutter.' A small group of second-home owners wanted to know why there wasn't a better organised protest against the new affordable houses – they were not in keeping with the medieval architecture of the village.

Margaret Byron passed round petition sheets and thanked the audience for their support. There was special applause for representatives from The Ramblers, The Campaign for the Protection of Rural England and The Friends of the Peak District."

Adrian Hucknall folded the newspaper and gave it back to Helen who was trying to concentrate on a colourful description of their latest holiday cottage. She had already read the newspaper article several times and did not need her boss to read it out aloud with a faint note of ridicule in his voice.

'I suppose it's not bad, for the Bugle. It serves its purpose at this stage and underlines the ecological importance of the quarry. What do you think, Helen?'

She sighed and saved her enthusiastic appraisal of the Old Pigsty on her computer. 'Disappointing. It could have been a bit more technical, given a few more facts and done some research into the Stonecraft company. Local readers need to know what we're up against. Joe did put in more detail but the editor cut it out. He thinks readers have the attention span of a gnat.'

Adrian rested a hand on her shoulder. 'Don't take this the wrong way, your Joe is a sound enough lad but as the main character in this quarry drama … well, could you drop him a few hints?'

Helen removed his hand. 'Inappropriate behaviour Mr. Hucknall. Staff might get the wrong idea.' She nodded in the direction of the glass-paned door to the outer office where one of the cleaners was busy filling in a time-sheet. 'Anyway, hints about what? Joe doesn't often take my advice.'

'All that stuff about Scandinavia and log cabins or something. And plastic bricks – it all makes him sound a bit of a wally. A bit flaky. Our limestone Peak District villages are a big tourist attraction, we can't afford to start changing their traditional character with fibreglass extensions and timber-framed new build.'

'You mean you can't afford to, Mr. Hucknall.'

Adrian took a friendly swipe at her with the rolled up Bugle. 'Nor can you, Miss Touch-and-Miss Typist, and nor can the army of cleaners and rip-off plumbers, electricians and gardeners that I keep in fifty inch tellys and holidays in Florida.'

Helen switched off her pc with a defiant click and reached for her coat.

Adrian helped her into it with irritating servility. 'I'd rather hoped you could finish that new brochure this morning and get it on the website at least.'

'Can't do. I need to check some more details on The Pigsty – I'll finish it after lunch. Besides, I've got an animal to look after.'

Adrian frowned. 'That's another thing. I hope you aren't taking it into any of our holiday cottages. Some people are allergic to animal hairs, and it isn't house-trained.' In the good old days, before dog, when Helen wasn't all the time dashing back home or leaving early, she would bring in a packed lunch and work through or he

would tempt her out with a business lunch to talk about plans for his next investment. He enjoyed those outings.

'He – Puppy – is now fully house-trained,' Helen lied. 'If you have a minute, Adrian, get online and see if the Bakewell meeting report appears in any real newspapers. Try the Derbyshire Times or Yorkshire Post.'

When she got back to her flat Joe was waiting at the gate.

'I gave you a key. Have you lost it?'

'I've only just got here. Saw you coming – look.' He flourish the Manchester Evening Post at her, 'a grown-up newspaper, and by a professional writer, though I say it myself. But let's get indoors because muttley is making a hell of a row, and Mrs. Bonsall is at the window upstairs with a face like a gargoyle.'

'Joe! You wrote the article yourself! Isn't journalism supposed to be unbiased? That's the government's pet obsession these days, isn't it? Cleaning up the Press?'

Joe grabbed her and swung her round several times. 'Bugger the article, I've got some real news and I'm taking you out to lunch.'

'Wait a minute, I love you when you're excited but I've come home to take Puppy for a walk.'

'I'm taking him out to lunch too.'

'It must be good news. Ok, we can go to my favourite pub at Over Haddon then walk down to Lathkill Dale. Then I'm inspecting a luxuriously appointed pigsty this afternoon, so there's no hurry.'

Puppy ensured that the walk came first and a swim in the icy water of a rock pool. 'You'd think that last swim in the quarry pool had put him off. I'm not fishing him out again.'

'I should have stopped him going in, he's too small to get so cold.' Helen wrapped him up in her woolly scarf and gave him to Joe to carry. 'Half an hour gone and still nothing about your great news, Joe.'

'It'll sound even better in front of the fire with a glass of cider, and the smell of fresh bread rather than wet dog. Just look at the sun on those wet limestone rocks in the river, they look as good as diamonds.'

Helen stopped and admired the dale. 'I think Lathkill is my favourite, especially now when the river doesn't disappear under-ground so much.'

'Let's get back to the inn to eat, and dry the mongrel and my shirt front.'

❧

'You remember I talked about the amazing numbers of different species of plants and animals in my quarry?'

Helen tackled a ferociously crunchy baguette. 'It's your favourite subject, you're always on about it.'

'At the campaign meeting, I mean.'

'Oh, of course. You said there were dozens of different things down there. In your quarry. All special.'

'You weren't listening at all. How many?'

'Well, hundreds then.' She gave Puppy an awkward bit of crust. 'He really does stink now he's hot. Everyone's moved away.'

'Right, over two hundred different species of trees and plants, making up a fair old percentage of everything in the country …'

'The view from up here is spectacular. Are those rocks over there Robin Hood's Stride? What's that stuff about percentage got to do with your amazing news?'

'A television company in Salford read my piece in the Manchester Evening News and rang me with an idea of a kind of challenge. They want to make a programme with a team of professors and wildlife celebrities to see if there really are hundreds of different species in my quarry. See how many they can find in an hour's programme.'

'And you agreed? I think it sounds great fun, but not very scientific, not your sort of thing.' Helen was impressed, but she could not imagine a television circus darting around Joe's sanctuary.

'The professors will do the scientific bit, with a posse of their post-graduates swarming about. You know how they always seem to get impossibly glamorous young academics as a sexy foil to the ageing oracles. Then later they may do another programme about all the nocturnal wildlife.'

Helen gave him an enthusiastic kiss, wondering if Joe himself hadn't been chosen as a sexy foil, and one that would be dumped if nobody watched the programme. 'That really is good news, then everyone will have to believe your *thousands of rare species* claims.'

'You mean you don't?'

'Of course I believe you, love. But you do get a bit … euphoric. These scientific programmes should be impartial. How much will they pay you?'

'A new roof on the farmhouse barn would be good. But that's not the point; if we can get the BBC involved and all those celebrities they get on Nature Watch and Spring Watch, just think of the publicity. We'll have the best of both worlds, big television names and scientific journals.' Joe stood up and knocked his cider over Puppy. 'The quarry will be famous and protected, safe from speculators.'

'Wet dog again,' Helen laughed, pulling Joe back into his chair. 'But I see what you mean – if Blackridge is a national treasure then no-one will ever get permission to blast it to bits. It's a good plan – when would they start filming?'

'I don't know, but I'm going to ring the producer this afternoon to explain how urgently we need the publicity. I was so overcome when she rang me that I didn't have my wits about me.'

'Those documentary telly programmes love a bit of drama, some sort of artificial suspense that they have to create, but there's no need for that at Blackridge because you've already got the drama. Get the cameras and profs in before the gelignite arrives.'

Joe stood up again, too excited to sit still. 'We'd better go. Someone's given the mutt a sausage and he's defending it to the death under the next table. I've never heard him growl before. Quite impressive, I think his voice has broken.'

'You're too much of a celebrity now to come and inspect a four-bedroom converted pigsty with me, so I'll get back to work. Come on Puppy. He's famous now as well as gorgeous and he's got no time for us.'

❧

Holiday cottage was a misnomer and The Pigsty was a self-consciously ironic name. When Helen got there she was surprised to see her boss already at the site.

'Hello Adrian. Amazing place, isn't it? Someone has spent a fortune converting something the size of a tithe barn. Even the en suites have got en suites. I could have checked whatever it is you need to know without you coming over.'

Adrian did not seem to be checking anything, but stood in the vast kitchen running his hands over the cream marble work surface. 'What do you think of the place, Helen?'

'Palatial. It's like nothing else we've got on our books and I can't imagine which bit used to be a pigsty. It's from another world. Not exactly muddy Peakshire. Have you seen the swimming pool in the old vegetable garden? The owners must have spent a few hundred thousand.'

Adrian went to the window overlooking a walled orchard, then turned to look at her. 'I spent quite a lot; I wanted you to be impressed.'

Helen froze. After a few seconds she said warily 'You mean you own this one? But you know by now I'm easily impressed. The most charming little two-up two-down sends me into raptures, but anyone could tell you this place is the very top end of the market, superb craftsmanship. I thought you were just acting on behalf of some multi-billionaire. Though if you can afford this, why would you need to rent it out?'

'I haven't shown it to just anyone – only you.' Adrian came towards her and took her hand. 'I know our office relationship has been quite formal, but could you start to think of me with some affection? I was going to invite you to dinner here, music and outside caterers … but then thought it was rushing things a bit. After all, I've had months to imagine all this, but for you …'

Helen took her hand away and tried to see someone who wasn't her boss but was Adrian, rather nervous and stammering. She said slowly, feeling her way, 'It's a shock. You and all this luxury, and you saying it was a holiday let …'

'It can be whatever you want it to be, Helen. For holiday or home.'

'You don't know me at all Mr. … Adrian. My office person is not the real me. Most of the time I'm selfish, a bit neurotic and … bad-tempered.'

'That's the one. I'd enjoy the challenge.'

'And friends say I'm too demanding and very high-maintenance.'

'If something, someone, is worth having, then money is of no importance.' Adrian came close and took her hand again, his other hand on her back, pulling her to him.

There was a frenzied barking and a damp bundle launched itself down the pale oak hallway, claws scratching and slipping over the shiny surface.

'How did you get out of the car, you bad dog?' Helen felt like kissing him for the welcome change of mood. Puppy felt the same and jumped up to lick her so she picked him up, a wriggling, smelly barrier between her and an awkward situation.

'I'd better get him out of here, Adrian. So sorry. I'll clean up the paw marks. We must have a drink one lunchtime and talk about all … about what you said.' Shit. That wasn't nearly firm enough, just avoiding telling her boss to back off. She escaped to her car, but where to go? Not back to the office yet, that definitely needed a cooling off gap. Not round to Joe wailing about another man's advances and spoiling his obvious delight at making a television programme about his favourite place. She drove to Monsal Head and walked down to the old railway track and across the viaduct.

'You lucky hound, one walk after another but you've certainly earned your keep today. First charging in like the cavalry and saving me, now therapy.'

The dog, sensing waves of approval, took advantage by rolling in a mound of something dead and putrefying. She sat on a rock and looked down the dale towards Cressbrook and the mill. She thought, as she always did, how beautiful the valley looked when really the ghosts of wretched mill workers ought to have damned and blighted the place forever. Her workplace problems, her boss and his advances were a small worry next to a history of such relentless industrial slavery.

At last she felt able to focus on the scene in the kitchen – why had he chosen the kitchen? Why, if he wanted to impress her, not the vast living room with its arching beams and huge traditional stone Derbyshire fireplace that would never have been found in an animal shed? At last she felt calm enough to think about Adrian Hucknall and to wonder about the man outside the office. Poor Adrian, though he certainly was not poor. She had left him with some hope, and that would have to be dealt with. She knew nothing about him, supposed he was about forty – had he been married? Was he still married? Pleasant-looking and well-built, though slightly over-weight, he had always been a thoughtful and competent boss; now he had changed everything. Was it all tiresome and irritating – or was she a little flattered?'

Puppy had dragged the end of the lead from her and was taking himself for a walk. Time to go home – she'd treat herself to a cold white wine and a hot foaming bath to help her think about the way ahead.

❧

When Joe rang a few days later he was triumphant. 'I explained about opening up the quarry, destroying a unique site, and new houses in the village and that they are trying to force me to sell up and she was wonderful.'

'Slow down, Joe. Who was wonderful?'

'Kathy, the producer. She saw the whole picture at once, the whole programme, the wildlife experts finding as many species as they could, film of some of the rarer ones – she thought the owls and kestrels, and some night filming of the bat cave would make good television. She'll get an interview with the Minister for the Environment to discuss the importance of such sites, and she'll involve some of the more enraged villagers who think the village will be changed forever. She even said I could do a talk about some of my discoveries and promote my book ...'

'Not unreasonable, it is your land. But, Joe, it sounds wonderful, just the break you deserve. When is all this happening?'

'She's coming up with a couple of her film crew tomorrow, just to assess the potential. Stands to reason she can't take my word for

everything, and she'd have to pitch for funding. She … Kathy … sounds really dynamic.'

'Dynamite in the quarry. Well, I'm pleased it's all happening. But be careful, I get the impression those media people are unreliable. If your newts aren't lively enough and your orchids spotty enough they'll lose interest.'

'You sound a bit down, Helen. Bad day at the office?'

It had not been as bad as she had feared. She and Adrian had managed a kind of joking, awkward friendliness, though perhaps she had been a little too understanding – or was it cowardice? – because he reminded her about the lunchtime drink and asked her advice on garden design for the palatial Pigsty.

'Are you still there, Helen? Okay if I come round? There's lots more to tell you about all the ideas Kathy's got. I'd like to put you in the picture.'

'You mean Pup and I will be centre stage on the telly? Yapping to camera? Are me and Pup still part of your plans?'

But Joe had switched off.

Helen threw two giant potatoes into the microwave, opened a tin of beans and grated some cheese. She guessed that Joe had been too excited to think about shopping or getting meals and she had been thrown too off-balance to do proper cooking. He arrived clutching a wad of papers and notebooks.

'Helen! You look good enough to eat.' He gave her a long devouring kiss, then a firm hug.

'I guessed right, then. You've been too elated to think about meals.'

Joe gave a long sigh, 'You'll keep my feet on the ground, stop me getting ideas above my station, won't you? I might even make you proud of me. Just now all's right with the world.'

The microwave pinged. 'I expect that's the aroma of jacket potato.' She really must learn to accept compliments graciously, but admiration from two men in the same week was an unusual experience. 'Put your papers somewhere safe out of hound's reach while we eat.'

'I've managed to finish the article on the special scientific interest of Blackridge Quarry and how it ought to be a legally protected nature reserve.'

'That's good going, considering distractions by media moguls.'

'Well, Kathy the producer said it could form the basis for some of the script, so I was up until about two finishing it off. I'd like you to read it through, see if it convinces you that nature is more important than industry. Looking at it as a non-scientific viewer who …'

'Who spends the evening channel-hopping and could end up choosing QVC? You know damn well I think the critters come first, you know me well enough by now, surely?' Helen choked on some hot potato.

'I mean I want you to read it as though you were some stuffy blinkered financial jobsworth obsessed with budgets. Just pretend for fuck's sake. Why are you so ratty tonight?'

'Well, try explaining yourself a bit better. Tell me you value my sensitive opinion, tell me my English Lit. degree wasn't wasted. You know I'd love to read it – it needs to be out there as soon as possible in all the papers and Peak Living magazine and Country Life. I'll dish up some bananas and custard then settle down to a crit. You could even play with Pup while I concentrate on your prose style.'

'Do I have to be that grateful? But I'll do even better and take him for a walk so I don't have to listen to your snorts of derision.'

Helen settled down to concentrate. She was moved by the strength of Joe's passionate determination to convince his readers and viewers that Blackridge should be left in peace. His voice came through the writing with authority, with a depth of knowledge that could have sounded dry with so much botanical and geological information if he had not conveyed the excitement of sudden discoveries like Mouse eared Hawkweed and the surprisingly fearless Little Owl.

She ran to meet them both when she heard the gate open, 'Joe love, if that doesn't convince them that Blackridge Quarry ought to

be the centre of the scientific universe then nothing will. And it's a good read.'

'Thanks, but who's *them*? I'm still not sure who I need to persuade.'

'Whoever it is, your article will do it. It's a knock-out bit of writing. The only trouble is, what with that and a telly programme you'll have the whole world beating a path to Blackridge to see the amazing beasts there. An invasion could upset the rare species that are only just hanging on by their … claw tips.'

Joe put his papers firmly away and drew Helen down onto the sofa. 'I'm being selfish. I haven't seen you for three days and when I do get here it's all about me. How's work? Sorry I didn't get to see that luxury pigsty – was it a laugh?'

'It was impressive.' It was a shock to remember the scene with Adrian in the dream kitchen.

'You made it sound rather vulgar; even the pigs would turn their snouts up at it – I'll have an enjoyable sneer some other time.'

'I don't think it will be on our books for renting.' Helen stroked Puppy's head and hoped she could change the subject. 'It's too expensive. Not really our market. Do you want more butter on your spud?'

'So why did you pay it a second visit? I'm surprised your boss agreed to consider it. The owner probably expects a fortune in rent,' Joe said, feeling he was showing an interest in the tourist industry.

Helen took a deep breath, 'Well, it's Adrian who owns the house – the Pigsty – and he must have spent a fortune on renovations. I suppose he wanted my reaction when he showed me …'

'You mean he met you there? You didn't mention that when we had lunch at the pub. Just as well I didn't go along with you, I might have ruined your chances of promotion. Adrian must really value your opinion, and I can't say I blame him. I reckon you do more for Peak promotion than any Bakewell Tart, sorry, I mean Pud. Seriously though, keep him on board because he'll do wonders for our housing protest and he's got a useful amount of cash.'

Encouraged by Joe's admiration Helen said tentatively. 'It was all very strange, unexpected; I haven't come to terms with it yet.'

'Unusual modesty, Miss Seymour. We all value your opinion on a whole lot …'

'But he seemed to think I might want to live there.'

'That you might want to rent it instead of this flat? I thought you said it was hellishly expensive. And has he met your messy mutt?'

There were times when Joe was irritatingly slow-witted. He never could fill in the dots, and she was not sure what her next words should be.

After a while her silence prompted him to say jokingly, 'Or was he suggesting you should live there with him? Happy as pigs in … you know.'

Helen shrugged. Perhaps it was best to laugh it off. 'An indecent proposal over the trough. Poor Adrian.'

'Poor Adrian? You mean he was serious? You and him?'

Helen thought Joe sounded unflatteringly amazed. 'He said he'd been wanting to ask me for some time … it was like a kind of old-fashioned proposal, could I see my way to possibly …'

'And you waited three days to tell me that your boss has been leching after you for months and fancies you as a kept woman in a converted pigsty? Or have you known for longer than that? All those comfy cottages for the pair of you to shag in.'

'That's unfair, Joe. He just turned up at the holiday rental, or I thought it was a rental, and seemed to think I'd love the place and then, well, he almost went down on one knee.'

'And you fell for it?' Joe shouted, making Puppy bark at the sudden noise. 'Your boss, who owns dozens of properties, tarts one up and reckons he can install you in it so you're available whenever he feels a bit randy?' He stood up angrily, baked beans sliding off his plate. 'Get off my leg, bloody animal.'

'He's just cleaning tomato sauce off your jeans. Don't shout at him like that. Adrian had every right to ask me how I feel and you are being childish getting so angry.'

'He had no right luring you to a deserted ponced-up outbuilding under pretence of discussing work – that's exploitation. So, right, okay, he asked if you fancied him, what did you say?'

'I said no, of course,' she lied.

'He knows you've just left some penniless scribbler who lives in a hovel and he thought he'd flash some of his millions and his vulgar, gold-plated pigsty at you.'

'I turned him down because I've got my eye on a budding author and TV personality.' Helen resented trying to calm the situation with flattery and added 'who just might shape up one of these days and stop thinking that any sort of comfort is wasteful indulgence.' She took the plates into the kitchen. 'Coffee?'

'No thanks, I'd better be going.' He had intended to stay the night but now he needed to put some distance between him and the scene of his raw outburst. 'Big day tomorrow. Thanks for reading my article and the helpful comments.'

'Thanks for taking Pup out. I'm sure he enjoyed it. Good luck with your telly interview, or whatever it is.'

They were being so very polite.

Joe drove back to the farmhouse, parked the car and walked down to the village. He needed a drink, or a few. He turned and looked back at the house as it squatted on its crumbly old stones, its dark windows following him like eyes, accusing him of neglect. What a mess. And what hope would he ever have of treating it well, with the care it deserved, so that it could sit smugly like a real Peak property with handcrafted pine kitchen and Victoriana conservatory with eau-de-nil woodwork. Helen was waiting, foolishly optimistic, for him to shape up. She'd already waited three years. He turned away from the farmhouse and stumbled off to The Miners; he'd never needed its warm, shabby comfort and loudly bigoted inmates so much.

'Joe! Just the man!' Alan clattered behind the bar, setting up Joe's usual pint of dry cider. 'We were all wondering how you'd take it, news about the planning.'

'What news about what planning?'

'Stonecraft International have put in an application to re-open Blackridge Quarry. Barry here,' Alan nodded towards a jovial-looking drinker splayed across two bar stools 'works in Planning and he saw it this afternoon.'

Joe took two large gulps of numbing alcohol, 'Can't have. I haven't heard anything.'

'You don't need to,' Barry said triumphantly. 'That's the bloody beauty of the crazy system we've got. Anyone can apply for planning permission just for the fun of it. You don't even have to own the property. There's no paperwork or anything lying around, but I saw it all on the screen. I expect you'll hear in due course. They'll be putting up those little yellow notices in crafty places where nobody can see them.'

'You've got them over a barrel,' someone called out. 'Name your price, Joe. We told you last time you were in here you'd soon be a bloody millionaire.'

Barry said officiously 'It doesn't quite work like that. If the company can persuade the council to slap a compulsory purchase order on it, then you'll have to take what you're given.'

Joe tipped a packet of viciously acid crisps into his mouth and ordered another pint.

'I won't be selling. That quarry is my future.' He thought that sounded a bit wet, a bit off the wall, 'I mean, I'm writing a book about it.' That sounded worse, and there was a disbelieving silence.

Barry said slowly, as though to a half-wit 'You still aren't getting it, Joe. You wouldn't have a choice.'

'And tomorrow,' Joe announced grandly, 'they're making a television programme about it.'

Now there was a rumble of interest.

'They'll probably be interviewing some of you, getting your opinions.'

'What about?' Barry tried to swivel on both bar stools but they stuck, setting bulges of overhanging, wobbling fat in motion.

'About the old quarry being a wildlife haven, with lots of birds and plants that you can't find anywhere else,' Joe explained, keeping the detail to ten o'clock pub level. 'And wanting your views on criminally destroying it to build the new estate in the village with houses that no-one could afford.' No harm in feeding them their lines while he had the chance.

'My father worked in a quarry,' someone rumbled from the depths of the saloon. 'Worked there all his life, up on Harpur Hill. It was the only work there was, but the place was fair crawling with folks, chipping away, slicing the blocks, and loading and trucking.'

There was a sway of agreement. 'We could do with some jobs round here. My boy's done three government training programmes but no work in sight.'

Alan plonked another pint in front of Joe as if to soften his next comment, 'Hungry and thirsty quarrymen, that doesn't sound so bad. It might help to keep this place open. Otherwise you lot would have nowhere to go. You spend all night in here, just buy one pint and you still don't make sense.'

'I think you'll find,' Simon Gent the accountant spoke with the slow authority of a bottom line man, 'that talk of hundreds of jobs is a bit of a myth these days. I've got several quarries on my books, hardly any labour costs, it's all huge heavy-lifting machinery, vast articulated trucks, computerised crushing and sorting. Brilliantly smooth operations, and machines don't need unions and they don't go on strike. But they are terribly noisy, that's one thing that's got ten times worse.' He slapped Joe on the arm, 'I'll go in front of the cameras and tell them what's what any time.'

'For a fee,' someone muttered.

'How's that lovely girl of yours?' Alan asked. 'She got that mongrel under control yet?'

Helen. Joe felt a surge of misery and had another drink. Helen and Adrian. To have Helen sitting in your office day after day in her prim, demure, sexy skirts, cotton shirts with the necklace he, Joe, had given her with its green stone droplets hanging down between her … and her brown hair tied back in silky scarves. Why wouldn't Adrian want to lay his bloody marble wet rooms at her feet? She, sweet girl, had said no, and he'd lost his rag and behaved like an animal. Except no animal would be so stupid. Joe groaned aloud and Margaret, who had just finished her omelette and chips in the small dining room, offered him a coffee.

'There's enough for three in this great pot. Why is it you can't get a cup of coffee for one any more?' She had never seen Joe almost

drunk; the pressures of big business must be getting to him. He was better at understanding animals than people and she wondered how well Joe understood Helen. You could hardly blame the girl for wanting a few more comforts in life than Blackridge Farm offered and for concluding that his wildlife studies, his haven of a quarry and the thought of beautiful photographs bound into a work of art were more important to him than renovations and homemaking. It was time to change the Helen subject.

'Have you heard from the police about the fire at your farmhouse?'

Joe took a while to focus on what seemed a lesser problem. 'I told them that petrol can in the kitchen wasn't mine, but I don't think they believed me. When I made a statement and described all the unpleasant attacks and said someone was trying to force me out of the house they just thought I was paranoid. They probably think that living alone in a shack in a wilderness is driving me round the bend. Perhaps it is.' He groaned again. 'I'm in a mess. Why does everything come down to money?'

'How's your book coming along?' Margaret tried again for a happier mood. 'You are putting a lot of love into your wildlife work and that isn't about money.'

'Isn't it? If I can't find a publisher – and who's queuing up for a book about strange creatures in an old quarry? – then I'll end up reporting on well dressings and charity rambles for The Bugle.'

'But if that TV programme I heard you talking about gets you national publicity …'

Joe stood up, his gutful of cider drowning any notions of a cheerful media future. 'I'm not sure I want my quarry turned into entertainment. Not sure at all. Thanks for the coffee, Margaret. I'd better get home.'

The sympathy and encouragement had not worked, so Margaret reverted to character and said briskly 'Get a good night's sleep and snap out of the self-pity. It wouldn't look pleasant on the television screen.' She wanted to offer to walk him home, but she pictured her portly middle-aged figure propping up a six-foot-something thirty-something. It would be ridiculous, so she limited her advice to 'Mind how you go. Don't go near the edge.'

10

Fame at Last

Joe stumbled out of The Miners and up the track leading to the farmhouse. It was a cold, clear night with a clamour of friendly sounds that lifted his spirits as no human voice could – the barn owl that felt at home in his derelict old barn building and the snuffling and grunting of a rare hedgehog crossing the path at surprising speed on skinny little legs. He breathed deeply and smiled in the dark; there was always this. What a fool he was to have forgotten that the important stuff was always outside in the trees and hedges; the creatures going competently and single-mindedly about their business had no notion of black moods. The damp, earthy air mingled with cider fumes and doubled his pleasant intoxication.

As he came up to his front path he saw lights in the distance and by a brief flash of moonlight two figures walking along the grassy slope to the left of the quarry, torches flashing as though signalling. There was no sign of any vehicle, but something could be parked out of sight behind the small wood farther down the track. The lights went on flashing and Joe laughed, his laughter reverberating down into the quarry and back from the many rock faces. This was just more provocation from the enemies of nature, from the armies of machinery and relentless destruction.

He'd got the hang of it, the threats and acts of intimidation and he didn't care any more. If he laughed at them, turned his back on them and ignored them, they'd go away. He shouted as loudly as he could at the flickering torches 'Fuck off, bastards', then for some odd reason 'Get lost. Goodnight!'

He'd almost nothing to lose; his quarry was indestructible, his farmhouse beyond what storms and decay had already done. There was no Helen to fear for, no small dog to search for. Joe laughed at himself this time, trying to fit the key into the lock like a comic drunkard. He collapsed on the baggy sofa and slept.

His mobile chimes woke him and a bright, crisp voice said 'Kathy Messeter here, just confirming our rendezvous this morning, Mr. Wright … Joe.'

'Hell! Er … hello. Yes, of course, looking forward to your visit. Very excited.' Even if it all came to nothing there was no harm in playing enthusiastic and easily-impressed.

'It's just the two of us for this first assessment, me and Phil who's going to do a few random videos just to get the atmosphere of the place. We're in ... where are we Phil? Just left Buxton, so should be with you …soon.'

Thank the god of drunkards that he had slept in his jeans and sweater. It was a fine morning so he took a very quick-brew tea into the garden and drew up two more chairs to the bench, propping his spade against one of them. Like that there was no need to tidy the house or apologise for the threadbare furniture indoors – it just gave an impression of early-morning gardening. In any case, they were sure to get lost for the last couple of miles; visitors always did. His head felt clear and last night's depression had evaporated – he couldn't wait to talk about his quarry and the wonders to be found in and around it. Could he persuade Kathy and thingy to come back at night, he wondered, because the wildlife always hotted up as it grew dark, as if knowing that humans were at their most blunderingly useless at night.

'This is a real wilderness you've found for yourself! Hello Joe.'

'Miss Messeter. Welcome. I didn't hear your car … and in fact I can't see it either. I did think I heard a helicopter a few minutes ago.'

'I wish! We were intimidated by your rocky track and decided to risk our Jimmy Choos by walking a few yards. This is Phil Weston who's even terrified of spiders, let alone eagles and bats, so be gentle with him.' Kathy plonked a vast cream canvas holdall on the mossy

garden table and stared about. 'Is that your farmhouse? It seems to be frowning at me.'

Phil snorted and muttered 'Don't get fanciful. We need to get a programme out of this, if possible.' So far he thought the place looked an unpromising dump.

'I was just having a tea-break, can I get you something?'

Joe made a pot of tea and blessed his mother for the recent assortment of unchipped, unstained mugs. From the kitchen window he assessed his guests. Kathy was plumper than her telephone voice had sounded, with glossy black hair and very confident make-up. Her movements spoke of a controlled energy that would burst out into creative action. Phil was tall, thin and nerdy, fiddling with a minute video camera that he had almost doubled in size with an assortment of attachments. That pair could work wonders for the future of the quarry and its inhabitants, him included. He grabbed some cushions to cover the gangrenous garden seats.

'I've just finished an article for the local paper and I've done you a copy.' Joe put sheets of text and photos, safe in plastic envelopes, on the garden table. 'It's got lists of all the plants and animals in the quarry and I thought it would help you to decide what to film.'

'Geez, you've really got eagles here in the Peaks?' Phil's attention swivelled from his camera to one of Joe's best photographs.

'Falcons. In fact they are quite common everywhere these days. Real survivors.'

Kathy stared away into the distance beyond the quarry without looking at his carefully and lovingly compiled article. 'The great thing is, any story about the Peaks is good for viewing numbers. Just mention Peak District and you've got a captive audience nationwide.'

'But Joe here needs more than that. He needs the weight of public opinion behind him, and that's good for viewing figures.' Phil was scanning a description of the bat cave. 'We need to grab viewers first, as usual, but when we've got them hooked, make them concentrate. We need to get an hour's worth of material out of this.

Give us a guided tour, Joe, and show us what we've got to save from the diggers.'

Joe led them round the crater-like rim of the quarry, hoping that his wildlife would perform on cue, willing the visitors to see not just grass and leaves but delicate shoots of spring flowers.

'It's like looking down into a lost world, a jungle growing out of rock and stone. Are those silver birches jutting out from the rock face? What do they find to grow on?' Kathy had forgotten her viewing figures and was leaning over the edge, 'I can see two … three hares down there, leaping about. They look like small deer with those huge legs. Surely they prefer grassy fields, not the bottom of a quarry, Joe?'

'They've probably gone down for a drink but it wouldn't take them many seconds to get back up here to open grassland if they caught our scent.'

Phil spotted an owl motionless on a ledge. 'That seems out of place as well, an owl out in daylight.' He looked at Joe, who suddenly felt like an elderly sage dispensing wisdom.

'Owls can be diurnal,' he pronounced 'but we probably woke that one up by making too much noise.' He had been about to point out some early spring flowers, but sensed their need for the more dramatic. He pointed up above their heads to where a speckled arrow-like shape was hovering. 'There's a Peregrine Falcon up there.' He handed Kathy some binoculars as neither of them had thought to bring any.

'But that's huge! A falcon sounds so medieval – it's hovering now, its wingspan must be over a metre. Now it's coming … ow!' Kathy screamed and ducked, 'coming straight for us.'

'No, she's just checking us out. Spectacular but not that rare – they love the rock faces here, but there are breeding pairs in Derby and even in London.' Like an infant school teacher he used their sudden interest to point out something less dramatic. 'Now what is rare, Kathy, is that late green striped snowdrop, but perhaps we ought to keep that a secret.'

'It looks rather dull, I wouldn't have noticed it. It wouldn't show up too well on the screen.'

'That's where skilful photography comes in.' Phil bent down over the tiny plant and drew an even smaller camera out of a trouser pocket. 'I bet our celebrity professors won't spot this little darling. You have to get the light right – shining through the petals.'

'Tepals,' Joe corrected 'not petals.'

'It's a wonderful place, but we'd better get back to Salford.' Kathy was getting bored and the stony path of the downward slope was cutting into her shoes. 'I'll study your article, Joe, and then send you an outline plan for the programme, and in a week or so we'll come back to think about the nutty professors bit and after that focus on you giving us all the scientific data and scoring the profs out of ten or something. Viewers always hope that the experts will get things wrong and look foolish. Everything has to be a game or a competition these days.'

Phil noticed Joe's uneasy look. 'You can still get your serious educational points in, about how important it is to protect special places like this, but it really does help to make a bit of a game show of it, with a lot of chummy humour. Rather like that Springwatch, though personally I think a little silliness goes a long way.'

'Before we go,' Kathy slithered to a stop, 'where can we catch a few of the locals?'

She made them sound like another endangered species.

'Probably in The Miners Standard, though most of that lot have never set foot in the quarry and wouldn't know a snowdrop from a cactus. I'm guessing you'd want a bit of controversy …'

'Yes, before concluding that Blackridge Quarry must be saved for the nation we do need a bit of suspense.'

'You could try the pottery shop for a bit of local colour.' He could trust Lauren to put a passionate case against blasting wildlife to bits; she was especially obsessive about owls. She reproduced their simple outlines in clay, pottery owls with spectacles, owls reading books and smoking pipes. And if the producers wanted suspense, Lauren could also be relied on to embellish Joe's horrifying experiences: fire, burglary and night-time visitors … who was out to get him?

Joe overheard Kathy speculating about whether the Quarry story had legs: 'It certainly could work, especially if some of the locals would rather drive quarry lorries than build nature trails. Give the story a bit of an edge. But that Joe could be a draw – the hermit hunk, wild man. He seems so caught up in the spirit of the place.'

When Phil had given up trying to shut the front gate they lurched off down the track. Joe grabbed his phone. He felt as though he were losing control, those media types must be made to see things his way. Hunk indeed! The Quarry was the star and Kathy's comments had made him cringe.

'Hello? Margaret? A big favour please … the telly people have just been and are now heading down to the pub to see what the villagers think of the Quarry as a protected SSSI. Can you get down to The Miners and entertain them before the usual misery gutses round the bar start whinging? Their names are Phil and Kathy, though you won't have any problem identifying them.'

Margaret laughed, 'Can't you hear the noise? I'm already here. What did you say their names were? No, don't tell me or they'll think it's a put up job.'

'Please don't mention Stonecraft International and the vast cash offer – I just want them to concentrate on the unique plants and animals. And my professional knowledge as a naturalist.'

Margaret snorted 'I don't know how you can keep that sort of local news quiet,' then added more positively 'I'll do my best but they can't seem to make natural history programmes these days without a bit of drama and suspense, and if there isn't any then they'll invent some. Perhaps a few backhanders in the shape of pints of local brew will convince them that Stoneybrook is a little piece of Heaven.'

A few hours later Fred Marshall rang from The Bugle. 'I hear the telly people have been round – can you let me have a story? About five hundred words? I can use some of the pix you sent me last time.'

'I'd rather you didn't, Fred. The programme might not happen, but mainly I don't want the Stonecraft people (that name makes it sound so cosy, doesn't it? Like a group of hobby knappers), I don't

want that lot getting up to any more dangerous tricks in front of the cameras.'

'I'm running a newspaper here Joe, not a charity. You know how it works – news is news, even if it never happens.'

'Could you just hold off for another few days?'

'Which bit of *news*paper have you not understood? By the way, I got a quote out of one of the planning officers about the Stonecraft application. She said they "Would be minded to look favourably on any application that promoted industry and housing, but there could be other considerations"'.

'Like hell there are.'

'Forget it, Joe. I'll knock out a few words myself, just give me some names. After all, we don't often have real media people taking an interest in holes in the ground.'

'Thanks for nothing, Fred.'

Margaret rang back to say that the normally obtuse inmates of The Miners had turned up trumps and were unanimous in their support for protecting the quarry, especially after she'd bought them a few pints.

'And because the telly people were from over Manchester way there was a bit of local side-taking. The only sour note was from someone from Buxton chuntering on about the economic down-turn getting worse and how we needed jobs not wild flowers.'

Lauren rang sounding triumphant. Kathy and Phil had called in – your telly people she called them – and she'd been able to tell them that quarries had nearly two hundred rare species of trees and other plants … had she got that right? She had sold Kathy a framed photograph by Joe, the quarry in winter with the lake frozen.

Inviting Lauren round for a drink was the least he could do.

❧

Jealousy was, Helen thought, a bit flattering, or it ought to be. So why couldn't she enjoy it? She had been honest with Joe, but honesty had not been the best policy. The old adage had probably taken a few hundred years to mature, but it was a lie. Now they had got into the classic situation of pride and stand-off. What was she to do? Say sorry Joe, sorry you felt I'd enjoy being a kept

woman? Sorry you didn't give me the benefit of the doubt? Sorry some other man noticed me?

The atmosphere in the office was more relaxed than she had expected. Adrian had put flowers on her desk and said he felt wretched for having spoilt things by rushing her. He couldn't stop admiring her, she was calm and efficient and had a knack of handling even the most irate holidaymaker. If a mouse dared to cross the floor of their holiday cottage or strangers used an ancient footpath crossing 'their' garden, Helen soon had them agreeing that it was all part of Derbyshire life.

Adrian could never seem to handle his customers. The holiday-makers who rented his immaculate cottages and his lifestyle vision for a week then, he complained, behaved as if they owned it and the garden and the whole village. He could not bear to go into one of his properties soon after the holidaymakers had left for fear of cigarette burns or dog's hairs on the retro sofa. Helen knew that such desecration was rare – most visitors were in awe of the impossibly idyllic settings that Adrian created. She enjoyed their look of pleasure when she turned the key and let them in to rooms that no lead miner or farm labourer would have recognised or felt comfortable in. Holidaymakers were usually docile and harmless and did little damage but she liked to feel indispensable. Adrian had an instinct for buying or handling the right properties, ones that had brochure appeal, as long as Helen could go first into the danger zone once the visitors had left. Adrian could not bear the thought that his carefully chosen antiques might have been abused. She would leave a note telling the cleaners not to miss the wine stain on the coffee table or the grease on the marble worktop. They made a good team.

Adrian invited her out to dinner and she accepted because to both of them it seemed like a pleasant thing to do, a business-as-usual kind of outing. He did not ask about Joe, hoping that he would fade away, absorbed with his plants and insects at the bottom of his quarry. Adrian decided to explore other parts of Helen's life that intrigued him. What did she do when she left the office? Apart from walking that wild hound round the dales he knew little about her.

He had seen her name in the local paper doing the occasional column on country cooking. The latest recipe for apple and mint crumble – did she invent that or resurrect it from some ancient tome?

Helen was pleased to be asked. She loved traditional recipes but inventing her own concoctions was absorbing too. Apart from writing a few ideas for lifestyle magazines or local papers there were not many ways of sharing her interest. Joe ate whatever was put in front of him and seemed to think that any study or research into what went into your mouth was an unnecessary complication of life. Her mother was quite impressed after Helen had her second recipe published in The Derbyshire magazine, but thought it a huge joke. Her daughter's cooking usually produced an enormous mess in the kitchen and an eccentric, complicated dish that any traditional cook would have scorned.

'Apple and mint are quite old and trusted ingredients,' she explained, 'but I discovered that adding a few drops of vodka produced a really good sort of mulch. Of course, no cottage garden in the old days could have supplied all the ingredients. I do cheat.'

'Sounds delicious.' Adrian thought it might be a waste of vodka, but said encouragingly 'I'd love to try it.'

Helen did not offer to cook for him. She had enjoyed the meal at an inn high up in Youlgreave and felt that she had graciously repaid a debt in some way. She had never wanted him to fall in love or in lust with her, never encouraged it. Conversation was difficult because there were no questions she wanted to ask him; he could have been on his fifth divorce or living in a happy threesome, she really did not want to know. Even so, Adrian seemed to feel that revealing his personal life was a kind of intimacy and his unwelcome frankness came as a shock.

'We'd been married two years and my wife announced – no, that's not quite right, she told me quite gently and with some difficulty – that she was gay and having met her new partner she couldn't bear to touch me. She felt guilty that it had taken her so long to be sure. That was fifteen years ago and things like that were still a bit of a mystery to me. We had our daughter by then. I

couldn't understand why we had to have a complete upheaval of family life. There's usually some civilized arrangement ...'

Helen at last found something that she could sincerely respond to. 'That's so sad. Did you lose touch with your daughter?'

'Oh, no. We were living in an apartment in Sheffield, so when the flat below came up for sale I bought it for my wife and Ginny.'

'Virginia's a pretty name for a child, shame to shorten it.'

'Ginny's my wife's partner. The abbreviation suits her better. We all get on reasonably well if I keep out of her way.'

'But the important thing is that your daughter has always had you close.' Helen hoped that sounded suitably caring. She could understand now why Adrian threw himself so energetically into collecting picture postcard cottages that he lovingly restored, but she was not going to ask about the nameless and potentially wealthy heiress daughter. Too much shared information already.

Adrian went on, 'I like to think I've been a good father, but now it's time to move on, make a life for myself.'

She hurriedly changed the subject, thanking him for a lovely evening, feebly pleading the demands of an incontinent puppy and drove back to Bakewell feeling annoyed with herself. Why couldn't she at least enjoy Adrian's friendship, flirt a little, enjoy his admiration as most women would? He had never put a foot wrong, never been vulgar or insensitive – except, perhaps, when he came close to suggesting that Joe was an idealistic loser.

❦

The cream-coloured envelope that almost looked like linen had Joe hoping that it was from the television people, but did media types send letters these days? They were probably all doing Linkedin or skyping – he'd better keep an eye on his emails which were the height of his techno skills. Disappointment, because the silver lettering on the back had Stonecraft International's address and the fake heraldic emblem. It was probably some kind of threat or trick and he reached out to put it in the stove, then stopped. If it was a threat, then at least it would be in writing and it would be evidence; he imagined flourishing it dramatically in front of the

television cameras as proof of the danger that precious wildlife sites were in.

It was a formal and legally worded offer for his land and the quarry, an offer, this time, of eight hundred thousand pounds. Strange, because verbal offers had all spoken of millions, now in black and white or cream they were being more cautious and wrote, in some form of ancient italic print, as though they were doing him a special never-to-be-repeated favour. *"From our considerable business and development experience, councillors and planning officers look favourably on projects that will enhance both the quality of life for the neighbourhood and the economic prospects for the nation … we have decided to increase our already generous offer in the expectation of prompt completion."*

Joe hunted around for some presentable sheets of paper, then found a postcard of one of his photographs, the sort that Lauren sold in her shop. It was a conventional sunset shot of Blackridge Quarry against an orange, purple and navy-blue sky. That was dramatic in itself but was set afire by the reflection of those colours on the limestone rock face, the pool on the quarry floor was liquid gold, the birches and reeds black etchings. He copied the formal language in his brief rejection of the offer, stressing the *"… importance of quarries as national treasures and valuable wildlife habitats listed for protection"* put the postcard into a recycled envelope then drove into Buxton to post it and get rid of it.

His mother was in the front garden tying up some late, straggling daffodils. He had to admit that the villa and its neat garden borders looked comforting and prosperous, saved from fussiness by several bushes of generously arching winter-flowering jasmine. His mother had no such welcoming sight whenever she visited him at Blackridge Farm, only a bleak yard and drystone walls.

'Just the man,' she greeted him, 'look at this little darling, it must have made its own hybrid. Have you ever seen anything like it? Do you think it will make my fortune?' She was pointing out a miniature pale pink crocus.

Joe gave her a kiss that caught the top of her head as she bent down and he knelt beside her to examine her find. The solitary pink

crocus nestled among a bed of white ones. 'Not only pink, but it's got cream-coloured veins if you look closely. I think I have seen a pink crocus before, but that one is definitely worth a photograph. Where's your camera? I haven't got mine in the car.'

Joe was grateful to the tiny plant for diverting the usual questions of how are you, where's Helen, did you mend your front door after the break-in or your back door after the fire.

His mother took off her gardening gloves and found her camera. 'I'll put some coffee on while you load the photo onto my laptop. I might do a print and take it to the next Wye Dale gardening club meeting to see what they think.'

'And I'll email a copy to The Bugle with an article claiming your pink striped crocus as a first – *crocus sylvaticus* – though there's sure to be some old plant buff wanting to destroy your moment of triumph.'

Mrs. Wright smiled delightedly. 'Takes one to know one. I don't think we've got the Latin right, though. When those old Victorian botanists discovered a new plant they seemed to have to put a double *ii* on the end to make it theirs. I'll check with my gardening club.'

'And on that point Mum, my amazing knowledge of things botanical, I have some good news. But at the price of tea and your best fruit cake.'

Joe told her about the television programme. 'Don't broadcast it to the whole of Buxton yet, just in case it gets put on the telly shelf for months.'

'Will you be in it, or just providing the information? Even so, that would be wonderful, a kind of special adviser. It all sounds very exciting.'

'The producer said I'd be doing a tour of the quarry, showing rare plants and animals.'

His mother frowned. 'Plants don't all flower at the same time, and animals don't put in an appearance just when you want them to.'

'Which is where some of my photographs and bits of video will come in useful. And there'll be a separate programme with famous professors and wildlife experts chipping in.'

'But you will be the real expert on the wildlife in Blackridge Quarry.'

It was the first time since he had inherited the land that Joe had heard his mother mention Blackridge with pleasure. On the few occasions when her grandfather had taken her down the quarry she had hated it, the noise and dust, the exhausted workmen; no-one then had mentioned flowers, or bats or rare birds and her mother had started a bitter row about taking a child into such a dangerous place. Her father had died when she was twelve and her mother had lived on resentfully patching up the farmhouse but losing out every year to ice, rain and wind.

It seemed a good time to produce the letter from Stonecraft International and Joe handed it to her with a flourish. 'Take a look at that – I soon told them where to get off.'

Sylvia Wright studied the letter slowly, her mood changing from the pleasure of sharing her son's enthusiasm to disappointment, then worry.

'Don't act too hurriedly, you really need to think about it now they've put in an even better offer. You could push them too far and get nothing.'

'I didn't need to think and I'm not pushing them. I'm not selling. It's done, dusted and posted.'

'You were probably distracted by those television people, but you said they were fickle.'

'I didn't say that exactly.'

'That kind of money could change your life, but a television programme – if it ever happens – would be forgotten in a few days.'

'It isn't just a programme or even a couple of programmes, it's publicity for my book and for the quarry as a protected wildlife centre. It would be up to me to make sure people don't forget.'

His mother sighed and looked irritated. 'You never take my advice, but wouldn't it help your future with Helen to sell up and

have more security in the form of nearly a million pounds? You could do your bird and bat watching anywhere.'

Joe stood up and prepared to leave; discussing his messed up relationship with Helen was the last thing he wanted. 'She isn't the type to let money change her feelings, Mum.' An unwelcome image of Adrian the Pigsty magnate forced itself on him, a feeling that in the end money could change Helen's feelings, but not for him.

'Sit down again, dear. It's an afternoon for strange news. Do you remember Gerald, your father's partner?'

Joe cut himself another slice of cake. 'How could I remember him? You never let me visit ...'

'Well, he's just died, and the oddest thing is, someone has sent me an invitation to his funeral. As if I'd want to go after all the trouble he caused us. People can be so insensitive.'

'You must know who sent the invitation.'

'He says he's the manager at Gerald's hotel, where all the staff want to give him a good send-off. A manager and a friend. Probably another boyfriend.'

Joe laughed. 'Gerald must have been nearly eighty, he was about ten years older than dad. Past having boyfriends.'

'But they do, you know. They go on a long time, that sort.'

Joe got up again to change the subject. 'Send me a copy of your photo of that little pink beauty – the name *crocus sylvaticus* would be lovely, echoes of woods and Sylvia – and we'll find out how rare it is. Who'd have thought it? I must get my bumbling botanist gene from you.'

Joe slipped the Stonecraft letter into his pocket and out of sight. 'I'll keep you posted about the telly programme, and you must come down to the farm, the primroses in the quarry are quite spectacular, more advanced than yours in the garden here.'

'They always were, your grandfather loved them, and the wild violets on the top meadow.'

Driving home Joe wondered why his mother had mentioned Gerald and his funeral when she could easily have binned the invitation. His father leaving her all those years ago had been sad and humiliating, never referred to afterwards and surgically excised

from her mind. A sudden thought came to him that needed so much mulling over that he stopped the car in a quiet spot near Peak Forest to examine this new idea, an idea that should have been part of his thinking for many years.

His mother, talking disparagingly about Gerald, had been watching him closely for his reaction and he had failed to show any interest. She had prattled on about the crocus and in that he could share her interest, but why mention her dead husband's dead lover to her son? Had she expected him to offer to go to a funeral for someone he did not know, way down in Bournemouth? Why would he want to? The answer was suddenly so clear that it must have been part of him for years, buried deep and ignored in an efficient way that he had inherited from his mother. What would be so unusual about a son taking after a gay father? She had waited for his reaction to the invitation, perhaps expecting him to show an awakening interest in his father's life and loves, a way to explore the genesis of his own feelings, and he had felt only surprise.

Poor mother. She had a thirty-something son who seemed unable to hold on to a woman's love, who spent his time studying flowers and writing in praise of them, in love with hares and kestrels and other creatures that were no emotional threat. Being gay was nothing these days, almost a badge of creative honour, but to his mother, just thirty short years ago, it must have seemed a shameful curse. Had she been watching her son for signs and worrying all those years? And he had given her no reassurance. Joe nearly turned the car round and went back, but what sort of impossible conversation would he have with her? And would she believe him? It had taken his father miserable years of uneasy marriage to know that it was not right for him. Perhaps he should take Stonecraft's money, settle down with Helen in a house with cavity walls and a ride-on lawnmower in the double garage and breed a clutch of … Crazy idea, just to prove that his mother's fears were just that. She would soon understand that he was determined to make a life with Helen and never desert his family as his unhappy father had done.

A black mood had ambushed him from nowhere. Did success really come spelled out in the letter from Webster that rustled in

his pocket? However hard he struggled against the forces of big business that ever-increasing pressure would crush him like a beetle under a rockfall. His future with Helen was not yet secure; there was no clear way ahead. There was a gulf between his vision of a rewarding life with Peakland creatures safe, protected and captured only in his books and pictures, and reality.

He drove on distractedly for a few more miles then turned off the road and walked up to Eyam Edge. He needed the comfort of hills, open skies and distant views but there seemed no reassurance. Reality was what he now saw in the distance – cement works, tall chimneys, open-cast mines and quarries. It was heartbreaking; how had it been allowed to happen? Nature was assaulted everywhere by a tide of humanity, the demands of the country's millions relentlessly spewing concrete over the fields.

In his present mood he could only see glaring white chimneys and holes gouged by robot armoured excavators. Unstoppable destruction. He was powerless to stop the nightmare. He sank down onto a squelching, moss-covered pad of gritstone. Just minutes ago he had been cheered by the discovery of a pink-veined crocus and by the prospect of ephemeral images on a television screen.

Joe drove back to his farmhouse feeling as though ten, twenty years of thought had been crammed into a brief pit stop. Poor mother, he'd have to put her out of her misery soon; his quarry was the key to a successful future – his books and photographs would sell in their millions and admiring visitors would walk in awe round Blackridge Nature Reserve. He felt sorry for his mother and annoyed with her prejudices at the same time. And sorry for a father he had not really known.

11

A Bit of a Scuffle

Simon Gent strode into Lauren's pottery workshop, then stopped dead in his clay-spattered tracks, or tried to. It was like applying the brakes too hard and skidding. He steadied himself by grabbing the edge of a table full of bowls, vases and mugs in various stages of lively decoration.

Lauren stopped the pottery wheel and laughed. 'You'd better stay where you are Simon, and I'll come to you. There's a fairly clean bench in the courtyard.' She guessed that Simon thought he had dressed down to venture into the pottery, his smart jeans teamed with an open-necked shirt and incongruously well-cut jacket were his idea of casual. She often watched him next door greeting visitors to his accountancy offices, immaculately suited and making welcoming gestures as though his converted barn was a luxury hotel. Village gossips grudgingly admired his obvious success; at barely forty he already had two city centre branches in Sheffield and Manchester.

'I hope you didn't mind me cutting through a gap in your hedge, Lauren. It saves trekking down my driveway then back up again.'

'Not at all. I think some deer make it a regular evening run and you are just as welcome.' She thought he had a pleasant smile when he relaxed and did not need to impress potential customers; he certainly had no need to impress her.

'I won't stop you working for many minutes. I expect stuff dries out or goes off,' Simon said, waving vaguely in the direction of her workshop. 'It's about this estate of new houses. Some of us have appealed against the planning decision and I did a bit of research into the developers. It seems a surprisingly large construction

company to be bothered with an estate of about a dozen small houses …'

Lauren cut in, eager to show her political awareness in spite of being spattered with clay and paint, 'That's because the builders are probably in league with the company that wants to open up the village quarry and it's a way …'

'Not just in league with. I found out that Stonecraft International own the construction company. It's called Village Cottages, which sounds deceptively comforting, doesn't it?'

Simon was looking more animated than usual and seemed to relish having a trail of intrigue to follow and a cause to fight. Lauren supposed it made a change from staring at columns of figures on computers, or struggling to balance books, if accountants still did that sort of thing. She fetched two cans of lager from her workbench to encourage Simon's enthusiastic neighbourliness, and reached for two newly finished mugs that were nearer to hand than foraging in her untidy kitchen.

Simon went on 'I went up to the quarry a few times to talk to Joe but he was never there. Probably out all hours communing with nature. I know he's a friend of yours, Lauren, have you got his mobile number?' Simon dusted clay off the new mug and poured his lager into it.

'I sell his photographs in the shop, and they've all got his details on. I'll get his number in a moment,' Lauren said evasively, though she knew Joe's number by heart.

'There's a group of us who are dead set against this new housing, and, as you said, having the quarry in use with limestone on the doorstep would make life too easy for the developers. We want to have a meeting with Joe, we know he's been offered about a million for the quarry and we want him to stand firm. He mustn't sell out.'

'He wouldn't. There's no need for a meeting, Simon. I just know Joe won't sell the quarry to that company. They've been hounding him, the mercenary bastards. They couldn't tell a kestrel from a … a something else.'

'A canary?' Simon suggested helpfully.

'Those moronic cretins certainly couldn't. And I'm sure they've been putting the frighteners on him with burglaries and fires. Trying to convince him the place isn't safe as though he were some little old lady.' She banged her mug down and the handle fell off. 'Oh, shit. Back to the drawing-board.'

'Shame,' Simon smiled, 'I was just about to order a dozen of those lovely objets d'art. He was intrigued by this suddenly fiery Lauren, looking even wilder, like a tribal queen with woad-like clay stripes down her face. 'You mean he won't sell because he loves the quarry, and he's working on a book about it that will make his fortune?' He just managed to keep the mockery out of his voice and to set his face in an understanding smile.

'All that, and what's even more exciting,' Lauren hesitated for a second trying to remember whether she had been sworn to secrecy under the Official Secrets whatsit, or whether this was a case of the public's Need to Know, 'is that there's going to be a whole wildlife series on the telly about Blackridge Quarry and it being a national treasure, an SSI.'

'A what? Oh, you need another S – a Site of Special Scientific Interest. But how do you know?'

'Because the producer called on me. She wanted to know the villagers' point of view. It could become a tourist attraction and there'd be more traffic. I think she expected me to be dead against it, but instead I bored the thong off her by going on about how it would be the making of the village and would put it on the map and what a great naturalist Joe is.'

'Just you? She only interviewed you?'

'Well, no,' Lauren admitted. 'She and her assistant called in at the pub, but it was a bit early for the locals. You don't keep your ear to the ground, Simon. Too wrapped up in spread sheets.'

'Lauren,' Simon put his hand on her shoulder and gave it a friendly squeeze, 'thank you. That's great news about the programmes, the best yet. But it may not be enough to protect the village. The thought of large sums of money can do strange things to people, especially as I hear that gorgeous girl friend of Joe's is playing up. We don't want her persuading him to cash in, do we?'

That was cruel, but jealousy was a great motivator. Simon saw that he had pushed the right buttons; the effect on Lauren was electric.

'I'll get you that phone number right away. Where are you thinking of having a meeting? Have you hired the village hall?'

'Good lord, no. That would be too formal, a bit intimidating. Joe might feel it was them and us, or rather us and him. No, the pub will do. It's just a friendly gathering of encouragement.'

'I think you are all wasting your time – and Joe's. He's more against quarrying in the village than anyone, there's no need for a meeting.' Lauren added tenderly 'It would break his heart to have his bats and kestrels disturbed.'

'Well, he hasn't done much to support the village in its appeal against the new houses. He does work for the editor of The Bugle; he could have gone to print and spoken up for us. Talking of broken hearts, it would break mine to have half my field requisitioned for an access road.'

Simon followed her into the shop, noting that it was professionally set out with shelves full of Lauren's pottery and the walls closely hung with work by local artists – a whole wall given over to Joe's large photographs. There was no tat, no candles or local produce, just striking images and confident pottery that made, as interior designers say, a statement. Simon was not sure what statement was being made, but he looked towards the end of the shop to Lauren's living room where uncluttered expanses of oatmeal tweed were shocked into life by lime green cushions and rugs.

'That's lovely.' Simon had been drawn to the living room doorway and pointed to a large vase decorated with sunflowers and a bee in bold relief. 'Are those on sale in your shop? I'd love one.'

'I can soon knock up another one – I mean, of course, it would take weeks of skilful artistry to repeat that unique piece. I'll sell you that one and do myself another one. Here's Joe's number.'

'You must come over and look at my barn conversion. How's that for a chat up line? But talking shop, the barn hallway has turned out larger than it needs to be, would you consider a small display

of your work on the hall table? Some of my clients have got a fair bit of money, but they wouldn't know original artwork if it bit them – they need their noses rubbing in it.'

'What persuasive sales talk, Simon. No wonder you are so successful. It's a great idea – you'll have noticed that there hasn't been a rush of customers for the past half hour. And you could probably stay for another few hours with the same result.'

'Best be off, Lauren. You sort out some work that you want displayed then give me a ring. What will I owe you for the vase?'

She named an inflated sum, quite sorry to see the piece disappear from her table.

Simon set off, and Lauren could hear him talking to Joe on his mobile and saying he'd be along to the farmhouse in a few minutes.

Lauren went up to Blackridge the following day; she had a plausible excuse and it was too good an opportunity to miss. 'I've come to apologise, Joe. I've been worried I did the wrong thing.'

Joe had been about to set off down the quarry to clear nettles that had got a head start on a delicate clump of early purple orchid shoots. Vigorous though the nettles were another hour or so would make little difference and Lauren looked distraught.

'Not like you to worry about much, Lauren. What's up?'

'I'm disrupting your work, Joe, I should have phoned.' But phoning might have made her visit unnecessary. 'Shall I come back later?' Later could mean a friendly evening visit, a few drinks, an understanding.

'I was only about to murder some nettles. I ought to let nature take its course, but I can seldom resist a bit of interfering. Do you want to help?'

Joe welcomed the interruption because he was waiting, and at the same time trying not to wait, for Kathy the television producer to get back to him. When she did, if she did, he would use that excitement to visit Helen to tell her the news, slipping in an apology for his unreasonable jealousy, an apology that on its own, bare and unprotected, seemed impossible to utter. The thought that the media people might keep him waiting for months was unbearable.

143

Lauren had answered his question and was staring at him. 'I said I'd love to help. Stinging nettles seem an appropriate sort of penance.'

'Sorry. I was just wondering whether I've got another pair of gloves. You can tell me about your hideous crime while we're walking.'

'I loathe people interfering, and that's just what I've done. Simon Gent came to see me about the link between the new estate and your quarry, wanting your phone number. He wants you to come to a meeting in the village.'

'Yes, he came up a short while ago. He declined my offer of a nettle-clearing session.'

'Well, I told him there was no need for a meeting, that you'd never take the money and run and that you'd think they were ganging up on you in the village.' Lauren slithered on the scree leading down into the quarry and clutched at Joe's arm. 'When he'd gone I realised that it was none of my business and that you might welcome a discussion to clear the air. Some of the villagers think you've been less than helpful about the new estate.'

'This is the patch that needs clearing, but don't yank up any grass because it helps bind the stones together. Watch out for the orchid shoots, I'll show you what they look like as they come through.' What made Lauren think that Simon would take any notice of her when he had his valuable property to protect? Her apology was a feeble excuse for a visit, just as his would be to Helen.

'Look out, you're treading on some aconites. My critics are probably right, I ought to have joined in the protests but I feel uneasy when it comes to denying people decent homes.'

Lauren sat down on a rock. Weeding and thinking at the same time were proving difficult. 'You wouldn't need to oppose housing, just tell everybody very loudly a hundred times you will never sell the quarry for new extraction. Put it in the newspaper again, say how you are being victimised by Stonecraft.'

'I've got no proof of that. Pile up the nettles over there, they'll rot down beautifully. You mean that if I make a big noise about not selling, and especially if I tell the Park Planning Department, they'll

144

realise that stone will have to be brought in from miles away and the village will win its appeal?'

'Yes, it ought to work like that. They'd have to build miles and miles of new road because all we've got now are glorified farm tracks.'

'I thought all that was obvious weeks ago, but I'll come to the meeting and say it all again.'

'The trouble is, Joe ...' Lauren could not believe that she was coming close to criticizing this tall, capable, desirable man. She was pushing her luck. 'The trouble is, you are a very quiet person, writing, taking photographs, hidden away in the quarry or in your farmhouse, so because you don't talk there are rumours ... They think Helen may persuade you to sell. We ... *they* say she'll never settle at Blackridge Quarry Farm.'

'I don't see why I have to explain myself. Who to, exactly? To that bunch of old women in the pub who have nothing better to do than drink every night and gossip? To Simon Gent who has a cash register for a brain?'

Lauren gave him an agonized look, 'I came to apologise and now I've made things worse. Made you angry.'

To her surprise Joe put his arm round her and kissed her cheek. 'No you haven't – I won't be explaining myself or my love life to the rest of Stoneybrook, I'll just go to the meeting and reassure everyone that the quarry is safe even if they offer me ten million. Now we've given those nettles something to think about, just come over to the lake. There's a resident pair of grebe – look at the clever way they make a floating nest out of almost nothing, just a few twigs and leaves.'

The birds left their flotsam collecting and swam towards them, hoisting themselves up on the shore on huge weirdly jointed feet.

Lauren was delighted. 'They seem to know you. Have you been feeding them?'

'Certainly not. They only arrived a few days ago; I don't want them relying on me for food. They must have come over from Bakewell, all the waterfowl there have got the tourists well trained.

The visitors sit cowering on riverside benches while the birds stride up and down demanding fish and chips.'

They climbed up the slope and out of the quarry, Joe pointing out tiny shoots of early spring plants that to Lauren looked like nothing more than weeds.

'I ought to be more adventurous in my pottery decorations, no more sunflowers or daffodils on vases, more Hoary Mullein and Jacob's Ladder to intrigue the customers. Simon wants me to display some of my work in his offices so I must develop a new range. He is being really encouraging.'

'That's good news. The village needs to support its tradespeople and artists all it can, like you display my pictures in your shop. Simon is a good sort, a bit of a control freak but his heart is in the right place.'

No hint of jealousy there, Lauren noted sadly, but perhaps with a nature as generous as Joe's …

Joe turned away from her at the sound of crunching tyres. 'I recognise that bloody vehicle. He's asking for a black eye.' They were coming down the track leading to Blackridge Farm and Joe strode angrily ahead past a silver personnel carrier squatting in his driveway. 'Hey, Webster, get off my land before I call the police. You're trespassing and you've caused me enough trouble.'

Frank Webster, apparently deaf, continued along the path to the farmhouse and was already peering through the grimy windows. 'I'm just replying to your letter. Thought I'd come in person because I'm sure you're already regretting turning down such a fortune.'

Webster smiled and held out his hand to Lauren, 'you must be the lovely Helen. I've heard a lot about you. This young man here is about to become very rich if he plays his cards right, and you, young lady, deserve better than this pile of …'

Joe caught hold of Webster's collar and swung him round. 'Piss off. I've done talking and writing to your mob. No more words.' He gave the man a hefty shove that sent him off balance, skeetering along the unforgiving gravel then falling on his hands and knees.

Webster examined the grazed palms of his hands in exaggerated agony; wonderful – a violent attack and a useful witness. He

stepped back towards Joe to provoke him even more and Lauren put her hand on Joe's arm to restrain him.

He shook her off and stood glaring at Webster, so Lauren ran off down the track to find help. Someone needed to stop Joe before he got hurt. She guessed that beyond a bit of pushing and shoving he was no fighter. Joe stepped back, still facing Webster squarely and expecting attack. He was shaking. He had never punched anyone before, but that seemed to be the next step. He did not know what else to do because Webster wasn't moving.

Webster held up a bloody hand in front of Joe's nose. 'That was your last chance. I'll be bringing charges for assault with your girl-friend as witness. As far as this shit-heap is concerned,' he gestured towards the farmhouse 'the next thing you'll get is a compulsory purchase order. You small-minded little people make me sick.' He got into his car and drove off, slowing down as he went past Lauren. She refused his offer of a lift down to the village.

Joe was shaking too much to pour himself a glass of Helen's brandy, so he drank it from the bottle. To calm himself he opened his laptop and read the last page of his writing. A new title for his book came to mind nearly every day, but *A Hidden World* had stuck for several days, so perhaps that was the one. His quarry was certainly not hidden, but to the untrained eye most of its birds, beasts and plants were almost invisible and for the impatient visitor bored after a few minutes silent waiting, its residents remained watchfully out of sight.

Joe was soon pleasurably lost in the world of brown hares, part of his third chapter. They lived in the grassy meadows above the quarry but sometimes came down to the lake to drink, loping down the slope like miniature kangaroos but keeping cautiously to the sparse shelter of shrubs. Unlike the grebe and ducks there was nothing they wanted from man, but they were not exactly frightened of him. They seemed to have made a shrewd assessment of his pathetic turn of speed.

Webster was eventually forgotten, and when the phone rang Joe snatched it up eagerly, tolerating the intrusion in the hope of

television stardom, or at least the protection of publicity that the media could provide for the wildlife in the quarry.

Margaret said 'About that meeting you're having in the pub ...'

'Good God! How did you hear about that? Was it native drums or pigeon post?'

'I just wanted to apologise because I won't be able to come. My cousin in Manchester is ill and she needs my homespun country wisdom and a lecture on her disgraceful lifestyle. But to get to the point, I'd like to have a word with you before the meeting. Okay if I pop up now?'

Joe hoped she didn't hear his frustrated sigh. Why did just popping in make disturbance acceptable? He would have to scribble a few notes before Margaret arrived or he'd forget those last few minutes of happy inspiration. He would leave his laptop switched on and open at his brown hares to show her the depth and seriousness of his concentration, a hint to make her visit short.

'I've hesitated quite a while and hope you won't take this the wrong way,' Margaret began, settled in with tea and shortbread left over from Christmas.

It was bound to be a well-meaning lecture about Helen, and how he ought to buck his ideas up. The vision came to him of a randy buck rabbit leaping on a flat-eared doe. Disturbing.

Margaret took a sip of tea and cleared her throat. 'When we were at the meeting in Bakewell Town Hall, you told us your views on quarrying, and it was in the papers, and it even got reported on Radio Derby.'

'Yes, I was pleased about that, more publicity than I had hoped for. You'd think all that would have convinced the locals ... ' Joe looked longingly at his laptop where two hares stood on hind legs as they thought about boxing.

'Please don't mention log cabins and straw-filled walls in public again, Joe.'

'What? Oh, I think you mean timber-framed construction. There's a lot of difference these days, with cavity walls and thermal insulation and PV roof tiles. No more stone, timber-framed houses are the future, in kit form and off-the-shelf.'

'There you go. It all makes you sound a bit of a crank, a bit unhinged.'

'Speak your mind, Margaret, why don't you.'

'Don't mix up your way-out environmental theories with your campaign to save your quarry or you'll end up getting neither. As soon as you mention Scandinavian-type wooden villages in the Peak District people switch off, or start sniggering. It hurts me when people laugh behind your back because I think you could be on the right track. But keep it to yourself for now.'

'But I thought you wanted quarrying to stop. It can't go on forever – after centuries of it enough is enough.'

Margaret's cup rattled nervously in its saucer. 'I don't see how it can ever stop, Joe dear. The government reckons we need thousands of new houses. I personally think they've got their figures wrong, but where would all the wood come from for timber frames? We haven't got enough trees, even if we cut all the forests down.'

Joe smiled and looked relieved, 'It's just that I obviously haven't explained myself to you or to all the others. Quarrying will have to stop, but it may take fifty, a hundred years, to cover some of the neglected farmland with forests. It will have to be gradual, but we have to start now. I'm not a head case, Margaret. It's dynamiting the hills that's crazy.'

'But quarrying and building in stone have been going on for thousands of years. Stone *is* the Peak District, and the Cotswolds and the Lakes.'

'So it's time for a change, think the unthinkable. Nothing's set in stone,' Joe smiled, discovering a joke. 'Renewables are the future, Margaret. We can grow more timber but there'll never be any more stone.'

'There you go again, ranting and destroying your own cause. Even if I want to believe you,' Margaret's jowls wobbled as she shook her head in some distress, ' and I really do, it just isn't going to happen. Why can't you see that? And what about this place? You'd dearly love to renovate this old farmhouse but it would mean digging up more stone.'

Joe took away her cup and saucer then closed his hand over hers. 'I'd be happy to renovate using timber and glass if only the planners would allow it. But message received and understood, friend. I can do tactics – save Blackridge Quarry Nature Reserve first, revolutionize house-building second.'

Margaret stood up and gave Joe a hug. 'So I haven't wasted my breath? No more log cabins and lavs filled with waste-digesting bugs? Especially not on the telly when you'll be talking to millions.'

'Not for the time being.'

❧

Joe's pub meeting with the anxious villagers of Stoneybrook was brief and friendly with a lot of flat cider drinking and handshaking. He took along copies of his letter rejecting Stonecraft's offer and passed them round. He showed them copies of the chapter of his book about rare grasses and orchids in the quarry and assured them that it would make him and the village famous. The villagers were not convinced.

'What if that company up their offer even more? One even you can't refuse?' Alan asked. 'I'm not sure I could refuse a couple of a million. What if you could name your price?'

'Then we wouldn't see him for dust, limestone dust,' someone joked.

He did not mention his feeble attack on Webster as proof of his determination. It would have been cheered to the grimy rafters, but Joe was beginning to feel ashamed of it. A naturalist and animal lover, especially one about to be a television guru, ought to be a peaceful soul.

❧

There was a message from Phil Weston, Kathy Messeter's assistant, on Joe's landline. 'We think your quarry story's got legs. Great idea. Dog's bollocks. Can't go wrong with animals in the Peak District, especially those lizard-things. Weird. Give us a bell.'

Joe hoped the pillock would not have anything to do with writing the script, but he gave a cautious celebratory dance round the kitchen. He'd ring them in the morning to find out how much they

were prepared to do and how soon they could get Blackridge on air. The sooner the safer.

❧

Didn't everyone start work at nine? He tried ringing Seat of Pants Film Productions again at ten. 'I'd like to speak to Kathy,' he said firmly, then, when she was found, 'I got Phil's message – things sound promising.'

'Yes, Joe. I think you've got enough material for us to get our teeth into. Could be another *Springwatch* but edgier, less chat, more balls.'

Legs and dogs, now teeth and balls. Style was a little disappointing, but that was only a detail if it meant putting his quarry on the map. 'I'm feeling really excited about this.' Joe decided on another show of honest and naive enthusiasm so they understood what a responsibility they had. 'This could be a turning point for Peak District conservation. Impresarios really take notice of you television people. You get results.'

'Of course,' Kathy went on, 'we aren't the BBC, just a production company ...'

'Yes, you gave me your card – Seat of Pants Film Productions. I've often noticed some weird names on the credits ...'

'But don't let the humour put you off, Joe. I'm emailing you some links to programmes we've produced and I think you'll be impressed.'

'You said you aren't the BBC, meaning you do the filming then have to sell it to the television people?'

'That's how it works, but we shouldn't have any problems. And in your case, with loads of shots of eagles and cute fox cubs, not to mention all the hot controversy with commercial quarrying ...'

'About that, Kathy, I think we ought to stick to saving Blackridge and not alienate industry at this stage. I wouldn't want to give the quarrying company any publicity.' Or, he thought, a reason to turn even nastier and press charges for assault.

'We'll discuss that later, Joe.'

'When do you think you can start filming?'

But she had gone.

151

Fred Marshall inspected the floorboards in his Bugle office. The old mill where he rented the first floor and three offices over the millrace had just been condemned by some health and safety officer. His landlord would need to carry out extensive structural repairs in order to continue to lease it out. Fred jabbed at a crumbly patch just under his desk; he could see the rushing water though a gap between the boards. It had never troubled him before because the mill was three hundred years old and its upper floors had held mill stones and giant iron cogwheels, so what were a few desks and computers?

When Joe appeared with an article on the increasing popularity of Well Dressing, Fred was too distracted to comment on the fact that it was ten days late.

'I'm going to have to find some other premises for The Bugle while this place is being renovated, and by the time the conservation people have finished with their listed building demands for medieval bloody materials I don't suppose the paper will be able to afford the new rent.'

Joe was relieved. Obviously his scrap with Webster was not going to be headlines; he had reluctantly finished the well-dressing bit of reporting as an excuse to call in at the offices and forestall any unfavourable scandal.

'There shouldn't be any problem finding other – and more comfortable – premises. Plenty of offices in Matlock and Bakewell are empty because businesses can't afford the rent or have stopped trading.'

'Which is exactly our problem,' Fred snapped. 'The paper isn't making money, or hadn't you noticed? Newspapers and magazines are dropping like flies, falling off their perches ...' Fred hesitated, searching for a more convincing phrase.

'Going to the wall?'

Fred suddenly focused on Joe. 'And what the hell have you been up to? First I texted you about that cache of bootleg vodka in Winster story but you'd gone awol. Then you run amuck and start beating people up. Must say I never thought you had it in you.'

'What do you mean?'

'A Bugle reporter involved in a punch-up with one of the county's wealthiest and most influential businessmen!' Fred stopped gouging out bits of rotten timber and straightened up, distracted from the danger of his impressive oak desk falling into the Wye. 'Webster's been provoking you for weeks and you finally cracked.'

'He's been in here?'

'Worse. He's filed a complaint with the police to get it on record, but he's not pressing charges – yet.'

'I only gave him a shove and he collapsed deliberately. He took a dive.'

'My police informant says there was bruising and a lot of blood on his hands. I'll have to give it a few lines in the paper, got to be impartial. *"Bugle environmental reporter involved in violent attack on boss of international company. Terrified girlfriend unable to ..."'*

'Please don't, Fred. Hold off for a few days. I'm on to something important and you could ruin it. Besides, I'm not exactly a household name. Nobody will care.'

'Then if Webster decides to press charges because you don't do as you are told and won't accept his generous offer like a rational being, The Bugle will be accused of a cover-up. And what have you got to hide that's so important that we've got to put an embargo on your scrap with Webster?' Fred resumed his examination of the floorboards. 'We're going to have to move out of here in a couple of days and you think you've got problems.'

Joe calculated that news of plans for a television programme had not got to The Bugle newsdesk from the media hub in Salford or from the bar of The Miners Standard, though there were other good reasons for him to be squeaky clean.

'Listen, Fred. Blackridge Quarry could get a grant as an SSSI, and national recognition. But as its owner I need to keep my nose clean. Say the newspaper report on Webster's few scratches fell through the mill's rotting floorboards and got lost. Something like that could have happened.'

Fred was looking on the internet for offices to rent. 'I suppose we'll have to delay publishing for a few days while we move, so you're in luck. I can't really see you in a proper punch-up. A bit of playground shoving more like.'

12

Accident at the Quarry

It was impossible to concentrate on writing his chapter on hares. His picture of them on hind legs ready for a fight looked worryingly aggressive. Joe's hands were trembling with anger as he closed his laptop so he went out into the garden to sit and be comforted by the antics of jackdaws plotting to destroy a hanging bird feeder meant for blue tits. One canny monster had one leg on a branch and with the other shook the feeder until seeds fell to the waiting mob on the ground. A successful social operation.

Joe wanted to phone Helen. No, he wanted to go straight round to see her. He was ready to tell her how sorry he was, had been ready for days, but more than anything he wanted her reassurance that however he was ridiculed, derided, provoked or insulted she had never seen him pushed to the edge of violence. He was not an angry man, and at his worst Helen had only seen him hurt and jealous, spiteful even, he was ashamed to say. He wanted to tell her that he had been provoked to behave thoughtlessly and that now there was his name on some list, some document in the police station: Joseph Wright, well-known local nature lover, conservationist, guilty of assault. It wasn't really him; she would know it wasn't.

He needed more than jackdaws and blackbirds to distract him. He collected his camera and notebook, and the remains of a sandwich that he had felt too sick to eat, and headed off to the quarry. There was always that pleasant decision – to take the route up to the grassy slopes leading to the moors, or go down the crunchy stone path to the quarry floor – but surely he had picked up the sandwich with grebe in mind.

He went down towards the lake and sat by the water, soothed at once by the sparkling ripples, the most turbulence the sheltered expanse of water could raise. He set his camera to video because although grebe were not the most photogenic fowl their deliberate plodding on huge striped feet always amused him. The grebe did not come, though he could hear their frustrated chattering on the reedy island. To his left, ripples were silently spreading out from behind a clump of coarse grass on the bank where a stoat was taking a leisurely drink, its tiny pink tongue glistening in the sunlight. Sleek and beautiful, and worth any amount of film, it turned its intelligent face towards him then spent a few seconds cleaning specks of mud off its white chest. It looked towards the now silent reed island, but decided the fowl were not worth a swim, and when the camera gave a subdued click it loped away, scaling the vertical quarry face until it reached a ledge of overhanging shrubs and disappeared. The video sequence was stunning; Joe paused it on the tiny killer's confident stare. He lay down on the bank and kept still, but it was several minutes before the grebe, joined by a duck, headed for him encouraged by the sight of a paper bag. An egg sandwich seemed like an insult to a bird but they soon demolished it, lost interest and swam away.

Joe felt so calm next to the hypnotic little ripples that it took him several seconds to focus on the figure on the skyline above the cliff face. Whoever it was came dangerously close to the edge in a spot that Joe knew was sliced with fissures covered by grass. He was about to shout a warning when the man retreated, turning away from the edge so that only the top part of his body was visible. He seemed to be prodding the ground with some long instrument that he inspected from time to time, no casual rambler straying from the footpath but someone intent on gathering information of some kind.

Joe told himself to keep calm. He had not given permission recently for any scientific samples to be taken, nor for any field studies to be carried out, but even if this was another provocation by Stonecraft International what harm could one man and a stick do? The figure moved to the edge again. He would have to shout

loudly for the man to hear his warning. Was a raised voice in a friendly shout possible without it sounding like anger?

'Stay away from the edge, it isn't safe.'

The man seemed not to hear, so Joe picked up bag and camera and started to walk quickly up the slope, along the footpath then up on to the rough fields bordering the quarry. The man went on plunging his metal rod into the surface of the field then levering the samples into a canister. Joe shouted again, watching the man through the close-up lens of his camera. There would be no need for anger or violence because his camera would provide all the threat needed, proof of some activity that Joe had not sanctioned.

The man looked up and saw him, but continued to stab at the ground. It was not Webster but then a company director was not likely to go poking about in mud in person.

'Be careful! You're too close to the edge.' Then because this helpful warning produced no reaction, Joe started to video the man and his tube-like instrument. 'Stop that please, you're trespassing.' The pompous, old-fashioned word sounded ridiculous.

Joe was nearly up to the man now and he took a last close-up of the man's face and said calmly 'You're on my land. Please leave.'

The man dug the metal rod deep into a crevice and said, without looking up 'I need to finish this. It's got to be done.'

'I'm the landowner and I want you to stop whatever it is you're doing. I shall take these photographs along …' Joe hesitated, not wanting to mention the police station where he was a marked man.

The man suddenly lunged forward and tried to grab the camera, brandishing the pointed metal tube in Joe's face. This confrontation was going wrong and Joe stepped back, pushing the instrument away. The man slipped sideways, his foot disappearing down a hole in the limestone. He lost his balance and went over the edge, clutching at Joe's camera strap in a desperate effort to save himself.

Joe peered after him – it was a steep drop to the quarry floor, but surely not enough to kill a man? Wasn't there always a ledge or an overhanging bush that the victim could cling to waiting to be hauled up? Or was that only in films? He could see nothing, so he ran back down the field and down the slope. The man lay half in the lake

and half on a couch of reeds near the bank. Joe dragged him out of the water and felt his wrist and his neck, but he had never managed to find his own pulse, so not finding that small beat now surely didn't mean anything. The man did not move.

So close to home, Joe did not have his mobile. He'd come out to be alone and now there had been this intruder, this body that would need help not to be a corpse. Down here it would take an air ambulance. Joe started to run back up the slope, then down again in a panic to hunt through the man's pockets until he found a phone. No signal, so back up the slope until half-way up the phone came to life. Joe gave directions, Blackridge Quarry and a black sprawling figure against the white quarry floor. They would see. He went back to the lifeless figure to keep it company. Why had he not kept away from the intruder, just taken photos from a distance, not shouted and threatened with his camera? Why had he not just phoned the police? He knew why, and it did not feel good.

The ambulance crew worked on the body until it was stretchered aloft to the helicopter, swinging out of reach. It seemed like a television drama, but several weeks too soon and not the kind of horror that he wanted for his quarry.

❧

'Helen … oh, Helen, I need to …'

'Joe! I'm so glad you've rung. I meant to come over earlier, but Mrs. Bonsall had a heart attack and I had to wait with her while the ambulance came. We said such silly, unkind things about her …'

'I said cruel things,' Joe insisted, 'but now I need to …'

'It was heartless of me to let you go on being jealous when …'

'Helen, listen, I think I may have killed someone. I pushed him, and now … ' the words were almost impossible to form 'I think he's dead.'

Helen was silent. Whatever Joe had done, this was no time for explanations. Death by pushing? Had Webster died? 'I'll come over now, love. Are you on your own?'

'Yes. The police have just gone. They want me to go to the station and make a statement – they think it was an accident, but after the last time, when I pushed Webster over ...'

Joe was not making any sense. Last time? Was he making a habit of assaulting people? 'I'll be right over, then we'll see the police together.'

Helen threw some food into Puppy's bowl and left in the few seconds it took him to gulp it down. His cheerful cavorting had no place in this afternoon of horrors.

Joe threw his arms round her and buried his wet face in her hair. 'I want to tell you, but I can't seem to remember … everything's broken up like a jigsaw, jumbled up.'

'That's just shock.' Her bottle of brandy came out again. 'Drink that, it'll help you stop shaking.' She propelled him onto the sofa.

'I can't. The police said I had to …'

'I'll take you down later, and anyway, they know where to find you. Start at the beginning Joe. What did you mean on the phone when you said *the last time*? I only saw you a few days ago.'

'Webster came round here again. He took no notice of my letter rejecting his offer. He was wandering round the place and wouldn't listen. I've told him so many times, I didn't know what else to do.' Joe drank a mouthful from the bottle.

'So what *did* you do?' Helen took the bottle away from him and poured a small measure into a mug, taking his hand to steady it.

'I just gave him a shove because I wanted him out of my sight, and he fell over. There was blood all over his hands, and bits of gravel.'

'I expect he made the most of it.' Helen put her arm round Joe's shoulders and kissed his cheek. 'And then what?'

'Then … ' Joe struggled to get things in the right order. 'That was two days ago, but Lauren will tell them what really happened, she was here. He went to the police to lodge a complaint about me, but he didn't press charges.'

'Big of him. Lauren was here? Good, she'll tell it straight. Was it Webster you say … you say you've killed?' She wondered whether Joe was having a breakdown; she had never heard his speech so disjointed, nor seen his normally cheerful, sun-tanned face so ashen She'd have killed Webster herself for bringing about such a change in someone she loved.

'No, not Webster. Someone was up on the hillside overlooking the quarry, and he was searching for something, pushing a long metal rod into the ground.'

'Like taking soil samples? What did he say?'

'He wouldn't explain himself. He wouldn't stop … like Webster, he took no notice of me. I didn't know what to do next.'

'So you pushed him over the edge?'

'Christ, Helen! Of course I didn't.' Joe looked at her in horror, staring deep into her eyes for reassurance instead of her questioning look. 'You know I wouldn't … but I can't remember. I only remember the medics and then the stretcher swaying in the air.'

'I think you need to sleep, perhaps things will seem clearer when you wake up. You'll be no use to the police like this.'

Helen led him upstairs and put him to bed, lying beside him, willing him to sleep, then to wake and tell her the nightmare had gone. When she felt him relax she went downstairs, made some coffee and went out into the cold night of the back garden. Beyond Joe's rockery the moonlight picked out distant hills; it was as if the quarry did not exist. It was there all right, alive in the dark, alive with scurrying creatures haunted by the menacing beat of owls' wings. Black shapes crossed the white surface of the moon, small nattering bodies zoomed expertly past her head. Were bats awake so early in the year? Joe would know, but she felt a stranger here. The night sounds were familiar but at the same time mysterious.

Helen played back the messages on Joe's phone.

'Joe, it's Simon Gent here. Good news and bad news. My solicitor has been reviewing recent extraction cases in quarries similar to yours . He sounds very pessimistic. Even if the planning authority turns down the application for extraction the company will almost certainly take it to appeal and that's where they get you. The Council hasn't got any money these days, and the villagers couldn't afford barristers. He worked out that even getting surrounding villages involved, costs could come to hundreds per head if we tried to raise the money. And the good news … do you know Adrian Hucknall? Owns a shedload of holiday cottages, filthy rich … but

ring me back, Joe, and I'll tell you about it.' Helen deleted the message.

There was a message from Joe's mother about some plant in her garden and a funeral, and a message from Fred Marshall saying something was urgent and had there been more trouble at Blackridge?

It could all wait until Joe was able to face it. Except for Sylvia, she was a problem. They'd have to get to his mother before the rumour mill got grinding, before she got the wrong story. But what was the right story?

At 6am Helen rang Bakewell police station hoping they would be puzzled, say Joe must have been hallucinating. No bodies, no helicopter. What was worse – a mentally deranged Joe or a fatal accident?

'Yes, Miss. We're expecting Mr. Wright in for an interview this morning.'

Helen said that Joe would be in to make a statement as soon as he could, but he had collapsed, had a blackout, was asleep. She didn't want them to think that Joe was avoiding the issue.

'No chance of that,' the duty sergeant said cheerfully. 'We've had a car and two officers at the scene all night. Well, at the top of the slope not right down the bottom. They've been keeping an eye on things. Didn't you notice them? We saw you arrive yesterday evening, Miss Seymour.'

'How do you know who …'

'Registration number. Don't bother to come in, one of the officers at the scene yesterday said Mr. Webster looked in a terrible state. Two of our men will be over to interview him again at Blackridge in a few hours. Shall we say eleven o'clock? He wasn't making much sense yesterday.'

'I don't know what happened in the quarry,' Helen explained, fishing for information, a few details, 'I was at work until six. I gather there was an accident. Is there any news of the …'

'Of the victim, Miss? Latest from the hospital in Chesterfield said he's in a bad shape. That was at two this morning.'

'But you mean he isn't … '

161

'You know we can't discuss it with you, Miss. If there's any more news we'll be informing Mr. Wright when we interview him later.'

❧

Helen left Joe asleep at the farm and went home to release Puppy. Eight hours on his own had pushed his benevolent nature too far and a shredded Bokhara rug made the point eloquently for him. Helen had a quick shower then scooped up Puppy and hairdryer and went back to the farm, a short journey between two worlds that she still found difficult to bridge.

Released from the car, the dog made a dash for the stairs, then to Joe's bed and leaped on him.

'Sorry, love. He was too quick for me.'

'That dog needs proper training,' Joe growled, getting out of bed. 'Watch out, he'll have you downstairs arse over tit. If you get down in one piece put the kettle on.'

Joe looked out of the bedroom window and saw the police car and the incident tape across the top of the quarry slope. He felt sick with anxiety.

'I rang the police station while you were asleep, Joe, I hope you don't mind. It seemed best to get in an explanation first. I mean, tell them why you didn't go straight round last night. Two officers are coming at eleven to take a statement. The man isn't dead, Joe. He's in a serious condition but it can't be as bad as you thought.' Helen got on with the soothing tea-making ritual.

'I was too scared to ask how the fellow was. He looked dead to me, and I can't understand why they didn't cart me off and lock me up straight away, finding me next to the body.' Joe looked more aware of his surroundings than he had the night before but he still looked haunted, as if old quarry ghosts had drained his spirit.

'If you are feeling better, perhaps you could tell me what you remember. Go over it before the police get here.'

'Prepare my story, you mean?'

'Don't twist my words. I just mean that going over the sequence of events may help you remember. And I really want to know what happened, Joe. I love you and I know you, the good and bad stuff, all of it and if anyone got hurt I'm sure it was an accident.'

162

Joe got up and started to walk round the living room, Puppy at his heels pulling at his socks. Joe picked him up and held him close.

'It was such a lovely day, and I saw a stoat, a young one, terrific energy and leaping about practising hunting. Then the pair of grebe we saw the other day, they were after my lunch. I took it down there because I couldn't concentrate after that business with Webster. That's right, I'd tried to get on with my book because that usually works like magic, I forget myself for hours. But it didn't happen.'

Helen rescued the squirming puppy from Joe's tightening grasp as he tensed with concentration. 'After the grebe? What happened then?'

'The stoat had leaped up the rock face and disappeared, and I kept trying to see where it had gone. So I was looking up and saw this man poking about. I suppose I've been a bit edgy lately about Stonecraft and Webster and threats to the quarry, so I shouted but he took no notice.'

'Perhaps he didn't hear?'

'He looked up but went on digging. I climbed up to the top of the ledge and kept shouting at him to stop. Then he started to run away from me round the edge towards the gorse until he ran out of path. He was sort of cornered. I remember him waving that metal pole about and I thought he was coming at my face with the pointed end of it and I must have tried to grab it. Then he was over the edge, but it's all a blur.'

'He must have slipped. The police will have seen that, they've gone over the ground thoroughly. They take casts of footprints, and the edge has probably broken away.'

Joe stopped pacing and leaned his forehead against the cold stone of the old wall. 'I wish I could picture everything that happened. I think I've blanked it out because I lost my rag. I tried not to get angry, but he wouldn't listen. If I scared him …'

'It's dangerous to jump to conclusions like that. Just keep trying to remember the facts.' Helen moved to the window overlooking the front garden and the track. 'Those policemen on duty are moving off and they've taken the tape down. I suppose they've seen and recorded all they want to.' She watched as the police car jolted

slowly over the stones and boulders. No flashing blue lights and wailing sirens would ever be possible along that ancient track meant for sheep and geese, or for the treasured farm cart with iron-bound wheels. 'They aren't coming in, Joe. They can't be blaming you.'

Joe picked up a log that was drying in the hearth and gave it to Puppy as a better teething ring than the chair leg. 'Most of the villagers think I'm a reclusive nutter. The police probably think I've finally cracked.'

❧

When the police arrived at midday to interview him Joe went over the previous day's events again. They commented on the unexplained gaps in his account and stopped the recording several times to warn him about withholding information. 'We know you had issues with Stonecraft International, and the victim was an employee. If he dies ...'

'But he must have slipped,' Helen insisted loudly 'did you check the ground for tracks?'

The inspector waved her aside with a dismissive gesture. 'Don't leave the village Mr. Wright, we'll be back tomorrow. I'm sure you will have remembered more by then.'

Helen and Joe stared wretchedly at each other and Puppy choked on splinters of log.

'Helen, love, this must be your worst five star nightmare. Closeted in this soul-destroying place with a useless prat who can't remember whether he's nearly killed someone or not. Why don't you run like hell?'

'Not sure, I'll give it some thought. The worst thing about this place is that we can't ring for a takeaway because no-one will risk their scooter down this track. Oh, there are some phone messages for you, but I'd leave them for a while.'

'Who from? The outside world seems a bit hostile right now.'

'Simon Gent with, he said, some good news, but I accidentally deleted that. I was in a hurry to phone the police. Oh, and your mother about a crocus. So I think we'll prioritise and have some jacket potatoes.'

'I couldn't eat a thing while someone's dying, probably dead. And it's my fault.'

'Bottle of wine, then. I need a drink even if you don't.' Helen wanted to shake him out of his self-pitying melancholia, but any bracing up platitudes that came to mind sounded heartless.

'How can lives go wrong so quickly? His and mine.' Joe reached to switch on the radio, but stopped as though it had burned him. 'I'm even afraid to listen to that.'

'I think you should ring your mother, because she'll certainly be watching the East Midlands news. And Joe, don't say it was your fault when the police come. I'm sure it was an accident.'

'Let me get outside of a couple of glasses of wine first. Everything seems unreal. I'm watching myself as though it's someone else. If only. One minute I'm in the sunshine making the most amazing video of a stoat, with some stills that will look great in my book, the next there's a body on the ground, right where I was feeding the ducks. It makes no sense.'

Helen felt the best thing to do was to stay at Blackridge for a day or two in an effort to make Joe's life seem as normal as possible, though with a man lying at death's door in the local hospital their idea of normal was distorted. She collected Joe's clothes from the bedroom floor and put them in the stone sink to get rid of the mud and dust from the quarry floor. He must have knelt beside the man for nearly half an hour feeling for a pulse, for breath and a glimmer of life, waiting for help. He had admitted with shame that he knew nothing about first aid and had not dared to try any life-saving measures. She cleaned the grey slime and mud from his shoes so that nothing would remind him of yesterday's horrors. If only she could wipe his mind clear to give him some peace, but remembering every detail was the only way to get at the truth. There was no easy escape from mental torture.

In the early afternoon Joe fell asleep in front of the fire. Helen had never known him have an afternoon nap during the months they had spent together – did shock make you sleep? Over the next half hour Margaret and Lauren rang; several people in Stoneybrook

had seen the helicopter and its dramatically swinging cargo. Had Joe had an accident?

Lauren's enquiry was almost incoherent, but she tried to sound casual. She was sure that as an old friend of Joe's Helen was a good person to comfort him, but as a near neighbour and fellow artist she would call in soon to see if there was anything Joe needed to distract him. She had an excellent set of books on eighteenth century ornithological studies with beautiful paintings and she always found that leafing through those was very soothing. Helen managed a tone of sincere gratitude as she thanked Lauren, but felt that she was being regarded simply as a decorative nurse and daily help, with Lauren providing intellectual nourishment.

Helen knew there was an urgent job to be done. She went into the kitchen and phoned Joe's mother, first writing a little script on a piece of paper because getting words in the right order was important when you did not want to alarm someone. She interrupted Sylvia's expressions of pleasure that the two young people were spending time together and told her that a stranger had been taken to hospital after a fall in the quarry. It was a version of the truth and details could come later, but it seemed natural to say that Joe was in shock, was mercifully asleep and so could not come to the phone.

It seemed heartless to forestall his mother's visit, but Helen asked her to wait another day. She could hear in Sylvia's voice the half-spoken questions jostling for attention, but as yet there were no answers that she could give, apart from the reassurance that her son was fine. She could truthfully say that she had not seen the accident and she had not forced Joe to talk about it. Helen assured her that Joe would ring when he woke up.

Her next task was even more difficult. When the police came she had made a note of their names and now she asked to speak to Inspector Greatorex. Had there been any news from the hospital? No, she was not a relative of the injured man, but the inspector had met her at Blackridge Farm and her friend Joseph Wright was suffering great anxiety not knowing ... again she had struggled to find the right words.

The Inspector had commented abruptly that the man in the hospital bed was also suffering, although he was still unconscious. They had discovered his identity but it would be inappropriate for the police to give details at this stage.

Helen was not sure that any of this information would be a comfort to Joe. Puppy had also drifted into an afternoon nap, forgivable in view of his tender years, tender months in fact, but now he was awake and raring to go. He went into stalking pose, fascinated by Joe's toes as they jerked about in troubled sleep. Helen anchored him to his lead and took him for a short walk, away from the quarry and unwelcome thoughts and towards the village. In sight of the first few cottages and the Miners Standard she turned away from the grandly named Main Road choosing the shelter of Toad Wood. She did not want to risk questions from any of the villagers, questions about the helicopter and the swinging stretcher heading off to Chesterfield.

Margaret had scornfully reported that rumour would have it that Joe had been shot by a hit man from Stonecraft International, or had plunged down the rock face in dark despair, feeling powerless to save his beloved quarry.

Walking in the wood behind the pub, Helen could hear the familiar blaring music that announced the television news coming from the bar and hoped selfishly that there was more dramatic news to entertain the regulars than an accident in a quarry.

She wondered how many men had died almost unnoticed and unreported in the long history of Blackridge Quarry, some even from the terrace of five cottages opposite the Miners Standard. They were cramped little dwellings built by Joe's ancestor in the 1860s for lead miners and quarrymen and still owned, in three cases out of the five, by families who could remember fathers and grandfathers working underground or at the rock face. These were families who saw the quarry as employment, a secure future for the village. They were genuinely bewildered by talk of the importance of Great Crested Newts and Spotted Orchids.

13

Looking for Clues

Joe woke up as Helen and Puppy came in from their walk. He smiled when he saw her, then his body slumped as he remembered the day before. 'Why am I in this mess, love? I should be working on my book, taking great photos, making a name for myself, making you proud of me … making some money. Instead of which because of me the life of the village is under threat.'

'How do you work that out? I thought there was a chance you could put Stoneybrook on the wildlife map.'

'My quarry is causing all our problems. The police could say it's not safe and would be better off in industrial hands. The village will get churned up by juggernauts and there'll be blasting at all hours, dust, pollution, illness … people will hate me for doing the wrong thing but I don't know what the right thing is.'

He was spiralling so far into a black depression that he would make himself ill. Helen tried not to feel impatient.

'I rang the police, Joe,' she got in quickly, trying to focus him on their main worry. 'The man is still unconscious. I'm sure the hospital will bring him round, it wasn't such a great fall, only a quarry, not the Alps or …' she was talking drivel, but it seemed to work.

Joe got up and stretched. 'Let's hope you're right. He'll recover and he'll give his version of events. I just wish I could remember … it was never in my mind to hurt anyone. How could it have been when the day had been going like magic, the sun at the right angle for photos and critters seeming to want to pose and show off?'

'Joe, love, shut up. You keep talking about how wonderful the film you took is, but you haven't shown me. Where is your camera? It isn't here. Where are the photos?'

'They don't seem important when someone gets hurt.'

'But was that what started the fight … if there was a fight? You were a threat, not with violence but with your camera.' Helen had grabbed his arms and was shaking him, willing him to remember.

Joe nodded, unable to speak for a while, then managed a whispered 'Yes. That was how it was. The man would not stop digging or prodding the ground, he wanted me to see him, he was grinning, taunting me.'

'Enough to enrage anyone.'

'But Helen, it didn't. I felt calm, I was still ashamed of losing my rag with Webster and I walked towards the man filming him almost as though he was another interesting species to be studied. When he realised what I was doing he stopped probing and smiling and shook that metal thing in my face.'

Helen gave a shout, Puppy barked and capered, so she shut him in the kitchen to muffle the noise. 'Now it's coming back to you! You film his illegal activities, he panics and runs. He must have slipped and fallen.'

'No. It wasn't like that. Yes, he ran, but in the wrong direction, because the footpath ends halfway round the top of the quarry. It used to go farther, but now it ends in a jungle of brambles and thorn bushes, so he turned and came back towards me with that metal spike thing …'

'Have the police got that spike? Did they find it? They'd know it could be used as an offensive weapon.'

Joe seemed to crumple again. He was living the events of yesterday but it was like re-running an old and worn film that flashed then faded. 'They didn't say anything about the probe, but then they were concentrating more on the body … I mean, on the man. They seemed to be looking for bruises and cuts, probably because I'm now on police files for assault.'

'No,' Helen looked exasperated, 'there were cuts and bruises because the fellow had just fallen down a quarry face, probably bouncing off the rocks a few times. If you are going to be so defeatist you may as well just admit to attempted murder.'

'Sorry, love. I'm remembering more now, but that probe thing, I can't picture what happened to it. It will be on video, because I can't recall turning the damn thing off, I was so horrified at the thought of another punch-up.' Joe turned towards a row of hooks next to the battered old front door where his camera case usually hung, with binoculars, scarves, shopping bags and recently a dog lead. 'Not there. Must be upstairs next to my laptop.'

'It isn't – I checked while you were asleep. I just assumed the police had taken it. Surely that's the first thing they'd take off you? That's why I haven't asked sooner. They'd have given you a receipt, or at least mentioned it.'

Joe sat down again next to the fire and put his head in his hands. 'Christ! I'm being such a wimp, love. The blackouts must be because I've got a guilty conscience.'

Helen swore at him then went to the phone. 'Inspector Greatorex? No? Well, any officer that went out to Blackridge Quarry yesterday. Were any items removed from the scene?' She was talking like a TV police soap. 'I mean Mr. Wright has lost his camera …'

She handed the phone to Joe 'They won't talk to me. Bloody confidentiality that everyone trots out as an excuse for not explaining anything.'

Joe spoke briefly then put the phone down. 'Helen, my camera must still be somewhere on the quarry edge. I'm going up to look – at least that's got a good memory.' Suddenly energised he reached for his jacket.

'You can't go now, it's nearly dark and you won't find anything. Plus it's dangerous, we don't want another …'

'Corpse? I'll take my torch – that camera could solve everything, just like in the old films where the hero finds he has accidentally clicked the shutter at the right moment and the proof slowly emerges in the darkroom.' Joe managed a smile, given this new bit of hope.

'And the heroine throws herself in front of him to stop him going out into the storm. You're going nowhere tonight, Joe. I'll set the alarm then we'll go as soon as it's light.' Seeing he was about to shove her aside, she added 'You've caused me enough worry.'

Joe nodded slowly, then took off his jacket and hung it over the back of his chair in readiness for action in the morning. The mood of the evening had changed from despair to one of plans and preparation. Puppy was released from the kitchen because his howling had been adding to the tension, torch batteries were checked ready for hunting in crevices and another camera found to photograph the position of the camera that had recorded the events of the previous day.

'We ought to take a photo of where we find anything and one of the quarry edge to show where he may have slipped.' Joe was feeling less abject now that there was some course of action to be taken. 'Off the sofa, mutt. Don't think I haven't noticed.'

'I bet he could find your camera and case,' Helen said proudly, 'he's always digging things up, dogs are good at scenting things.'

'Except he thinks 'finder's keepers' and we'd be chasing him half way to Kinder Scout to get hold of anything he snuffled up. We ought to take some kind of long stick to fish around in holes and crevices. What have we got?'

'Poker? Not really long enough.'

'There's an old golf club in the barn. I don't know how it got there, but that bit on the end could be useful. And there are some bean poles that I'm saving for next year.'

'As you're going outside, get my wellies out of the car. There's bound to be a heavy dew early on.' She threw him the keys. It was still only seven o'clock, a whole evening of anxiety stretched ahead and Helen had no idea how to lighten the mood. They could make love, but it would be unkind to suggest it in Joe's worried state.

Joe came back in with an armful of clobber, an umbrella with a hooked handle, a curtain rod and the golf club. Puppy made a dash through his legs and nearly made it out of the door.

'Bloody animal. He's still totally untrained, Helen. You should have started as soon as you found him.'

'No time like the present.' She seized on the idea gratefully. 'Why don't you try now? He seems to take more notice of you. I think it's the deep, menacing voice.'

'Fine. No problem. We'll start with sitting on command, shall we? Or perhaps 'fetch' so he can go and find my camera.'

Helen walked into the kitchen to hide her amusement. 'I'm just getting some biscuits to train him with.'

Joe fixed the dog with a stern gaze as though trying to hypnotize him. 'I won't need any bribes, Helen. The trick is to be firm and consistent. Sit.' He pushed Puppy's rear as he said this, gave him another baleful glare then another push.

There was a knock on the door and Margaret walked in, tripping over the golf club. 'Good heavens! Are you getting ready for a car boot sale?'

Puppy escaped from the grip on his rear end and remembering cake and other treats leaped at Margaret with little yelps of love.

'Margaret, how good to see you.' Helen could see that the dog training was doomed to failure, not what was needed tonight. She just hoped that Margaret would be unusually tactful and not ask questions about the accident. 'We're in the middle of intensive dog training and are in need of a stiff drink.'

Joe grabbed the pup off their visitor. 'Sit,' he growled, and Puppy sat.

Helen scooped him up before he changed his mind and covered him with kisses. 'Celebration all round!'

'Complete fluke,' Joe insisted. 'He was just showing off.'

'I don't think so, Joe. Your voice had the ring of authority, so much so that I feel I ought to sit down myself.' Margaret accepted a glass of Armagnac and produced some papers from a baggy cardigan. 'About your nature reserve plans, I don't think a Site of Special whatsit is quite what you need. I printed these off.'

Margaret had been trawling about on the internet. Several quarries, such as Baileycroft, Duchy or Cawdor, had been awarded SSSI status and they were supposed to be protected by legislation, but most were privately owned so that monitoring was quite difficult and visits by naturalists or students were not encouraged. One protected site near Buxton was still owned by a quarrying company who carried on extraction in half the quarry with the other

half being a conservation area. Special permission had to be obtained from the company if anyone wanted to visit.

'Do you think the resident wildlife gets confused?' Helen wondered. 'Comfortable nesting boxes one end and earth-shattering blasts the other.'

Margaret stroked Puppy, who was now on her lap on the sofa and staring triumphantly at the other two. 'There was a lovely old quarry near Matlock, limestone from it built up the London Embankment and very grand buildings near Hyde Park centuries ago. That was supposed to be a protected site because of the wildlife that had gradually colonised it, now it's got a damn great supermarket on it, and a petrol station. There were supposed to be hundreds of houses too, but I don't know what happened to those.'

Joe shook his head sadly. 'People must think I'm a hypocrite, I love old quarries that have been reclaimed by nature but I'd fight like mad to stop any new ones being gouged out. Enough is enough, but you've heard me ranting on before.'

'What would be wonderful for the village would be a small-scale wildlife park where some of the bolder creatures, such as newts and toads, or bats even could be encouraged to breed.' Helen was inspired. 'Animals that don't mind being stared at for a while because the general public gets disappointed if it can't see action in the first few minutes. Then there could be hides, to watch out for the more wary critters like badgers and foxes. Rare plants would be easy, a special bit of garden …'

'Conservation doesn't quite work like that,' Joe interrupted. 'Animals don't turn up on cue, and wild flowers don't often grow where you want them to. I shall have to look at the categories of conservation to work out a compromise, something that doesn't disturb the wildlife but that interests people at the same time. I'm not sure that's possible.'

'But first we need to save the Quarry,' Margaret smiled encouragingly. 'Did you hear from Simon Gent? He told me he had tried to ring you.'

Helen looked guilty. 'Sorry, Joe, there was a phone message from him but it went straight out of my mind. Something about his solicitor digging up old quarry disputes.'

'And about your boss, Helen,' Margaret put in helpfully. 'He carries a lot of financial clout with all the properties he owns and he's threatening to sell up and leave the village if that new housing goes up.'

Joe shot Helen a look that said he understood why she had conveniently forgotten the message from her boss. 'Yes, it's the old argument – tourism versus local jobs, but it's often difficult to unscramble them. We've got two builders and several painters and decorators in the village and Mr. Hucknall gives them a fair amount of work with his renovations and extensions, but he pays them peanuts. I bet they'd love to get work on a big job like a housing estate.'

'Except small tradespeople wouldn't get a look in. We know now that Stonecraft International owns the development company behind the estate application, and a big outfit like that has its own builders, architects, plumbers, the lot. No work for locals.' Margaret got up, removing Puppy from her lap and placing him gently on the sofa. 'Don't puppies smell lovely? A bit like baking scones. I must be off, I've got to collect a sheet of our petition against new houses from Mrs. Fox in the end terrace. She promised to pass it along but I don't expect any of them will sign it. Those terraced houses are on three floors with stone staircases and some of the older people would love to get out and into new purpose-built flats at the other end of the village. Can't blame them.'

As she went out, the telephone rang. Joe answered it but said nothing apart from 'I see' and 'I won't'. He went back to his chair and sat gazing into the fire. He could feel the intensity of Helen's stare and her silent question.

'That was the police. They've heard from the hospital and the injured man has just died. They said they think he was a rambler and he must have taken the wrong path. They don't want me to leave the house.'

'Bullshit!' Helen sat on his lap and wrapped her arms around him. 'Why would a rambler run away then come back at you with a metal spike? We need to get your camera and we'll be out of here first thing to get to it before anyone else does. It can't have disappeared.'

⁂

They could not sleep. Filling the hours to daylight seemed like a challenge they were not used to, scared to touch radio or television, fearful of the speculation and questions on the regional news. They could not eat, so there was no joy in cooking up enticing little snacks in the kitchen. Puppy alone had no trouble in sleeping, snoring and grunting. His dream-state noises were the only sounds in the farmhouse apart from wind whistling down the chimney, using the stovepipe like a monotone flute.

'How much of your book have you managed to write?'

Joe made an effort to answer. 'Three chapters before all this happened. Now I keep getting disjointed ideas, then a few seconds later they've gone.'

'I'd like to read it. Remember how I used to proof-read some of your articles? You'd get so enthusiastic about a new arrival in the quarry the whole thing came out like stream of consciousness.'

'Is that a kind phrase for garbled rubbish?' Joe got up and found his laptop, switched it on and gave it to Helen. 'You read it back to me. It feels as though someone else wrote all that months ago. I need to hear it in your voice, love.'

'Ancient caves and caverns deep in the Derbyshire hills may once have sheltered beings who had no need of walls and a roof. They ventured out to snare rabbits or lay traps for deer, to collect firewood and pick berries. Gradually all signs of these ancient inhabitants faded with the relentless passing of time. The caves were inhabited after many centuries by sturdy people with pickaxes who hewed the rock and brought out serviceable chunks to build their walls, cottages and barns. When the quarry fell silent again, for decades the raw limestone rocks stayed exposed to biting frost, sun and rain, and most of all to the constant wind that coated them with dust and seed, filling up the jagged cracks with small deposits of soil. A dozen hardy varieties of grass and moss started the greening of the quarry,

catching and holding spiralling seeds and spores of ferns and mosses. Their constant growth and decay formed fertile beds for seeds of ash and birch that grew unrestrained, their roots and decaying leaves forming an ever more welcoming oasis of greenery ...'

Helen stopped reading and looked up, hearing a gentle snoring noise from Joe and a doggy descant of grunts and yelps. When she stopped, Joe woke up.

Helen joked 'If it sends you to sleep, just think what it'll do to your readers. It sounds good, but I'd like to know more because you trot through a million years in a couple of sentences. More research required.' She pretended to scribble a hasty rejection slip from an agent on a scrap of paper and flicked it at him.

'Well, how about you and your rivetingly exciting recipes. What have you cooked up recently that would send me to sleep?'

'I sent one off to Good Housekeeper a few days ago, nut roast moistened with mashed prunes in brandy ...'

'I might have known brandy would be in there somewhere, but surely you mean purée of prunes?'

'No, too runny, the nut roast is ground almonds, brazil nuts and hazelnuts, and the prunes just need to be roughly chopped to break the skin and let the juice mix with ...'

Joe let out mock snoring noises, then got up to make coffee as though in a trance. Someone had died and they were talking about recipes.

'Make mine cocoa, I do need to get a few minutes sleep if I'm going to go hunting evidence.' Helen sounded light-hearted but worry seemed to have seeped down from her thoughts to knot up her guts and paralyse all movement. What if they found nothing, no camera, no video, no weapon-like rod? Who would believe Joe then?

They set off in the dark just before seven.

'I want to get up on the cliff over the quarry by first light.' Joe checked their torches for the tenth time. 'It always gets light up there a few minutes before it does in the farmhouse.'

177

'Don't go so fast, it seems even steeper and the stones even looser in the dark. Don't you think we should have started down on the quarry floor?'

'No. I'm beginning to recall a little more of the scene, horrible though it was, and I'm pretty sure my camera didn't go over with …' Joe's words were lost as he hurried ahead, caught up in the wind and faltering as the memory hit him.

They could have started searching earlier, because although there was no moonlight and no light in the sky from distant cities, the frosty dew and white limestone rocks scattered about the sparse grassland seemed eerily luminous.

'Switch off your torch now and it will seem even lighter,' Joe shouted.

A white, softly fluttering wraith rose up from the quarry rock face. It gave a mournful hoot, disturbed in its patient observation of prey on the grassy ledges.

This could have been a leisurely nocturnal ramble on the look-out for badgers or hares, Helen thought. In the past she had been dragged out sleepily, encouraged by Joe's enthusiastic hunt for a rare species of bat, one discovered days before in Longsidings Quarry, so why not in his Blackridge caves? She had shivered for hours while he monitored his familiar shapes in the half-light, counting them in and out like pilots on a sortie, but no rare newcomers emerged. It was only a matter of time, Joe had remarked patiently, but whether he meant hours, nights or decades she had been too cold and stiff to find out.

That past night time vigil seemed like a pleasurable outing compared with this sinister hunt. Joe was a long way ahead now, but then he stopped and waited for her.

'This is where I turned on the camera. The man was still some way ahead, and still digging and probing, then he must have seen me filming him and he ran off round the rim of the quarry. He must have thought the path continued, and years ago I seem to remember that it did. But you see that black mass ahead? That's where the brambles have taken over, from that outcrop of rocks over to the quarry edge.'

'Where we picked blackberries last year? It was a good crop.' Happy days. 'Where did you actually meet him? That's where we need to search.'

'He tried to scramble over the rocks for a few seconds, then gave up and came back towards me.' Joe switched his torch back on to examine the ground, sweeping its beam along the quarry edge, then stopped at a pale, muddy streak that ended where the edge had broken away. He stood transfixed, the torchlight wavering over the edge, lighting up a patch of quarry floor and a silver rim of lake far below.

Helen said it for him. 'That's where he went over.' She took the camera they had brought with them out of Joe's jacket pocket and took several shots. 'There's no sign of your camera, or of that metal probe. How can they have disappeared? Come away from the edge, Joe, or you'll be going over as well.'

Joe had sunk to the ground, staring at the slide of mud and the patch of grass around it, bare of the hoped-for proof.

'There wasn't a fight, love. You do believe me, don't you?'

'I believe that you would never have pushed him over the edge for all your beloved bats and falcons and orchids. Never. But if he tried to threaten you and there was a struggle … it was an accident, Joe. You weren't to blame. We should go down and search by the lake.'

'There's nothing down there. I know. I was there for what seemed like hours waiting for help.'

'But you were not really seeing. All your attention was focused on the poor fellow lying injured. I say poor fellow because however evil he looked pacing around on your property with his pointed rod, he'll probably only turn out to be an underpaid employee of Stonecraft International and they'll have convinced him that re-opening the quarry is in the national interest. Something like that will have been going through your mind and you wouldn't have left him dying so that you could look for evidence. Now get up off that wet grass.'

Joe eased himself up onto his elbows. 'How logical you are. I just wish I could believe in your generous view of me, but I can remember feeling angry, so angry I couldn't think straight.'

'I thought you said you weren't angry, Joe.'

He shook his head, confused. 'Not at first, but when he wouldn't listen …' He peered over the edge, small stones and shale dislodging and cascading down, sending up an indignant pair of sheltering blackbirds resting on the ledge below.

'I can see something down there, something black on a ledge.' Joe wriggled closer to the edge, then shunted back again and stood up.

Helen grabbed his arm and pulled him even farther away from the void. 'Don't ever do that again, taking risks just because you feel guilty.'

Joe stood up and ran down the hill towards the slope of the quarry entrance, shouting back 'I can see something about three-quarters of the way down the rock face but I'll have to climb up from the bottom to get to it.'

At least they were going downhill now. If Joe wanted to go rock climbing from the quarry floor he would not have far to fall. It was light now, squawking jackdaws wheeling overhead. Surely that was the small black object Joe had seen, an injured or exhausted bird?

By the time Helen had reached the bottom of the quarry next to the pool Joe had climbed about thirty feet up the rock face. She heard an anguished shout.

'Oh, for chrissakes, no. No bloody use,' and when he scrambled and half fell back down again, he held fragments of camera, smashed into three main pieces but with smaller fragments breaking away in his hands. There was no sign of the metal probe the man had threatened him with.

The police arrived at seven-thirty to find Joe hunched by the stove in the living room clutching his second whisky.

'My inspector says he told you that things have taken a turn for the worse, Mr. Wright.'

'You mean he's dead,' Joe moaned. 'More than a bloody turn for the worse. As worse as it can get.'

'We've been up all night, officer. Mr. Wright has had no sleep. I gave him the whisky for the shock, and ...' Helen's explanation trailed off.

'In view of the serious turn of events, we need to ask you some more questions Mr.Wright. Down at the station, if you wouldn't mind.'

'What, right now, officer? He's had no breakfast. I mean, he won't make much sense with just whisky on an empty stomach.'

Joe stood up. He still had camera fragments in his hand but dropped them on to a table. 'We were out in the quarry trying to figure out how it had all happened. I thought that would help, finding the camera, but it's smashed to fucking bits.'

'Is that ... was that the camera from the scene of the accident?' The officer reached out for it, then stopped. 'I'll send someone with a container to collect it, though it probably isn't going to tell us much now. Shall we get going, Sir? Just a few more questions, and I'm sure we can find you a cup of coffee at the station.'

Helen released a howling Puppy from the kitchen and hugged him to her, burying her face in his fur then collapsing with him onto the sofa.

14

Helping with Enquiries

There was chaos at the new Bugle offices in Bakewell, but a kind of evolving chaos that would soon resolve itself into just a muddle. Fred Marshall thanked technology for the hundredth time that week; in the old days moving newspaper offices would have taken six filing cabinets, a roomful of cardboard boxes and a hazardous mountain of archives and back numbers. There was still a filing cabinet, and some boxes of old material that he knew would never find its way onto a computer, but with the three office pcs and his own laptop he felt that things were almost under control.

Gillian, his part-time secretary, was comfortably installed in the next office, pacified by discovering that there was a small kitchen with appliances instead of the plug-in hotplate at the mill. The move from the old building had taken about three days and as she had not been expected to heave furniture and boxes about it had provided a good excuse for a peaceful time.

Most phone calls received the recorded message *'We regret that due to relocation The Bugle offices are closed until Monday'* although with the careful use of a few news stories, some nature articles from the files and the usual assortment of small ads, the next edition of the paper would be out the following week. Even the news story was an elaborate account of the dangerous state of the old mill and the narrow escape of The Bugle's editor and staff from being pitched through rotting timbers into the raging torrent of the Wye. A photo of the river taken this year was rejected as its sluggish waters were at their lowest level since records began. The trusty archives provided a shot of the Wye in flood six years ago, its white water splashing impressively over gleaming rocks. Bugle readers were a

genial, unquestioning lot, in fact Fred would have welcomed a few vitriolic letters to the Ed along the lines of 'Your article on the miracle cures of Bugsford Spa waters was a fanciful load of bullshit.' He usually had to write controversial letters himself.

Gillian jumped when the phone rang. She had to let it ring while she mopped up nail varnish remover that was eating into the cover of her paperback. Did she know that one of The Bugle reporters had been arrested? The caller was a resident in the flats next to Bakewell police station and he'd recognised the reporter, he'd seen a picture of him in the paper, he was the one who wrote about wildflowers and bats and suchlike. Not that he'd been handcuffed, but he did arrive in a police car out of office hours.

Fred Marshall felt that events were overtaking him. Out of the kindness of his heart he had held on to the story of Joe's punch-up with Webster of Stonecraft International, now it seemed likely that Joe had gone ape and pushed someone over the edge of the quarry. The man was dead, Joe was arrested and it would look as though The Bugle had done a cover-up to protect a member of staff. Not an actual staff reporter of course, just a contributor.

'Joseph Wright is only an occasional contributor of wildlife articles,' Fred explained to BBC East Midlands Television when they rang asking for news of the accident. 'No, we don't have any photos of him available as we are just relocating our offices. Sorry, there isn't an online edition of The Bugle for you to search.' It was the least he could do for Joe, a few delaying tactics, but now he would have to put an article together that gave Bugle readers the facts, told the truth. Bored bystander of Bakewell might be short-sighted, could be lying, could be nurturing some insane grudge against Joe. Perhaps he was a passionate twitcher and Joe had thrown him off his land at some time, or he was a builder at odds with Joe's wild ideas on conservation. Who knows? The truth was out there, probably down at the Old Black Bull Inn in Bakewell when the duty officers at the police station changed shifts. Fred decided that he would have to buy a few pints if he wanted to get nearer the truth.

≈

Helen dreaded phone calls. There was sure to be someone in the village who had seen Joe driven off in the police car, and soon there would be calls from local radio and television wanting information that she knew the hospital and the police would not provide them with. Joe's mother would call back today, placated for a short while by her reassurance that her son was fine but anxious to find out about the accident. Helen could hear her now. Hadn't she always said that the quarry was a hostile and dangerous place? Now Joe would have to take her advice and sell up.

Helen felt paralysed by worry and uncertainty, a state that Puppy had no hesitation in dealing with. He needed a walk even if *she* seemed unwilling to move. A threatening squat on the rug would soon move her. They were not in their usual home, but for a dog the old farmhouse held no end of delights: frayed ends of rugs to tug, deep holes in chairs where he could scent the comings and goings of mice, chewable logs within easy reach, cupboard doors that did not fit and could be flipped open with a paw. Added to all this fun, the large person, the one that growled a lot, had disappeared so the house was his to explore. After a walk.

Helen got her coat and gathered up dog lead and poo bags. That was a Bakewell town centre habit that she could probably forget about out here in the wilds where everywhere was covered in cow pats and assorted droppings. She got to the gate and turned towards the quarry and towards the track leading past it; she certainly did not want to go anywhere near the dreadful place, nor did she want to go near the village. Drawing level to where the rough limestone path sloped down to the quarry floor, she stopped. She felt sick, and although Puppy was choking himself on the end of the lead in an effort to get free, she sank down onto a rock and put her head in her hands.

'Helen! Are you all right? What's the matter?' Lauren came running up from the direction of the farmhouse and put her hand on Helen's shoulder. 'Can I help you back to the farm?'

'Thanks, but I've got to take him for a walk. It's just that after yesterday's accident it makes me feel sick going past the place, and

now someone's died I can't bear to look. I didn't want to go the other way, into the village in case …'

'In case people like me asked questions? Well, I'd love to take your dog for a walk, he's adorable. What's his name?'

'Puppy.'

'Mmm. Still Puppy? You go back and put the kettle on and I'll take him for a brisk canter up the hill. I take it you don't let him off the lead?'

The phone stopped ringing as Helen got back, and Sylvia left a message asking Joe to ring her as she'd got some interesting news. Helen reflected on the fact that whatever the news was, the news from the Blackridge end could probably top it.

Before Lauren took a sip of tea she said 'Poor Joe. He must feel terrible, that dreadful accident happening in his beloved quarry. I mean, hideous that the poor fellow died, but as the landowner I expect Joe will have to answer all sorts of questions.'

'Did you see him go off in the police car?' Helen was in no mood to be diplomatic. 'Is that why you've come up? Did you think he'd been arrested?'

Lauren picked up Puppy and put him on her lap before she answered.

'Alan Wood in The Miners saw them go past, then his wife rang me … we only know what we heard on the news. That someone had fallen and then he died. I was worried … did you know about the row Joe had with the man from the quarry company?'

'He told me last night. I hadn't seen him for a few days before that, but when this accident happened he said …,' Helen paused. It was not really the time to score points, but there was only one truth. 'He said he needed me, needed to talk to me.'

'I can understand that. Going down to The Miners for a pint would have meant facing an inquisition. Better to talk to someone from outside the village. But I really was worried, Helen, about that man here at the farmhouse, the one Joe was supposed to have pushed. Was he the manager, or director? Somebody important.'

'His name is Webster. Managing Director of Stonecraft International.'

Lauren nodded. 'I saw what happened. He got Joe riled up, then deliberately fell over when Joe took his arm. He said he was going to the police, he'd got a witness – me – and I thought I'd have to make a statement, but nothing happened. I *wanted* to make a statement. That's why I've come round now, do you think I should tell the police what really happened, just in case they think Joe had something to do with the accident? They may think he's an aggressive person and get the wrong impression.'

Making an effort, Helen could see that Lauren was being irritatingly public-spirited, and as she plainly lusted after Joe then who could blame her for scoring double points. 'That's really thoughtful of you, dear Lauren. But hold that thought for a while, because I'm expecting Joe back soon, once he's told the police all he knows. If we do,' (the *we* was a bit difficult to spit out) any special pleading for him it may look as though we have something to hide.'

Helen took their cups and stood up 'Thanks for coming, but I'm going to lock the door and get some sleep for a few hours. We couldn't sleep last night.'

Lauren paused at the front door. 'Don't feel badly about going near the quarry. Just think how old it is, and how many accidents and poor labourers dying there must have been over the years, but those lovely flowers still grow and the birds and bats still make their homes there. It sort of heals the wounds.'

The woman was nearly as sentimental as Joe. Helen slept for two hours, but Joe did not come back. She left a message for Adrian at her office saying she was taking a long weekend. He would probably guess why. She read through the chapters of Joe's book again, hearing his voice through the loving description of newts and dragonflies. She scrubbed bleach into the old pine kitchen table so that its honey-coloured surface shone through the tides of tea and coffee stains. She stacked more logs round the fire and brushed dog hairs off the sofa, but there was really nothing she could do to help Joe. Except, if she was being such a busy housewife, why not over-act the part? She rang the police-station.

'Mr. Wright's helping you about that accident at Blackridge Quarry. Well, Inspector, I've just cooked his dinner because I

expected him back by now, but I don't know whether to dish up or leave it in the oven. The price of food these days, I don't want to see it ruined, so could you find out when he'll be home?'

The officer said he would find out, not surprised by such an innocent domestic demand being made on the centre of law and order, agreeing that the ruin of a good meal would be a crime in itself. He thought there had been a new development in the case and he would ring her back.

Inspired by her fictitious hot meal, Helen explored the ancient fridge that was usually just a storage cupboard but that shuddered into action from time to time to protect three vegetarian sausages and open tins of chickpeas. Perhaps it would be better to go home to her flat because there seemed nothing she could do to help Joe at the farmhouse. Even so it would feel like desertion. At least dog-walking expeditions were easier in the countryside than in Bakewell town centre. She would take some bread to feed the friendly grebe in the quarry pool and they would help her to exorcise the nightmare.

The birds overcame their suspicion of a cavorting dog when they heard the familiar rustle of a plastic bag; the sun was shining, its warmth intensified by the surrounding rocks and Helen sat at the edge of the water and relaxed, feeling closer to Joe there than she did in the house. And Lauren was right, whatever horrors had taken place in the quarry only humans were to blame, not nature, and it had all happened many times before.

Once the bread was finished the birds lost interest; she couldn't expect to see real, untamed wildlife because she was an amateur intruder and snuffling Puppy pulling her round on a lead and following trails of scent was a threat to wilder nature.

High on a ledge a shadow moved and stretched to form the outline of a huge bird that roused itself from sleep. Wings wide, it fixed bright, unblinking eyes on the creatures below. Helen had no idea what it was, but it was the biggest bird she had ever seen, and it was beautiful. An eagle, perhaps? A hawk? It had an elegantly grey striped chest and the underside of its broad wings had more

delicate bands of grey. The bird fixed intelligent orange-rimmed eyes on her then settled down to observe the intruders' behaviour.

Why hadn't Joe protected this place better instead of wandering silently and thoughtfully about, keeping it to himself? It did not need fences and gates, but it needed the protection of the law enforcing a public right to preserve it. That was how she could help him.

She stood up slowly, pulled Puppy out of the rabbit hole he had enlarged and went back to the house.

No message from the police station, but another one from Sylvia angered by her son's thoughtless silence.

Helen switched on the laptop; what was the difference between nature reserves, sites of special scientific interest, wildlife sanctuaries, designated sites, conservation sites and trusts? Blackridge Quarry and its surrounding hills deserved to be all of these, but where did you start? Did they wait to be chosen, all the while at the mercy of unscrupulous developers? Where were the forms to fill in, the societies to lobby? She sent emails requesting forms, asking for visits from experts and for advice, sending map references and some of Joe's photographs. She remembered the promise of a television programme with its professors and wildlife celebrities. When they came they would know, they would see for themselves.

She fried the sausages, found some pickled onions and made a sandwich, an unidentified guilty feeling at the back of her mind. It was those messages left by Joe's mother; poor Sylvia may have heard about the accident victim's death. She could well be on her way from Buxton right now. Helen dialled her number, but there was no reply. She left another reassuring, stalling message. Joe was fine, still fine and had got her message about the exciting news. He'd had to go out again for a few hours. He had mentioned calling in to see her. Was that a lie too far?

She had expected a few visits from sympathetic villagers, or phone calls from locals curious about the police car, but none came. People were being unusually tactful. Helen kept the doors locked and the lights low, with only the glow from the stove and the laptop. She had to admit to herself that it wasn't just nosey villagers or

reporters from the media that made her cower in the dark, they would just be a temporary nuisance.

Images of Puppy paddling in black water in the dark quarry came back to her, and returning to the farmhouse after the break-in with cut-up photographs and scattered fragments of Joe's nature articles in the mud. If Joe could not prove his innocence, and she'd heard of far worse miscarriages of justice, then the dirty tricks campaign could have a field day. She imagined bulldozers, diggers, excavators eating relentlessly away at the birch and bracken-covered cliffs. Where was it, somewhere near one of the famous Edges, that the giant machines had continued their destructive progress in spite of legal decisions and injunctions? Month after month after year more rock face crumbled to the diggers, in spite of the rational protests of villagers, their eyes full of dust and ears ringing with blasting. The relentless, onward march of the machines went on, simply because they could.

At Blackridge the peaceful lake would be churned to mud and all signs of life dead and buried. That was too lurid a spectre, of course. Her eagle-like bird would simply glide away gracefully to another sanctuary, to be admired by someone else. Of course the old farmhouse was in the way of progress and would need to be gone, crushed back into the limestone hills that it came from.

Puppy wriggled free of her grasp and stood by the door, ears pricked as far as they would go, head on one side in classic dog concentrating pose. He had picked up sounds of tyres crunching gravel before Helen saw wavering headlamps away down the track filtering through the ragged curtains. She switched off the pc and hid it under the dog-bed then in time-honoured fashion picked up a poker. You were not supposed to injure intruders these days, only assault them with sweet reason and logic so she put it down again and pushed a Windsor chair under the door handle. In the kitchen she heaved the heavy pine table against the door, then realised to her horror that the back door opened outwards.

The car drew up but kept its engine running. Voices, two men she judged, but over the noise of the engine and Puppy whining she could not hear what they were saying. She upended the kitchen

table against the back door to block the hole, jammed the log box against it, started to ring the police then hung up. Difficult to ask for help when the owner of the premises was already at the station being interrogated and possibly under suspicion of murder.

She could still hear voices; whoever wished Joe harm would realise that he was safely out of the way, his property unprotected and vulnerable to their next intimidating stunt. She rang The Miners Standard, imagining a group of lusty, tanked-up villagers coming to her rescue. No reply. She left a message. 'Please help, as soon as you get this. I'm at Joe's place, Blackridge, and there are strangers in a car outside. After all that's happened, I'm very worried.'

15

The Camera Didn't Lie

'It's filling in the forms that takes the time. Are we nearly there, Sergeant?' The Inspector came into the interview room, his arrival finely timed to miss four hours of questioning and the printer trundling out a dozen sheets of rambling description of a sunny day that turned to sudden horror.

'You'll appreciate, Mr. Wright, that when a death occurs and there are no other witnesses, we need to go over the facts several times. We need a thorough account on file.'

Joe nodded in a daze, but said nothing. What was the point? They would either believe him or not.

The Inspector hovered near a chair, looked at his watch then walked back towards the door as though more important matters were waiting.

'Have you brought Mr. Wright up to date with the results of the search, Robertson?'

'Just about to, Sir. First Mr. Wright needs to read his statement and sign it.'

'Good. That's the ticket.' The Inspector left, looking unreasonably cheerful.

Robertson piled the papers up evenly and pushed them towards Joe. 'Check through those carefully, Sir. If it is an accurate account of events, then please sign each page.'

Joe speed-read the papers then signed them, pushing them away from him as quickly as possible. He leaned back in his chair, staring warily at the officer who had given no clue to his feelings apart from incomprehension that any upright citizen should have nothing better to do than wander about in a quarry on the off-chance of

spotting some furry or feathery creature. He had treated Joe as gently and sympathetically as he would have treated a disturbed six-year old. He had read reports of Joe's Bakewell Town Hall speech, something about living in log cabins and shitting in holes in the ground so that you didn't need miles of drainage pipes. Crazy stuff. Unbalanced. Obsessive. Even if he had murdered a trespasser, no judge would convict him. Officer Robertson smiled benignly.

'What now?' Joe asked. He had no idea whether he would be locked up for the next few years, an inevitable progress from police cell to court to prison, or whether he could go home. He had signed those wretched papers admitting that he had been angry, that hatred and frustration had exploded like a blinding headache so that he could not remember the sequence of events. Two men, a chase, one falls.

'Well, Sir. While you were kindly answering all our questions, our men were running some checks. They sent through part of the information we needed about twenty minutes ago,' he nodded towards the computer screen. 'The deceased, Adam Perkins, was an employee of a company called Stonecraft International.'

'I could have guessed as much.'

'We don't do guessing, Sir. The fact is, when you had a break-in at Blackridge Farm some weeks ago we dusted everything.'

'Gold stars all round, but you never caught anyone.'

'The fingerprints we got then match the prints of Adam Perkins. He wore gloves most of the time during the break-in but for some reason he took them off when it came to shredding up your photographs. Perhaps he thought paper didn't count.'

'So he broke into my place and he worked in an unprincipled industry, but I didn't push him over the edge.'

'The fingerprint check was easy, Sir, couple of minutes, but the technical boys have been working on those bits of camera you gave us. It looked a bit suspicious. You could have smashed it up yourself, but then why hand it in?' The officer stared out of the window that from the first floor gave a calming view of the hills towards Chatsworth. He was enjoying his leisurely conjecture, which was the nearest he got to sleuthing. 'Unless, of course, you

thought that a camera bouncing down the rocks for a hundred feet or so would be smashed beyond repair. In which case …'

'What are we waiting for now, then? How long would they take?'

The computer announced an incoming message with a grunt and at its command Robertson held up his hand to silence Joe.

'Looks promising. The camera's memory is better than yours, Sir, even if it is a bit smashed up. They say they are "… retrieving some images that need some digital enhancement." Sounds like my holiday snaps.'

Joe jumped up and swivelled the screen round towards him. 'That'll show you! Now you'll see! Where are they? Those enhanced images?'

'Oh, I won't get them on this pc, Sir. Evidence like that will go into the Inspector's office first then over to Chesterfield for interpretation. Sit down for a bit longer, Sir and I'll send for some more coffee.'

Joe was about to swear in frustration for the first time that day, when the Inspector came back in.

'Looks like we have the proof to substantiate your version of events, Mr Wright. Would you come in to my office? The video you took gets rather erratic after a few minutes and cuts out when the camera hit the rocks, but they've salvaged some sections. Did you tell him about the fingerprints on the metal rod, Robertson?'

'You found that thing? Helen and I looked for hours last night but of course we never found it.'

❧

Puppy was sniffing along the bottom of the front door and growling. Helen heard footsteps on the path, then the phone rang. If she answered it, whoever it was outside would know she was there, and she did not know whether that was good or bad. The old doorknob turned and the door rattled against the bolt.

'Helen! It's me, open the door.'

'Joe! Wait, I've wedged a chair under the handle and now it's stuck.'

'I'll go round the back to the kitchen door.'

'No, I've done it now, and in any case I've shoved everything I could move near the kitchen door to block it.'

'Everything but the kitchen sink.' Joe's spirits were rising and he turned to wave at the police car and watched it drive off before he hugged Helen and kissed her. 'I'll need a few hours of this before I feel human again. God, you feel wonderful. You must have been scared though, sitting here in the dark and wondering what the dirty tricks brigade would do next.'

'Are you back for good? Did the police believe you?'

'Yes, they believe me now. I'm a free man!'

'Before you tell me everything I'd better ring The Miners in case they are sending a rescue party up.'

'You do that while I get us some of your brandy. If there's any left, we've been knocking it back like squash recently.'

Joe dismantled the back-door barricades, then made up the fire. He told Helen about the fingerprints on the metal probe and the camera's memory card.

'The video wasn't much good, but it did show the man, Perkins, running at me with the metal probe, holding it like a spear. My fingerprints were on the pointed end of it, trying to keep it off my face.'

'And when he fell?'

'I'd stopped filming because he grabbed the camera. His prints were on that from when he threw it down the cliff.'

'So they can't say you pushed him?' Helen insisted. 'That still doesn't prove …'

'My finger prints were not on him. I think that's what took the time, checking his clothes and the ... his body. I suppose it was only about five hours I was at the station, but it seemed like a week.'

Helen nodded. 'It was horrible, and I was a real coward. Went to pieces, especially when I heard the car and Puppy growled.'

Joe pulled her onto his lap and put his arms round her. 'Listen to him sounding off now. He probably knew it was me outside. Muttley always growls at me. He's jealous.' Joe gave her a long, hungry kiss, 'and that makes him even more jealous.'

'That's cruel, Joe. He's not had a good start in life and he's only small. Perhaps you're both jealous?'

'Well, I didn't have a good start in life either, but he gets more of your attention.'

'That reminds me, Joe. Your mother rang three times. You'd better tell her you're home.'

Helen printed off forms and advice from Natural England and the Wildlife Trust that had arrived by email. 'I needed to keep busy while you were … out, but I think we ought to try to ignore Stonecraft and concentrate on doing practical things.'

'I wish I could, but it's difficult to ignore fire raising and fatal accidents.'

'I mean, leave the police to deal with all that and concentrate on getting official government recognition and grants for Blackridge Quarry. There's a lot of help out there, Joe, but it just seems to me that all these trusts, campaigns and agencies are so fragmented, dozens of them, that it takes time to find out how they can help. We need a Blackridge Quarry file – the first chapters of your book would be a good introduction, then a stunning set of your photos, and plans for how the public could be involved.'

The printer was chugging out application forms and copies of emails and Helen squared them into a neat pile then searched for a clean, new folder. 'That television programme should help, we ought to put a bit of pressure on them tomorrow. I thought if we saved up enough money for materials, you could renovate the barn enough to use it as a public information and education centre.'

That was about the tenth time she'd said 'we', and each time Joe felt more confident, felt the vision of the fallen body and the police interview room fading. 'You've been thinking great thoughts, love. The critters of the quarry will love you for it, and I certainly do.'

'We went down there for a walk, Pup and me – I needed to exorcise the feeling of death and evil – and I saw the most wonderful bird, a goshawk I think. I looked it up in your bird book. It seemed to keep watch over us.'

'A fanciful notion, you little Romantic. More likely it was sizing up fresh pup, and it was probably not a goshawk, they prefer deep woodland. Perhaps an eagle.'

ӕ

The email from Kathy Messeter came the next morning.

'She didn't have the guts to ring and tell me,' Joe said bitterly. 'They are pulling out. Have pulled out, in fact. No television programme. Nothing.'

'That's sickening. It would have been so exciting, but why have they? Because of the accident?'

'Yes, listen. "Really hate to have to come to this decision, Joe, it would have been such a worthwhile project. But making an entertainment programme in a place where there has been a recent fatality simply would not be right. Viewers might find it a bit ghoulish. Perhaps in a few years time ..." She must think I'm responsible for the death, guilty of something.'

'Ring her up now, Joe. Tell her the facts. Do you want me to?'

'It won't make any difference. There was a body there, and it's spooked them.'

'He didn't actually die there, and as Lauren pointed out, there must have been several poor souls who died in Blackridge Quarry over the centuries, in rock falls or explosives gone wrong. That's if the dust didn't choke them. Seat of the Pants Productions, my fanny. I'll bet there are loads of tinpot outfits making wildlife films; we need someone with more integrity. That Kathy woman sounded obsessed with viewing figures.' Helen kissed the back of his neck. 'Poor love, I'd take you to bed right now to take your mind off the disappointment, but I'm starving hungry and too weak for sex. Let's go to that posh supermarket in Buxton and get some extravagant retail therapy. And think positive, you've had – we've both had – a horrible few hours but the cops let you out of the nick and at least you got a free sandwich and two coffees.'

'I ought to call in on mother while we're in Buxton. If she's heard the local news she'll think her son's doing time for murder.'

Helen groaned. 'In that case I'll have to insist on having a gourmet pizza in her immaculate front room as some compensation. I ransacked your kitchen and found nothing to eat.'

The two bottles of cava, three bags of groceries and a lemon meringue pie were a consolation, not a celebration.

'I wanted to be famous,' Helen said sadly. 'Puppy and me would have featured prominently in your programme. You'd have provided all the scientific data, of course, but those nature series always have an attractive woman presenter drifting elegantly through the orchids or whispering huskily about owls at dusk.'

'Thank god it all got cancelled.'

Sylvia was not at home. Her neighbour was staking tulips in urns placed symmetrically at his gate on the terraced Gladstone Villas.

'Hello, Joe. I think your mother's gone to the Opera House, they've got another Gilbert and Sullivan on. Or is that tomorrow night? Anyway, she's not in. I'll tell her you called round.'

Joe stuck a note through the door and, reprieved, they drove back to Blackridge Farm and the instant delights of the grocery bags. Jolting up the track they found Sylvia's small Renault abandoned halfway up. She was standing at the farmhouse door and she brandished a bottle of champagne aloft when she saw them.

'There you are. I got tired of listening to recorded messages and I just needed …' Sylvia threw her arms round her son, nearly knocking him out with the bottle, then burst into tears. 'I know how angry you've been about the Stonecraft company so I thought there had been a fight. People sometimes stay in police custody for years with nobody believing them…'

'I'm fine, Mum, really. I was just helping with enquiries, as they say. Let's get indoors before the hound demolishes the door. In fact, we came round to you at the villa to celebrate, though we can't quite work out what we are celebrating.'

Helen took the champagne and gave it to Joe 'Get your thumbs working on that before explanations. I'm afraid this classy booze will have to go into mugs, Sylvia, because we couldn't find any flutes in the kitchen cupboard you gave Joe.'

They let the Krug take hold before tearing into pizza and garlic bread, though Sylvia was too upset to eat. 'I can't believe someone has just died in our old quarry, it brings back the horrible stories Dad used to tell us. He said the conditions men worked in years ago weren't fit for animals, so they suffered poor health and early death. They had miserable lives and so did their families. Down the road in the cottages in Stoneybrook there would be two or three families in one cottage, and they were the lucky ones. He told us how some men died in rock falls and in accidents with explosives.' Sylvia drank more champagne, then opened the cava. 'That all seemed like ancient history when I was a child, sad but unreal. But this death … it's horrible. It doesn't make sense because there was no need for it.'

'Just as there was no need to put the frighteners on Joe with the break-in and the fire.' Helen sounded indignant; Sylvia was making the whole thing sound like an unfortunate accident, another chapter in history. 'And we didn't tell you about the assassination attempt on Puppy, poor love.'

'But, Mum, you turned up here with the most expensive bottle of fizz as if you had something to celebrate …'

'And we haven't told you about the bloody telly programme,' Helen interrupted, taking another gulp of champagne. 'They've pulled out because the accident might upset the viewers. Well, fuck them, I say.' She held the champagne mug up high, 'here's to Joe's book, and the wildlife centre and the SS thingy with eagles and boar and wild cats and loads of other stuff out there.'

Joe eased her into an armchair and gave her a kiss.

'Mum, you must have been worried sick when I was at the police station, so why the champagne? And that message about good news, we certainly need some. Did you hear about your crocus discovery, is that it?'

'*Crocus Sylvaticus* – no, not yet, but I've got high hopes. My good news is even stranger. Wake Helen up, she'll love this. Do you remember the funeral?'

Joe shook his head, looking puzzled and wondering whether his mother was now deliriously drunk. 'I thought you said good news, I can't bear any more death. Whose funeral?'

'I told you last week. Your father's so-called partner ... that Gerald person.'

'I forgot about it,' Joe lied. 'Not surprising really. I thought it was odd to write and let you know, then I wondered if, after all, I might go. I know so little.'

'That Gerald person had no children, being an old queer, though your father just about managed to produce...'

'What's the good news, Ma?' Joe insisted, to forestall his mother's bitter rant.

'He's left you some money, that Gerald person. He wrote us a letter to be sent after his death saying that your father had often said how much he missed you.'

'So how was it he never bothered to come and see me? Or write, or phone, or anything?'

'I think he was ashamed at leaving us, and quite right too. Anyway, this Gerald person says in his letter that he always felt guilty, responsible for taking away your father, and looking back he wished they could have worked something out, something that included you.' Sylvia's voice wavered. 'Your father was always weak, sweet natured in a spineless way but swayed by whoever he was with at the time, anxious to please. He cried sometimes when he couldn't satisfy me in bed, said he didn't feel ...'

'Too much information, Mum.'

Helen was awake now and opening the second cava. 'How much money did he leave Joe?'

'Eighty-five thousand. Not much for ruining two people's lives, but a comforting amount when Joe probably doesn't earn much from those nature photos and hasn't even thought about a pension fund yet. Of course the real money is in this place, half a million at least when you put it on the market and let big business fight over it.' Sylvia fished about in her handbag then handed Joe Gerald's cheque. 'But that's not bad to be going on with and I thought it deserved a bottle of champagne. Did we finish it all?'

Two days later Joe had a phone call from Natural England asking for Miss Seymour, owner of Blackridge Quarry. Helen had gone back to work, but Joe explained that he was the landowner.

'We were quite excited by her description of some of the rare species that have colonised your quarry. These old quarries are proving to be a valuable refuge for many endangered animals and plants.'

Joe searched for the email Helen had sent them, wondering what amazing creatures she had claimed to be roaming about Blackridge. 'Miss Seymour is a great enthusiast, but not always scientific.'

'She says you have albino bats? Those are unheard of in Britain.'

'But we do have them. I have some fascinating photographs, taken, of course, at night, when these creatures flit about like tiny ghosts. I knew they must be rare ...'

'That's an understatement Mr. Wright! I'd never heard of such a thing, but when I ran a check on it, it seems there was just one discovered in Australia, and you say you have a whole family of them? When could we arrange to visit Blackridge?'

❧

'Joe! Great to see you!' Fred Marshall looked genuinely delighted. 'I feared for a few days that our celebrity wildlife correspondent would be penning his musings from the slammer! Though that, of course, could be quite a feature.'

'What nasty new offices, Fred. 1970s brutalist. Worse than Bakewell nick, but at least they'll keep your feet dry. Four miles upstream, north of Ashford, the Wye has gone berserk and it'll probably take the old mill with it. It's a shame I'm too busy to get any photos, but I've been writing a piece about the accident at Blackridge, to set the record straight. I sent the email about half an hour ago, so if you check your inbox instead of hankering after poetic musings from Bakewell gaol your humble rag could get its facts right for once. Details of the death have been in all the media across the Midlands and I want people to know about the provoca-

tion and the criminal assaults I've had to put up with to get me to sell the quarry.'

Joe was handling a paperweight, a chunk of jagged Blue John, as though he'd like to smash his enemies with it.

'It isn't an exclusive for The Bugle, Fred. It's going to go in The Derbyshire Times and four other newspapers to get a good coverage. I've had a bloody awful few days, and so has Helen, and I'm determined to get the facts out into the open. These big companies think they can get away with murder. I'm just glad it wasn't mine.'

Fred was looking uncomfortable; he'd never known Joe be so forceful. Perhaps he had never really known Joe and perhaps he *was* capable of that punch-up with Webster, or of scaring a trespasser into losing his footing. He sat down slowly behind his desk looking unusually apologetic.

'It isn't quite that easy, Joe. You see, there have been developments. You may not have heard if you've been working all morning. Of course I'll handle your article – making it quite clear that it is your version of events. '

'It isn't a *version*, Fred, it's the truth.' He was grinding the purple crystals into his hand and Gillian was peering through the glass partition to see what Joe was shouting about.

'Have a seat, Joe, you need to hear this and then we'll decide how to play it. Stonecraft issued a press release early this morning saying that you'd only been let out on bail. Not true, of course, it only took me a second to check that with the police, but it'll do a certain amount of damage of the mud-sticking variety. The company is considering going for a charge of manslaughter. They said you'd given permission for their employee to carry out soil tests knowing the cliff was unsafe, so what may look like an accident ...'

'Rubbish, absolute lies. I thought that a death would put an end to all this harassment. Nothing was worth that wretched employee dying.'

'Why are they still going for you?'

'Because I still won't sell.' Joe sat down and put the Blue John back on the desk where it performed beautifully, sparkling pink, blue and purple in a shaft of sunlight. 'But I don't understand it

either. Chunks of limestone are not worth the sort of campaign they've mounted against me. Especially as hardly anyone is building much round here these days.'

Gillian came in with mugs of tea. 'I heard you talking about limestone and saying it isn't worth anything. What they usually want is fluorspar – like that stuff I think,' she pointed a long silver fingernail at the chunk of Blue John.

Joe shook his head. 'Surely we've got enough of that. Places like Chatsworth and Kedleston are stuffed with it – vulgar vases and monstrous mantelpieces, and the tourist shops round Castleton are full of tiny bits of it.'

'No, perhaps it's a bit different, because it's used for making hospital equipment. I only know about it because my aunt lives in Wirksworth and some company got permission to open up a quarry there because they said it was in the national interest. Anything medical and the powers that be just roll over. Bugger the countryside.' Gillian tipped some digestives onto a saucer, took three then went back to her section of the office.

Fred was tapping the word fluorspar into his computer search engine. 'That still doesn't make sense, because there's deposits of the stuff everywhere. All over Europe and tons in China, so it can't be all that valuable, plus the boffins are coming up with a substitute made from industrial waste to use in refrigeration. I like that, keep your food fresh in a fridge made from shit!'

'What else could Stonecraft be looking for? Or think they have found in Blackridge? I've never seen any fluorspar.'

Fred studied the screen and read '"Limestone uplands in Derbyshire ... lead ores in Peak District ... silver-bearing lead ores mined by ..."'

Joe leaped to his feet sending biscuit crumbs onto the computer keyboard. 'That could be it! Silver!'

'"Mined by the Romans and more extensively by the Normans in the 12th century." I think you've missed it, Joe, by nearly a millennium.'

'No, they're wrong, because my grandfather had a lump of silver on the mantelpiece that he said he'd found in one of the caves –

except no-one ever believed him, or just thought it was a fluke. It was embedded in a larger piece of something and it all looked very dirty. We never took much notice. But what if there's a whacking great vein of it, and that was what that poor dead bugger was prodding about for? At least it would explain Webster and Co's criminal behaviour.'

Fred grunted and stopped searching. 'It would have been found centuries ago. That grimy chunk your grandpa had was probably left in the cave by the Normans. Silver rush and saloon bar brawls in Stoneybroke? I can't see it.' He changed the subject: 'Your article is here in my inbox. Looks a bit longwinded, I may have to prune it back a bit.'

Joe had gone, but then he came back and said in a dramatic whisper 'Don't you dare breathe a word about silver, Fred, or my quarry will be full of idiots digging about. Just when Natural England and The Wildlife Trust are beating a path to my door expecting tranquility, except for screeching owls and snuffling badgers.'

❧

The farmhouse seemed dead again. When Helen was there she lit it up, trying to civilize the old place with a pot of snowdrops or curled up in the chair next to the stove, the runt jumping up and pulling at the toe of her tights. Now they were both gone again and the silence seemed deeper every time.

Joe went down to The Miners Standard. Not that he was in search of company, he'd got his book to write and official forms to fill in, forms that would go off and be rewarded with other forms saying that Blackridge Quarry was protected forever, a refuge for bats and owls and newts and any other creatures drawn to its safety. He wanted to tell the village what had really happened, and the pub was the nearest you could get to the heart of the village. True it was a weakened heart drained of the energy of labour, of wealthy farms, trade, wage-earning and old families and lucky to get a few dozen customers a day. The village shop clung to the side of the pub and begged inhabitants not to pass it by, their own convenience store that boasted a post office two hours on a Wednesday afternoon,

selling stamps that were no longer used because the postie only collected from the post box three times a week.

Joe was on a mission – his quarry could not only save its rare inhabitants but it could help the village to survive. Alan had only just lit the coal fire in the bar and he was fanning it with old copies of The Bugle. 'Good to see you, Joe. I've been waiting to buy you a drink after that dreadful business up at the quarry, and when we saw you carted off in the police car … disgraceful. And I told them so next time I saw one of the officers doing his weekly shop in Bakewell Co-op. Ought never to have happened.'

There was a murmur of agreement and chairs were scraped over the stone floor closer to the fire.

Joe joined them. 'No, I'm buying a round and if Sandra is cooking tonight then a stack of sausages and chips for everyone.' That enormous cheque was still nestling comfortably in Joe's pocket; he'd imagined, nostalgically, a thronging Miners with roaring fire and a few bottles of whisky passed round but he'd have to make do with the five of them huddled round smoking coals. They'd think he was just celebrating his escape from the latest of Webster's dirty tricks – they didn't know about the manslaughter accusation which seemed so wildly off the mark that Joe had decided to ignore it. His poor father's sort-of-inheritance would stay a secret and if he dared mention Natural England, rare bats or Mouse-eared Hawkweed as a cause for celebration, the locals would think his hermit life-style had addled his brains.

Simon Gent came in with Lauren. Joe ordered more drinks and judged his audience large enough to be told of the tragic sequence of events at Blackridge and the proof of his innocence that the police had pieced together. Word would get round to the rest of Stoney-brook soon enough. He felt a sense of relief and comfort in the telling.

'Horrible. Just a shame it wasn't that Webster that fell instead of some poor sap he sent to do his dirty work.' Lauren helped herself to whisky and a brace of sausages.

Simon took it upon himself to load up the grate with more coal. 'Talking of Webster, there's something odd going on about the plans

for the new estate in the village. You know we appealed against the approval, and sent in our petition about three weeks ago? Well, we expected Stonecraft's legal team to slap us down straight away, but so far … silence. What can they be up to?'

'Did you ask the planners?'

'They said the contractors, owned by Stonecraft, had been informed of the appeal, but there had been no response.'

Lauren filled up everyone's glass and pressed a button on the ancient jukebox for some reggae music and Joe went home to the beat of 'No Woman, No Cry.' He took the cheque that his mother had brought round out of his pocket and smoothed it out, then looked up central heating boilers on his laptop. Or would it be better to fit new triple-glazed windows first? Where was it best to start? A few calculations told him that he had plenty of money for both, and bespoke hand-crafted kitchens that looked like something from a life-style magazine. He would need Helen's advice on those. And on sturdy, plump sofas with not a hole, bulge or mouse's nest in sight. Sending off for a few brochures felt like starting a new life, joining a buy-it-now society that he had never felt part of before, though most of his new wealth would be spent on the old barn.

With relief he switched to his documents folder and opened up a fresh page of his book, pasting into it a photograph of the small intelligent face of the stoat that the police had retrieved from his smashed camera. The creature stared at him triumphantly, sure of always being a survivor. That instant now seemed a hundred years ago, a moment of warm, sheltered sunshine and friendly grebe.

He started to write, making each chapter a log book of sightings of individual creatures and the ease with which they had made Blackridge their home and the unique surroundings it afforded them. Joe was soon lost in a comforting, absorbing world; it was the only way he could put the spectre of the inert, disjointed body out of his mind for a while.

After a few satisfying pages Joe allowed himself some practical progress. He wandered out into the barn to take stock of fallen slates and stonework, soon satisfied that there were enough to make the old building weatherproof. Some he had collected in piles over the

years and more were still covered in long grass and ferns where they had fallen. It was important to him that no new material should be used, no new stone or slate quarried from Blackridge or from anywhere else in the world. He would try for planning permission for new windows and skylights, but that was as much of an insult to the old barn as he could allow. Tomorrow he would go into Buxton for mortar and then make a start on fitting back the old limestone into the walls – Helen had promised to come back at the weekend and with glossy brochures and building in progress she would see ... but would she really come? It was all little enough, his few pages of book, the promise of a new kitchen, white bats and Peregrine Falcons, but over everything there was still the horror of death, the threat of powerful enemies and their ruthless determination to get him out of the farmhouse. Back in her comfortable flat with the hound for company, would she be tempted to stay there?

The next day the regional manager from Natural England rang to make an appointment – could they come that afternoon? Perhaps at first they may have doubted Joe's sanity, he imagined they must have no end of wild enthusiasts claiming to have spotted ospreys or large striped wildcats. He had sent them photographs of the albinos, and some surprisingly endearing shots of palmate newts in a sensitive courting ritual, and now their eagerness to visit the quarry came as no surprise to Joe. It was an excitement that any naturalist would understand, an intoxicating hunt for the rare and undiscovered.

'I'm Sebastian Parker, Regional Co-ordinator, and this is Andy our research assistant. I wanted him along so they didn't think my judgement had been shot to pieces at the sight of your newts! We're all a bit batty, off the rails at the sight of a rare orchid – in fact we're a rare breed ourselves. Can I dump some paperwork on you, then get down to the quarry?' He handed Joe a sheaf of papers explaining SSSI selection criteria and landowner agreements and responsibilities.

'Plenty of time to study those later. Is it off in that direction? I did study an aerial view of the quarry and hillside, but if you've got time to show us round, Mr Wright ...'

Joe grabbed binoculars and led them up the slope. This would be the conducted tour to end all tours, and he just hoped at least a few of his inhabitants would perform to order though no doubt Mr Parker had the patience of a saint in spite of his excitement. One small fear at the back of Joe's mind – if Stonecraft International really wanted to hurt him, this was the time to do it. He just hoped that bats and newts did not register with men like Webster.

As they went out of the gate, Margaret arrived. She seemed excited and almost ready to join the party.

'Got these specialists from Natural England, Margaret' Joe whispered. Their verdict could mean a lot for Blackridge conservation and for the village. Very exciting. I don't know how long we'll be so I'll call in to see you this evening and let you know what happens.' Helen would be the first to hear the news. She was the one who had sent in the application forms.

'I'd rather wait, Joe. It's important. I'll go in and make myself some tea if you don't mind.'

Sebastian Parker set off at a businesslike jog. 'Of course we can't expect to see much on a first visit, but we've scheduled in at least five over the next few weeks, and we'll be here until late this evening to try to get a shot of the bats.'

When Joe got back to the farmhouse about two hours later, Margaret was still there, asleep next to the stove.

'Can I make you some soup?' he offered, hoping to wake her up. 'Only tinned, but I'm too excited to eat much.'

'Where are the nature people you had with you?'

Joe laughed. 'It's OK, I haven't done away with them in the quarry. They've gone down to The Miners for a meal, then back later to go bat hunting. Leek and potato sound good? And did you say you were excited too? High spirits all round then.'

'Soup would be lovely, but I need to check the Footsie first. Can I use your computer? I need to check the news.'

'I'll find the news channel for you before I heat the soup. I'll even use a saucepan in your honour.'

'No, not that sort of news, I mean the financial markets. I was checking my online shares this afternoon and noticed something

intriguing. South African Minerals Inc. has lost about forty percent and still falling. The miners have been on strike for nearly six months and investors are pulling out in case the government sends troops in.'

Joe looked puzzled, but he was hardly concentrating. He liked Margaret but would have welcomed the evening to himself, to dream about Wildlife Trusts and Protected Status and Areas of Special Scientific Interest, and to wash the dishes and change the sheets in the hope of a weekend visit from Helen. Why was Margaret banging on about her shares?

'I do hope you haven't lost too much money' he soothed vaguely.

'No, I haven't lost anything. South African Minerals owns Stonecraft International.'

Joe slopped the mug of soup as he set it down beside her; now she had his full attention.

'Oh, Margaret, are you trying to tell me that you've been investing in Stonecraft shares all along? Well, I suppose that's all part of playing the stock market. Make a quick buck wherever you can.'

'Shut up, Joe, and just watch the screen.' She had tapped expertly into her account then into its international search engine. More columns of figures, mainly red. 'Down even more. It isn't sustainable … their markets are still open for another half an hour. Down seventy-two percent, look!'

'I don't really know what I'm supposed to be looking at.'

Margaret pointed to the screen to where a flashing light was now saying "Trading Suspended."

'That means that Stonecraft and its parent company are going under. Down the pan. Broke. Your troubles could be over, Joe. Let's switch to the American financial channel and see what they are saying, their markets will still be open. '

There was a knock on the door. 'I'm going to have to leave you and go looking for bats with Natural England. Stonecraft have gone bankrupt? Just like that?' Joe seemed stunned as he opened the door. Too many events were crowding in on him and it was difficult to sort out what he could trust from what could be yet another

disappointment. He could depend on bats and their frantic evening hunt for food not to let him down.

Puppy hurtled in first, then Helen came in and slammed the door behind her. 'Joe! There are two men in the garden with a load of dangerous-looking equipment, didn't you hear the noise? Puppy tried to take a lump out of one of them. What could they be doing in the dark? Shall I call the police?'

Joe threw his arms round her and smothered her in kisses. 'Three in a row and I'm not talking about ducks. I almost believe my luck is changing.' He stopped kissing her when there was another knock on the door. 'Stay and keep Margaret company for a while, see if you can make sense of what she's been telling me. Those men are the ones who have come to see our white bats … remember you told Natural England about them? They could hardly believe you but after checking me out to make sure I had all my marbles they came straight round. They seem to think Blackridge is one of the wonders of the world and it'll be safe, so wonderful and special and scientific that it'll be safe and protected.' Joe could hear himself babbling insanely, so he stepped out into the night, shutting the door firmly before Puppy could escape and ruin the night's vigil.

'Hello Margaret. Joe certainly isn't making sense. Why didn't he let me know that the scientific world was beating a path to his door? Isn't that the most amazing news?'

'I don't think he trusts anyone bearing good news right now in case they turn round and bite him, what with being arrested, then the telly people chickening out. I just hope his beloved critters in the quarry perform on cue for their VIP guests.' Margaret took the teapot off the stove and settled back into the dingy depths of the sofa. 'Let me tell you the good news I brought him. It seems that Stonecraft International have gone down the tubes. Bankrupt. Shares suspended. Look, I'll show you online. They are finished.'

'Just like that? They'll have to stop work?'

'Just like that. The excitement of the Market. Someone pulls the plug and …splat!' Margaret's tea slopped over onto the dog's complacent head; his eyes were riveted on her biscuit, wobbling promisingly on the arm of the sofa.

Helen stood up, circled the room then sat down again, staring at the screen on Margaret's lap. The rows of flashing figures had meant nothing but the financial news running across the bottom of the screen was clear enough: "Mining disaster … Stonecraft collapses … rumblings spread panic across minerals sector … about to implode." The financial news hacks were having fun.

Helen frowned. 'It doesn't seem real, can't be trusted. It could all change tomorrow, another company, another investor.'

'No, it doesn't happen like that. It'll be liquidation.'

'It isn't the answer, it isn't safe.' Helen started pacing again. 'There are hillsides under threat everywhere, woods and meadows and cliffs. Real birds and animals, not just flashing figures on a screen. We can't rely on stock markets and thoughtless people with shares … sorry, Margaret.'

'I agree, dear. It isn't safe enough.'

'And we can't even rely on whether the telly people think enough viewers will be interested. Or on the dreadful shock of a fatal accident. There has to be something safer than all of that.'

'Sadly, Helen, I don't think there is. Our best bet is with Joe and his albino bats or those newts of his that look like tiny dinosaurs. All the special things that make the countryside so precious. I hope the critters in the quarry are putting on a good show right now for those scientific adviser big wigs.'

❧

Joe proudly led the other naturalists down into the silent quarry again. It was a clear night where no creature stirred yet but where hidden eyes watched and waited. Furry bodies snugly curled in dens. Softly feathered wings protected nests. They were all out there, you just had to be patient and they would come. They always did.

Other books by Lynda Aylett-Green

An Aztec in Spain - novel
The Emperor Moctezuma thought that Spaniards were white gods. His daughter found no gods in Spain, only the Inquisition, a warring King and gold-hungry adventurers like her lover Cortés. The Princess would take revenge for her father's death and destroy him.
Paperback ISBN 9780755204779 and ebook

A Topiary Garden - novel
The actress, the aristocrat and the gardener. A story of Elvaston Castle, Derbyshire in the 1820s
Paperback ISBN 9781844269952 and ebook

I Hate Books - novel
When the old Norwich Library burned down they thought it was an accident. Chris knows a different story; getting rid of so many books was sweet revenge.
Kindle ebook

Thank you for using Derbyshire Libraries.

To renew items www.derbyshire.gov.uk/libraries

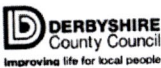